HIT ME

PETER J THOMPSON

PETER J THOMPSON

1

I step up on the platform as the train pulls into sight. The sun is just starting to rise and it's still dark. Commuters stand beside the tracks, some strewn out, others in tight clusters. It doesn't take me long to find my quarry, Alan Silverman. The guy's exactly where I expected him to be, in a group of commuters at the far end of the platform. He's easy to spot because first, he is a creature of habit and second, has a distinctive look.

I'm about average height, five foot nine, but he's at least a head shorter than I am. In his slick, black Italian suit he looks like an oversized bowling ball with a shiny human head and stubby legs.

The train barrels in and screeches to a halt at the last moment, its brakes squealing and hissing loudly. The commuters bunch up and as the train shudders to a stop they surge toward the doors. I stroll to the far end of the platform and wait in line, well back from Silverman. The doors of the 6:10 inbound to Chicago slide open with a pneumatic *whoosh*. I move with the crowd as we surge up the few steps and into the train. Silverman turns to the car on the right, as I knew he would.

I follow discreetly behind. He walks halfway up the car and takes an empty seat by the window. The car is already half full and most of the double seats have at least one occupant. The seat next to Silverman is empty and for a moment I consider sitting next to him. What better way to keep track of him and appear innocuous than by planting myself right beside him? But that would be too bold. I work best unnoticed, and, although he probably wouldn't give me more than a passing glance as I sat down before returning to his paper, it's not worth taking the chance. I move past him and slide into the seat across the aisle a few rows ahead, making sure I can still see Silverman in my peripheral vision. I don't even bother looking. The guy's not going anywhere.

The last few people scurry to find seats as the train starts moving and picks up speed. I slip in my earbuds and settle in for the trip. I have my music on shuffle. The randomness, not knowing what music to expect helps me stay focused on the moment. I close my eyes, lean back in my seat and relax. No need to even think for the next forty-three minutes.

The train starts and stops every few minutes, gathering passengers at stations in Evanston, Davis Avenue, Ravenswood, and Clybourne. Our car soon fills up and the later arrivals have to stand. I mostly keep my eyes shut and focus on the mix. First Wilco, then the Shins, then some electronica. As we pull into Union Station, it's some bad Gangsta rap I don't even remember uploading. The train pulls to a stop and everyone rushes out of their seats and herds toward the door. I'd like to hang back, but my seatmate is impatient. He stands and shuffles his belongings around. I take the hint and step into the aisle, even though the doors haven't opened, and no one is going anywhere yet.

I steal a look back and Silverman is in the aisle, too. We all stand together in a tight scrum. The heady mix of cologne, deodorant soap, sweat, and coffee breath makes me want to gag. We're much closer together than strangers should ever be. We stand this way for a long minute before the outer doors open and the scrum pushes outward.

Now we are a river, flowing out of the train car, down the steps and into the noisy bustle of the main terminal. The river keeps flowing toward the escalator, which carries us up to street level. I try and slow to let Silverman pass me, but short of dropping down to tie my shoe and risk getting trampled. I'm caught in the flow. Fast food joints and convenience store kiosks line the path. I step off the escalator and duck into one and pretend to scan the headlines of a newspaper. A moment later, Silverman marches past me without a glance. I give him a little space before stepping into the river behind him as we flow toward the street.

The stream of commuters still flows outside as we move along the sidewalk and cross over the Chicago River. The sounds of traffic and the smell of diesel fumes add to the ambience. Now the sun is moving higher and reflecting off the glass of the skyscrapers that line both sides of the street. If I were a tourist, I'd hang back and take in the beauty and energy of the city. But I'm no tourist. I have a job to do. I keep walking.

My job. I consider myself a problem solver. Sometimes the problems are small and require a small solution, and other times the problems are so big the only solution is drastic. Such is the case with Silverman. Although I don't know the specifics, Silverman is an attorney, a prominent one. He's had problems with various groups in the past and isn't the type who'd win a popularity contest. These aren't my concerns. I don't want to know too much about him, good or bad, or it may affect the way I think of my quarry and introduce emotion into what should be a pure business transaction. My employer is an agency that does all the due diligence beforehand. If Silverman's on the list, he deserves his fate. I have scruples. I trust the Agency to do the research, but I do have my standards.

It's hard to keep track of Silverman because he is short enough to blend in with the crowd and I'm not tall enough to see over it. No matter. I know where he's going and how he will get there. I've made this same trip four times now—I know what to expect. He works on LaSalle Street, but, by habit, he takes a short-cut through an alley that cuts on a loose diagonal between the two streets, past the trash bins and various service entrances, before connecting back to the main drag. It might save a minute or two, maybe, but it's part of his daily routine. It's also the one spot along the way where he is out of the crowd and the most exposed.

Sure, I know where he is going, but I needed to make sure he wouldn't get sidetracked along the way. Now I know he is on the right path, I want to reach the spot before he does. I adjust my gait and walk a little faster. I weave between the pedestrians and pass Silverman, who is huffing and puffing and doesn't pay me the slightest attention. I hurry on and, by the time I arrive at the alley, I figure I'm at least half a block ahead of him.

The alley is busier than I hoped. A truck is backed up to a loading dock, delivering supplies, and two young guys are manning their hand trucks while the driver supervises them. A little further on, three Hispanic men stand near a dumpster, smoking cigarettes. One is telling a story, using his hands to sketch out the details, and his buddies laugh. Compared to the street scene this is quiet, but for my purposes, it's Grand Central Station. I pass the men and turn the curve which leads to LaSalle Street. It's quieter here. Up on the sidewalk, maybe twenty yards away, the street traffic is a blur of motion. But right here it's isolated, and this is the place I need to be.

I position myself on the side of the alley and make myself ready. I don't think he'll see me until after he turns the corner, and I doubt he'd think twice if he does, but a man standing by himself doing nothing is naturally suspicious. I pull out my cell phone and start an imaginary conversation with myself. Now, I'm perfectly normal and fit in completely.

I'm well into my conversation when Silverman rounds the corner and bobbles into view. He probably hears me talking before he sees me. When he notices me, he swings his head in my direction for maybe a microsecond, long enough to categorize what type of alley life I belong to, and to decide I'm not a threat. Then he is back to his mission. I don't know why he's walking but he has plenty of money to take a cab, and the way he is huffing along, he doesn't seem like he is walking for enjoyment. He must be walking for his health. This strikes me as ironic.

He passes me when I call out his name and take a step toward him.

"Silverman? Alan. Is that you?"

He turns in my direction, a baffled expression creases his face. He stops and gives me the full once over. "Do I know you?"

I take another step forward.

I don't have the kind of face you'd remember. In fact, there is nothing about me you would find memorable. I've been described as doughy, nondescript, a normal kind of guy. I've been told I look like an accountant or maybe a truck driver. I'm of average height and average weight. My hair is starting to thin, and I carry a little more around my waistline than I used to, but that's not unusual for someone in their late thirties. It's considered ordinary, which I appear to be. And it's not surprising that he wouldn't be able to place me, if he ever knew me.

"Alan, remember me? Dick Olson." I take another step toward him, holding out my hand.

He's stuck to his spot, but he's not really buying it. Doesn't matter. All I need is another few seconds and a few more feet. I keep moving.

"At Gibson's. You were with Jerry, Jerry Calhoun."

I'm basically babbling, throwing out names and places I picked up from my research on him. From his expression, I can tell I oversold it. Again, doesn't matter. This is routine and it will all be over in short order. I am not a big fan of weapons. Guns make too much noise, knives are way too messy. But if you know what you are doing, and I do, hands are all you need. I'm almost within reach.

His hand dips into his pocket and he's pulling something out. It might be a cell phone, or maybe he wants to give me his wallet. But I don't think so. The time for subterfuge is over. I lunge toward him.

His hand jerks from the pocket, holding a small can. Mace or pepper spray? I grab for his neck and pull him toward me while I reach for his hand. He gasps. His chest heaves. The guy might have a heart attack before I can kill him.

The spray hits me. Sudden pain. Intense, shattering pain. My eyes tear, my lungs burn, and I can't breathe. Pain is everywhere. My grip loosens and Silverman twists free. I drop to one knee, but I grab for him again, or at least where I think he is, because I can't see a thing. I grab at the air and his heavy footsteps pound the pavement, running now. His locomotive breath is so loud it seems to echo off the walls.

I lurch to my feet and head after him. He's heading toward the street. I have to stop him before he reaches the safety of the sidewalk. This is a disaster, a royal fuck up and I don't even want to think about what will happen if I botch this job. He's running, but even in full panic he's no runner. I stagger after him. My vision's blurred, and the pain is just as intense as before, but I force myself to run though I can hardly maintain my balance.

I hear him in front of me as much as I can see him. I'm gaining on him, but even as I bridge the gap between the two of us, the street sounds grow louder still. We are nearly out of the alley and close to the sidewalk. The busy street means safety for Silverman. Surrounded by people, I can't do a thing, and all he has to do is yell and a crowd will form, police will come, and it'll all be over. If he makes the street—and he's almost there—the only thing I can do is slink away.

The truth is, I can't make it. My lungs are stuffed with hot coals and my vision is shot. He's too far ahead. If I had a gun I might shoot, but I'd surely miss and only make matters worse. I keep moving but I already know it's too late. I blink back the tears and I get a cloudy look at what's ahead. He's out of the alley and on the sidewalk now. I've lost.

Silverman jerks his head back for a look at me. I can't see his expression, but I'm guessing it's one of joy, or relief, or maybe even anger. Or is it still panic, and fear? But he turns again and keeps running, bumping into people but still running, past the sidewalk and right into the street.

A screech of brakes.

A loud thud.

A chorus of yells, screams and gasps break through the background hubbub. I slow to a walk, cross the sidewalk and join the crowd forming around the scene.

A lady lets out a wail of lament. The taxi driver leaps from his cab, his hands aflutter. In his thick Pakistani accent and high voice, he tells the crowd it's not his fault. The crowd isn't listening, their eyes are all on the broken body nearly underneath the wheels.

"Call an ambulance!" a woman yells.

"Too late for that," someone else says.

I push through the gapers for a good look. The last voice was right. Blood is everywhere, and Silverman is not my problem anymore. The lady lets out a wail again, and I try not to smile with relief. I can't believe my good luck.

2

It's two weeks since the Silverman fiasco, and I'm sitting inside a Chuck E. Cheese theme restaurant. It's my son Jason's seventh birthday party, and I'm here with eight of his friends from school, my wife Jen, three other moms, and David. David is the one dad who came along. The moms are all off shadowing the kids as they run in six different directions, playing games, so David and I are alone at the table. We sit across from one another, a few slices of leftover pizza and a pitcher of root beer between us. Video bleeps and ringing bells, corny theme music and screaming kids are all so loud it's hard to talk. This suits me fine, but not David.

"So, Chuck," he yells across the table. "What do you do for a living?"

First of all, my name isn't Chuck. It's Charles, or Charley. He's already losing points for calling me this. I now know he sells insurance. And that loses points, too.

"I'm a consultant," I say.

"What?" he yells. "I can't hear you."

A group of six-year-olds run past our table pretending to be airplanes. Their motor sounds aren't authentic, but the decibel level is.

"I'm a consultant," I repeat, louder this time.

David smiles slyly. "I know, Chuck. We're all consultants. I'm an insurance consultant myself. It says so right on my business card."

I know this is a fact because David has already given me one of his cards.

"Really," David goes on. "What is it you do?"

This is always the point where I am tempted to tell them the truth. Sometimes I do, and it's always good for a laugh. Sometimes it's even enough to stop them from asking more questions.

"Basically, I take care of problems," I say. "Whenever someone has a problem they can't solve any other way, they call me."

I can tell from the look on David's face he's only hearing part of this. It doesn't matter. Clearly, his mission is to keep this conversation going.

"Yeah, yeah, I understand." He nods deeply and slowly, as though I've said something profound. "So, what made you get into this line of work? Why do you do what you do?"

I have, of course pondered this question before. Why do I do what I do? But then that's like asking why birds sing or bees buzz. I suppose I do what I do because it's what I've always done and what I'm well suited for.

I shrug. "I kind of fell into it. It was the family business."

I don't say it, but this brings up the whole nature versus nurture debate. Do I do what I do because my father started taking me out on his jobs long before my voice changed? I knew what my dad did wasn't normal, but it was normal in my family. Or is it because, by disposition and character, I fit into the job so well that even when I think about quitting—which is more often lately—I can't imagine myself in any other line of work?

"The family business. So how does that work? You work with your parents? Brothers and sisters?"

"No. It's just me. My dad started in the line of work, but I work for myself these days."

"Hmmm," He nods his head. "You like what you do?"

All the questions. Do I like what I do? Yes, I do. Don't get the wrong idea. I'm no psychopath. I certainly don't get a thrill from offing people. Let's say that I get satisfaction from a job well done. I go into each contract with a goal in mind. When I accomplish the goal, I feel good about it. Moral issues aside, it's a good job. I am reliable and professional, and near the top scale for my line of work. I get paid well enough that I only need to take on eight or ten jobs a year, most of them local. This is enough for a solid income and provides my family with everything they need, as well as a strong retirement and rainy day fund. That doesn't mean I love everything about what I do, or that I don't have feelings or even second thoughts. I do, but this is my job. Under different circumstances I might have become a banker or a lawyer, but if a fish had wings and nested in trees, it'd be a bird. This is what I do, but it doesn't define me as a person. This is what I do, not who I am.

I'm struggling with how to answer when I sense movement behind me. Jen drops her hands on my shoulders and leans close, so we are nearly cheek to cheek. Her hair touches my skin and I smell her scent. I don't know if I smile, but I'm smiling inside. She's the love of my life and with a touch I feel the connection.

"How are you boys doing? The kids are having a great time together. David, you should come on over and see what Tommy is up to."

David slides his chair away from the table and stands. "Yeah, I should see what the little man is up to." He smiles again and nods at me. "We'll catch up later, Chuck."

A moment later, he's gone. "Thank you," I say.

"You looked like you needed rescuing." She kisses my cheek and wraps her arms around my neck.

The roles have reversed. She's my protector now.

"Are you going to join us?"

I should. A better dad would join the party, but all the noise and flashing lights are starting to get to me. Besides, when I checked my phone, it showed a message from the Agency, and I'm anxious to hear what they have for me.

"I have to get out for a few minutes. I need a little fresh air."

Her arms stiffen, but she doesn't say anything.

"I'll be back. I just need a few minutes."

After a moments' hesitation, she says, "Okay. Don't stay out long, though. This is for Jason."

I get outside as quickly as I can. Stepping out from the dark interior to the bright sunlight is a shift into another universe. I'm on a busy street in suburban Naperville, but even with the cars rushing by, it's quiet out here compared to the bedlam inside.

My hands are damp and I wipe them on my jeans. I haven't heard from the Agency since the Silverman contract's completion, and it pains me to think of how that could have turned out. The method wasn't ideal, but it worked out and I've been paid for the job. The payment went into my account in the Caymans, and through a series of automated transactions set up to launder and insure that no one can trace the money, it ended up in my normal business account. Just like always. Though the details were messier than expected, I fulfilled the contract. And the Agency doesn't know about the messiness. At least I hope they don't.

I've dealt with the Agency for almost fourteen years now, and my father worked with them for decades before that. As you can imagine, my line of work is specialized. Sure, you hear about people who arrange contracts through Craigslist or who set something up with some stranger they met in a bar, but you hear about these cases because the morons get caught. These are amateurs. I am a professional. The Agency is my go-between. They find the contracts, do the due diligence and arrange all the details. It's my job to execute the contract in a professional and expedient manner. In my case, they also screen the job to make sure that it fits my moral criteria. As I said before, I do have scruples.

One more advantage of the Agency is almost total anonymity. When I take on a job, I don't know who takes out the contract, and they don't know who I am. This has obvious benefits for everyone. I am completely anonymous with the agency, too. Even though we have worked together for years, they know me only by my code name, Martin, and I know them only as the Agency. This was the arrangement my father set up all those years back, and as my dad's apprentice, I inherited the same protocol. The process is more high-tech than it once was, but to them, I am nameless and faceless. To them, I'm an operative who gets things done, but not a threat to them. And vice versa. This is protection for us both.

I stroll to my car and take my encrypted laptop out of the trunk. This is technology at its finest, a satellite hookup that, for all intents and purposes, can't be traced and is invisible to all the surface networks. I glance around to make sure no one is watching before climbing inside the car, where I connect to the internet and enter the deep web. A twinge of anticipation tightens my stomach as I wait. It seems to take forever, but I finally get the connection, enter the site, and authenticate my credentials. I have one new message.

I click it to open. There's a new job available. It's mine to accept, if I so choose. The information here is bare bones, a name, an address, and the contract price. I note the details of my new target, and as I do, my heart starts to race. I click to accept, and write down the access key for the dossier. Then I cut the connection. My hands shake, and I start to sweat as I stare at the name I've written on the paper.

Charles Fieldner Jr.

God, that's me!

3

I'm in my home office, my heart pounding, sharp pains in my head, trying to read the dossier, but the kids, Jason and my daughter Emily, are in the next room playing video games with the volume too loud. It's hard to concentrate, and completely surreal, reviewing the details of my life as the cartoon music plays in the background. I wouldn't normally do this while the kids are still up—but I've never had a contract like this before.

I think everyone has thought about killing someone at one time or another. Maybe it's a bitter breakup, or over a business loss or because, for whatever reason, they think their life would be better if a particular person were gone. People might not want to admit it, but I'm betting this is a common fantasy. Usually that's all it is, a fantasy. Most people won't go through with it because they have second thoughts, or they're afraid of getting caught, or they don't know how to find a competent hired killer. While it doesn't surprise me that someone might want me dead, it's a shock they want it badly enough to put up the money and take out a contract. It's ironic that they hired me to kill myself.

The dossier comes as a code-locked computer file on the deep web. I've already run it through the encryption program and scanned the contents. Now I go through it again. It's clear they know more about me than anyone should. The obvious things, my name, address, birth date and education, they have all those right. They have my profession as *consultant*, which is half right, but it's the little things that surprise me. They know I'm left-handed, even though I do nearly everything right-handed. They know my favorite books and music and that I'm allergic to penicillin. They know about the time I went to the casino and lost twenty thousand dollars in an hour of blackjack—something I never even told Jen about.

"That's no fair! You can't do that!"

That's Jason. Emily is almost two years older than him, and in his view, when she's around, most of life is unfair. If this follows the normal pattern, within a minute or so it will be a full-blown fight. If I was in the room I might say something to diffuse the situation, but it's best for the kids to work it out on their own. I have more pressing concerns.

I return to the file and look at the pictures. These disturb me. They are pictures of me, but some are of me with Jen, and the kids. These aren't the grainy clandestine photos I often see in a dossier, the ones taken by a professional with a telephoto lens. These are pictures from past vacations, and candid shots taken when no one else was around. They have one of me dressed in a suit and tie, dancing at a friend's anniversary party, and another where I'm playing with my kids in our back yard. Where did they get these pictures? They must have come from someone with access to my home, or someone who knows me well. Someone close.

"Come on, it's my turn!" Jason's whining is picking up steam.

"No. I get a longer turn because I'm older."

This time it's both of them. The next step will be Jason grabbing for the controller and Emily pulling it back to show her power over him, and it will escalate from there. It's best to end this quickly, both for fairness, and before someone gets hurt. But I can't pull myself away from the computer screen. The pictures are too intimate, too personal. How did they come into the Agency's possession?

And the question enters my mind, not for the first time, who wants me dead? I stare at the pictures. They were taken by someone close to me. Now, that someone could have broken into our home and robbed us, only taking a few personal pictures. Or, maybe someone who worked in our home—a plumber or cleaning lady, maybe—took the pictures and sent them to the Agency. These things are possible, but I learned a long time ago the simplest answer is usually the best one. This means someone who knows me well, a close friend or maybe a family member, gave the pictures to the Agency as part of the contract.

Yelling erupts from the next room, right on schedule.

"Give me that, jerk!"

"No, stupid!"

I don't even have to get up. All I need to do is open the door and call out. But I don't even do that. I sit rooted in my chair and yell at them through the door.

"Emily, Jason, stop it right now!"

They keep arguing. I click on the next picture.

This is a picture of me and Jen on vacation a year ago. We are at a street side café in Madrid, posed together, smiling. I look at the picture of us together and the contrast strikes me. We are an odd couple. Jen is a beautiful woman. I say that not because I'm her husband and I love her, I say it because it's true. She is tall, nearly my height, and slim, but well proportioned. Her hair is a soft blonde, her smile is warm and winning, and her eyes are those of an angel. She could have been a model or an actress—she's got that look. And then there is me. Average. The contrast is striking, and I know that strangers look at us and wonder what she sees in me. And as I look at the picture I wonder the same thing. Does she think she can do better?

My heart races, and I realize I'm afraid. I'm thinking the unthinkable. I push myself out of the chair and stand up. I need to move. I'm breathing hard and my hands are shaking. The kids are still fighting in the next room, yelling, and I throw open the door and charge out. Suddenly, I'm angry. Almost enraged.

"Stop it!" I scream. "Stop it right now!"

As I storm into the room they stop their arguing and freeze, both gripping the game controller. I snatch it away from them and fling it across the room.

"You're acting like animals! Can't you behave?" I'm yelling at the top of my lungs.

I look at their faces and see the fear. I'm not the kind of dad that yells. I've never spanked my kids and I try to deal with them without using threats or fear as a motivator. They've never seen this side of me and it clearly frightens them. But momentum takes over and I'm too far gone to stop.

"You're both grounded! No more TV, no more video games!" I'm shaking my finger at them and waving my hands around, acting like a wild man.

Jason starts crying, and this upsets me more. I grab his hand, rougher than I mean to. He tries to pull away, but I hold on tight.

"Don't be a baby!" I yell in his face.

He cries harder. I'm a monster. And all at once I realize I'm channeling my father. Before I fully stop, Jen is in the room.

"Charley! Let him go right now."

She's not yelling, but the tone is urgent. I do what she says.

She takes Jason's hand and guides him away. He wraps his arms around her. Emily moves close to her, too. Jen looks at me as though she doesn't know me, and maybe she doesn't. I drop my hands and my rage is gone, replaced by an overwhelming sense of guilt. Bile rises to my throat, but I swallow it back. How could I act that way to my kids? How could I even suspect Jen?

"Next time choose a game you can play at the same time," Jen's voice is soft and reassuring. "Let's go kids. It's about bedtime anyway."

"Are we really grounded?" Emily asks.

"We'll talk about that in the morning. Let's go now."

I hang my head as she herds the kids in the direction of their bedrooms. She hangs back a second and moves close to me, glaring.

"What is wrong with you, Charley?"

I don't ... I can't answer. She shakes her head and moves away, following the kids. What's wrong with me? I'm supposed to be the hunter, not the prey, and someone close wants me dead. That's my problem. I need to turn things around. I need to be the hunter again.

4

The temperature at home is suddenly too chilly and I need to find a place to think. I need a drink, but I'm not the drinking type. Instead, I head to the local coffee shop. I wouldn't normally drink coffee this late, but I don't expect to sleep much tonight, anyway.

It's after nine, but the place is hopping. The crowd is mostly college age with a few businessmen on laptops and a middle-aged couple who act as though they're on a date. Piped in music and conversation fill the air, but not in an intrusive way. I order a tall latte and take it to a corner with a clear view of the door.

I've brought along a notebook and a pen, and the first order of business is to start a list. Who could want me dead? I write the number *one* on the first line and next to the number I write, *Jen*. It feels like a gut punch, but I do it without hesitation. The genie is out of the bottle, and I need to fully consider the possibility. I'm not sure why she would want me dead. We have a great marriage, and she is truly the love of my life, but she also has the most to gain if I'm gone. I'm well insured and she would gain a fortune if I die. The pictures point to someone close to me and she is as close as it gets.

I mark a *two* on the next line and write *George Lansing*. George was the best man at my wedding, my closest friend, and I've known him for years. Maybe I know him too well. We see George regularly and he has been in my house too many times to count. I know he's cheated on his wife, and I know he has had fairly serious money problems. He asked me for a loan recently. and though I've given him money before, this time I turned him down. He's the type to hold a grudge, but would he really put out a contract on me? Maybe.

I write a *three* on the next line, but then I have to think. Who else would want me dead? Brendan Kelly, maybe. At least he did at one time. Kelly was a bully and a big thug of a football player who thought he would have some fun at my expense. I broke his nose, leaving him crying on the floor and gurgling blood as all his friends looked on in shock. I caught hell from my dad for showing my skills and, after the incident, I made it a point to avoid calling attention to myself from then on. Okay, Kelly wanted me dead, but that was way back in high school and I hadn't even thought of him in years. Besides, he wasn't close to me in any way, so he couldn't have taken the photos.

I look at the number three on the paper and try to think of anyone else who might fit the bill. There are plenty of people who had access to our pictures or were at least in the house and could have taken them. Jen is social, and with two young kids, people are in and out of the house all the time—neighbors, my kid's friend's parents, Jen's friends—too many people. The photo albums are in plain sight. It would be possible for most anyone to slip some pictures out without anyone knowing. So, in a way it could be almost anyone.

I look at the paper again and without even thinking, next to the number three I write a name: Dad. There it is. His name should have been first on the list with a star. Does he fit the bill? Yes. Not only is he close, but he knows all about the Agency and how to set up a contract, so there was that. But does he really want to kill me? I'm not sure, but he'd tried it once before. So, I guess the answer is *yes*. I love my dad, but I can't think of a time when I was younger when I wasn't afraid of him. Not so much now, but as a leopard can't change his spots, he remains who he is, no matter his current condition.

I add a few more names to my list. I write down my sister Beth, as she is close, but I can't think of a motive for her. I also add Jen's brother, Adam. He has a temper and we've argued over little things, but this doesn't seem right. I'm grasping here. I write down her parents, too, and I know I'm reaching.

I'm not sure if it's because of the coffee or my suspicions, but I'm suddenly shaky, and my stomach is uneasy. I glance over my shoulder and scan the room. All these years I've been the hunter, and now I see things from the other perspective. Did any of my targets know they were on a list? Did they feel paranoid, thinking someone was out to get them? Did those around them scoff at the claims and tell them they were crazy? Or did they feel they were in control of their lives and didn't see their reality until the last instant when it was too late, and they knew they were going to die?

Across the room, a man is sitting in a chair, reading a book. He is big and rough looking with a shaved head and a broken nose—a casting director's idea of what hired muscle should look like. He seems out of place here in this coffee shop. He is holding the book in front of his face, but it doesn't look like he's reading it as much as using it as a shield. He reminds me of a gorilla pretending to read. Is it my imagination, or has he been watching me?

When I look at the man he buries his head deeper in the book and doesn't look up. A thought occurs to me, could there be more than one contract on me? I know there were times where I was brought in after someone else had failed. Could I be the backup on my own hit? Fear tickles the back of my neck and my stomach tightens into a knot. I take another sip of coffee and look down at my paper. I can't show alarm or act any other way than normal. If the man is here to take me out, it will be when I leave the shop, out in the dark of the parking lot when no one is looking, and no one will notice. It's how I would do it.

I take a breath. Am I'm reading too much into this? The man looks out of place, but it doesn't mean he is here because of me, and it certainly doesn't mean he is a hired killer. My imagination is getting away from me. If I want to solve this problem I need to calm down and keep my focus. I stare at the paper again and try to concentrate. The man isn't a threat here in the coffee shop. Getting worked up about it won't do me any good. I pick up my pen again, but my mind is buzzing and I can't even think. I glance up again and the big man is staring right at me. Our eyes lock for a moment. He knows I'm on to him. He quickly breaks the gaze and covers his face with the book again. My heart thumps like the kettle drum in a marching band.

What can I do? I fight the urge to walk over and kick the big gorilla's face in. Killing a man in public, in a crowded room in my own home town, may keep me alive for tonight, but it isn't a good long-term move. I can leave now and take the action out to the parking lot. Knowing he is after me will give me an advantage, and it might be my best option. Before I can act, the big man stands up, leaves his book on the table and quickly heads for the door.

My mind is racing, but I'm slow to react. Does he know he is compromised? The man was clearly here to keep tabs on me, at the least, but he was too easy to spot and got too flustered when I spotted him. He is clearly not a professional. But who is he?

I jump up and head for the door, too.

It takes me a second to adjust to the darkness as I step outside the coffee shop and into the shadows to avoid making myself to big a target. He's been gone less than a minute, but I don't see him right away. He could be around the corner in the parking lot, in his car, or hidden somewhere, lying in wait. I scan the front parking lot, but it's quiet. There are a few cars, but no one is around. Hugging the shadows, I creep toward the rear parking lot. He could be hiding in the bushes or between parked cars. He has a slight advantage on me, because he's had time to hide. But I'm in hunter mode and it gives me the edge. As I walk I'm tuned in to any sound or movement, but I see nothing and sense nothing. I reach the back of the lot and spin around. How could he have disappeared so quickly? As if in answer, an engine fires up in the lot next door.

I run toward the sound, hopping over a low hedge that separates the coffee shop from the bank next store. As I round the corner, a green Toyota pulls out of the lot and onto the street, tires squealing as it roars away. I ball my hands together tight and try to slow my breathing.

Who wants me dead?

5

I don't sleep well, and I'm up early in the morning. I make coffee and breakfast for the family and try to put on my happy face. My outburst last night is forgotten or at least, unmentioned. I tell my goofy jokes and pretend everything is okay, but the truth is, I'm reeling inside. I keep thinking about the pictures and wondering how they got in the file. Who can I trust? I kiss my wife tenderly. I show my kids love and affection, and I race from the house as quickly as I can.

In the car, my hands shake against the steering wheel. As a rule, I'm all about control. I plan everything. I know everything there is to know before I make a move. This is how I am, whether it's going to see a movie, or planning my next job. Control is an illusion, I know this. I think back to how I botched the Silverman job, and how disastrous that could have been. Still, I do what I can to maintain control, but now I'm at sea in an open boat. The waves take me where they will, and I'm adrift.

Who wants me dead?

It's still early, but I need to do something. I speak George's name on my Bluetooth and dial him up. I know he won't answer this early, but I call anyway. When the voicemail kicks in, I leave a message asking if he is free for lunch. I hang up, and drive, heading west, away from the morning traffic.

I drive aimlessly, lost in my thoughts. The traffic is light as I head out of Naperville and the western suburbs into what used to be the country. Only there is no country anymore. Everything has built up. Subdivisions and strip malls sit where farmers used to grow corn and soybean. Now the sprawl extends out further and further. Traffic going in toward the city is heavy. Heading west, I have an open road.

I try to clear my mind and consider my options. Last night, I accepted the contract, which buys me time. I have almost two weeks to finish the job. At the end of two weeks, if the deed isn't done, the agency will turn over the contract to someone else. I think this through. Even if I find the person who put out the contract and get this reversed, the Agency now has my name.

Who has the motive to want me dead? And, as I think of it, the list lengthens. It could be most anyone I know. Humans are a violent and petty species. People kill for love or money, out of anger, as revenge for past slights, and sometimes just because someone thinks their life will be better if a person isn't around anymore. People lash out for the silliest reasons. I could have been targeted for most anything by most anyone. I think this, but I immediately know it isn't true. We might have thoughts of violence regularly, but they're only thoughts. Most people don't act on their whims. Someone went to a lot of trouble to put the target on my back, and there is no getting around it.

I have been driving for a long while now, and I suddenly realize the sprawl has cleared away. I'm out in the country now, with fields of corn on either side. The road is clear and I'm driving fast. As I follow the curve of the road, a town appears in front of me. The green sign at the edge of town tells me this is Holton, Illinois, population 8,384. I slow down to the speed limit and keep both hands on the wheel. I pass a John Deere dealership and a seed store. I'm not that far out from the suburbs, but this is a whole different way of life here. I stop at a red light across from a small high school. On the wall there's a mural of the school's mascot, a cartoon hornet, angry-looking with an exaggerated stinger. With a start, I realize I've seen this before. My heart beats a little faster as the light turns green. I follow the road and it leads past small frame homes on the side of the road, into the downtown business district.

I park in one of the many empty spots and look around. This is an old town along a river, and it's hilly here. The business district is only a few blocks long, and there is a bank, a diner, an accountant's office and a whole lot of empty storefronts. There's a big brick building, a brew pub, that looks like it has been sandblasted to look new and old at the same time. But that's the only sign of new life in the town. Everything else is old and faded. A water tower above me is painted with the town's name and that Hornet mascot. Now I know it, I *have* been here before.

The memory floods back. I'm five or six years old and out for an afternoon with Dad. It's always a special treat to be with him, and we talk and play little games in the car as we go. We have a contest and we're counting cars. I count red cars and he is counting blue to see who can find the most. We talk about baseball cards and monster movies. We laugh, and I'm happy. We come into town, and Dad turns the engine off and looks me in the eyes.

"Charley, I have to do something here, and I need your help. OK?"

I nod but say nothing.

"This is important. I need you to do exactly what I say. You need to be a good boy here. Can I count on you?"

"Yes, Dad."

"You have to be very quiet. This is an adult thing, and I need you to be quiet, and not say a word. If you're good, we'll go get ice cream afterwards."

"The kind with the flavors?"

"Sure, you can get any flavor you want. Let's go, and remember, be extra good."

We get out of the car, and that's when I notice the water tower. That hornet is big and angry, bright yellow and jet black, and it scares me. I was stung by a bee once, and I know how much that hurt. I stare up at the water tower and I'm afraid of that hornet, thinking it might fly down and sting me, even though I know it's not real. Dad takes hold of my hand and we move on down the sidewalk. We enter one of the storefronts, and it's an office of some sort. There is a counter at the front and a few chairs for people to sit in. The place is old and dusty.

No one is at the front counter, and Dad calls out a greeting. I look around and notice a poster on the wall, it's a shiny red car with a woman standing in front of it. I walk over and look at it closely. I like the car. It looks fast, even while it's sitting still. Dad calls out again, and a toilet flushes. A voice calls from the back of the store, and after a minute a big fat man comes out and greets Dad. They talk. This is grown up stuff and I'm not paying a lot of attention. Dad introduces himself, but he doesn't say his real name. He puts his hand on my shoulder and introduces me too. I nod but don't say anything. I promised to be good, so I don't say a word. The man is friendly and offers Dad coffee and leads us to the back of the store. We pass an open door to a bathroom and it smells really bad. I hold my breath as we go past it, into the fat man's office.

Dad sits in a chair and the fat man sits behind his desk. I sit in another chair and try to stay still. There is a small model car on the man's desk, the same car as in the picture. I want to pick it up and play with it, but I sit on my hands. I promised to be good.

Then, Dad spills his coffee on the man's desk. They both jump up and Dad apologizes. The man moves his papers away from the stream of coffee spreading across the desk. Dad tells me to go to the bathroom to get some paper towels.

I get up to go, but I don't want to go in that bathroom. It smells awful. I walk out of the room and I take a big breath and hold it as I walk into the small bathroom. I look around for the paper towels and there is a big stack of them on the counter. As I grab a bunch of them, I hear a noise from the other room. A thud, then a gasp, and more thudding. I grab the paper towels and hurry out. I take a big gulp of fresh air as I step out of the bathroom. I stop in the doorway to the office. Dad is on the other side of the desk, behind the fat man, with his arm locked around his neck. The fat man's eyes are bulging, and his mouth is open like he's trying to talk, but he can't make a sound.

"Turn around, Charley. Don't look!" My dad calls out, as he continues to squeeze.

I spin around. I'm not sure what to do with the paper towels so I squeeze them tight. I'm scared again, but I try and think about ice cream, and what flavor I'll pick. I always like the pink one, peppermint, but lemon custard is one of my favorites, too. There is more thudding as the man kicks against the ground and struggles. I want to turn around and look, but I have to be good. I stare out in front of me and think about ice cream. And then, everything is quiet. The only sound is Dad's heavy breathing.

"It's okay, Charley, you can turn around now, and please bring me those paper towels."

I turn, and Dad is standing, still breathing hard. The man is back in his chair, slumped over with his head on the desk. Dad takes the paper towels from me and starts to wipe things down.

"He was a bad man, Charley. A very bad man. He had it coming," Dad looks up at me. "Do you understand, son?"

"Yes, Dad," I say. I don't feel well, and my stomach is turning, but I try not to show it.

"This is our secret. OK, Charley boy?"

I nod. The man is slumped over in his chair and I wonder what he is thinking now.

"You can't tell anyone about this. Ever," Dad said. "You understand?"

I nod again. "Yes, Dad."

"Good. Let's get out of here and go get that ice cream."

Dad finishes wiping things with the paper towels and heads out of the room. I grab the toy car from the desk and put it my jacket pocket before I follow.

I snap out of the past and am back in the present. I pant and my heart races as I look around me. This is the same town, but I can't tell which storefront it was. They all look the same. I shake my head at the audacity of my father's actions at the time. What if someone had come in? What if someone saw us and noticed our license plate or the make and model of the car? It all seems needlessly risky to me now. I try and think back. It was the first time, I'm sure. Or, maybe, it was the first time I realized what was going on, and what my dad was doing. It had been an initiation of sorts, and as time went on, I became more of an active participant and partner. This was our secret.

The sun is higher in the sky, and without looking at my watch, I can tell it's mid-morning. I suddenly feel tired. The weight of the past lies heavy on my shoulders. I still don't know what to do, but I do want to get out of this town and head away. I stare up at the hornet again and I just want to get away from here.

My phone rings and I check the screen ID. It's George.

6

George is already seated when I reach the restaurant. It's an old steakhouse near Schaumburg, oak paneling, red trim and lots of leather. It's masculine, dark and very old-school, the kind of place people go when they are on an expense account and want to impress a client. It's not the kind of place I normally eat at, but this wasn't my choice. The hostess weaves through the room as she leads me to George's booth, back in the corner.

He is on the phone when I arrive, and he keeps talking, even as he stands up and gives me a hug, pulling me in tight with one arm. George is a big man. He stands over six two, with broad shoulders and a large frame. He is thicker around the middle than he used to be, but still looks trim in his suit. George is handsome. With his full, dark hair and strong features, he looks like someone you would trust. He's the type who'd play the heroic fireman, or the battling district attorney on TV. I release the hug and take a seat in the other side of the booth.

"Yeah, Bobby. I know," George says into the phone. "That's got to be tough for you."

I take a sip of water and settle in. I'm still trying to figure out what

I feel, and what I can accomplish here. George is like a brother to me. I have known him since my college days, and he has seen me in good times and bad. I have my secrets, of course, but George knows more about me than most anyone else. He doesn't know what I do, of course, but we have been in situations, and he knows what I'm capable of doing. I know loads about George too.

Still, how much can I trust him?

"Listen, Bob. I feel for you. I really do, but you need to make a decision. If this isn't for you, tell me, and I'll give it to someone else. I don't want to make you do something you're not comfortable with."

George falls silent as the voice on the other line starts to talk. George smiles and takes a drink from his glass. It's brown and on the rocks, and I know he is drinking scotch. He listens for a minute without saying a word. With his eyes, he clues me in that the guy is a talker. I smile back and wait. At length, George finishes his conversation and puts his phone down on the table.

"Sorry," he says with a smile. "Some people don't know what's best for them."

I nod and keep the smile plastered to my face.

"Listen," I say. "I've been thinking. About the money, I was wrong to—"

"No," George interrupts me. "We're good. I don't need it."

"I just wanted to—"

"Seriously," George breaks in again. "It's all good. I don't need it." He looks at the water glass in front of me and scowls. As if on cue, the young waitress arrives, order pad in hand.

"Get this man a drink," George says.

"Not today," I reply. "I have some things to do this afternoon."

"Me too, but I'm celebrating. I need you to celebrate with me."

He says this with conviction, and I nod slowly.

"Ok. I'll have a gin and tonic," I tell the waitress. "Tanqueray is fine."

The waitress is young and cute with long dark hair. She looks like an athlete, maybe a gymnast. She marks the order down and hurries away. George follows her with his eyes but doesn't say a thing.

"Celebrating?" I ask. "What's up?"

"You know how I was telling you about that union pension fund? It's official, they sent over the authorization and wired in funds the other day. They're switching everything over to me. This will almost triple my funds under management. I'm going to need to hire people to keep up with this. This is huge."

A genuine wave of relief flows over me. "That is great news! Congratulations, you've been working on that for a long time."

"Tell me about it, brother. I made the first contact over four years ago. And they signed the contract at just the right time. I have to tell you, things were getting tight."

"Well, that is great news. You deserve it. I know how hard you worked for this." I'm genuinely happy as I say this. George is close to me and I'm excited for his good fortune. But it's more than that. If George has money coming in, he shouldn't hold anything against me, I think. I can trust my best friend.

The waitress returns with the drink in hand and sets it in front of me. She asks if we are ready to order. I haven't even glanced at the menu. George takes charge.

"Yes, we are ready to order," George says. "Bring us some shrimp cocktails to start with, and then we each want your biggest steak—"

'No," I protest. "I'm really not that hungry."

"The porterhouses," George ignores my interruption and keeps going. I'll have mine bloody rare."

She looks to me. I shrug and tell her to make mine medium. George orders a few side dishes, more food than we can possibly eat, and another scotch.

After she is gone, he leans back with a sigh of relief. "I got to say. This feels good. I was planning to call you today, I'm glad we could get together. This feels like a huge weight has been lifted. I can breathe again."

I nod and smile. But I feel my own weight now.

"I mean, I would have made it through, but Christine's been acting crazy lately. You would not believe how she spends money."

This is a recurring topic when we talk. Christine, George's wife, grew up on the North Shore and her family came from old money. She grew up having the latest and best of everything. George launches in on a story of how she recently bought over $18,000 of designer clothes while out shopping with friends and made a big pledge to a local charity. George does well and has always made good money, but he also lives the high life. This new money may not be enough.

The waitress arrives with George's scotch. He orders another drink before even taking a sip of this one.

"Come on, Charley. Drink up, we're celebrating. You're already behind."

I sip my gin and tonic. How far behind him am I? Is this his second, or third?

He finishes the story, giving it a twist so it's funny, while showing the troubles he goes through with his wife. I like Christine. She is smart, pretty, and a good mom. She was a big spender from the beginning, though. George knew what he was getting into long before they were married.

"You are lucky, my brother." George raises his glass in a toast. "You have the perfect spouse."

I raise my glass to his toast. I've always thought that was true, but my gut tightens and now I'm not so sure. I may be jumping to conclusions, and Jen has given me no reason to suspect her, but I can't help the way I feel.

"Seriously, man. I envy you. I wish I had what you have."

I look into George's eyes and see he is sincere. It is heartfelt, and I know what he is saying. But I can't tell if he is happy for me and wishes his marriage was like mine, or if he truly means he wants what I have. Again, my stomach churns.

The waitress returns with the shrimp cocktails, the shrimp so big this could be a meal in itself. It feels decadent to be eating this for lunch. The waitress sets George's new drink down, and she is right on time as he has just finished the last one.

"And bring my friend another, too," George orders.

"No, not yet," I say. I haven't taken more than a few sips of the drink I have. The girl hurries away before George can make it a bigger deal or order another one for himself. George likes to party, but he doesn't usually drink so heavily during the day. Is this really all about celebrating, or is something else going on?

"Hey, do you remember that time when we were down in Key West and we rented that boat?"

"Yeah," I laugh as I think back. "How could I forget? You were Captain George and you convinced them you had your own boat and had been sailing for years. Neither one of us had ever sailed before. I was sure we were going to sink. I kept looking for sharks in the water and couldn't decide whether we were going to drown or be eaten by the sharks, first."

"I was on my knees and praying. I was sure we were going to die when that old fishing boat came by and towed us in."

I relax as we laugh. This kicks into a round of stories about our past adventures. These are all from long ago. Our lives are different now. I'm happy and have almost forgotten my troubles when the waitress returns with platters of food. She sets the massive steaks in front of us, and the sides fill up most of our table. George orders another drink and I do the same.

We dig in and eat, concentrating on our food. The steak is juicy and primally satisfying. Jen cooks healthy meals and has cut down our red meat to once or twice a week. I feel like a caveman as I chew on the delicious steak. It's great to be with George. He is a good man and a close friend. We are truly like brothers and I don't know how I could have ever suspected him.

"Listen," George says between mouthfuls of food. "We need to take a trip again. A boy's trip. No wives, no kids, just us. We can get out and go wild, like in the old days. What do you say?"

I nod. It's appealing. We had fun in our single days, and we made a good pair. I can't imagine doing it now though. My family is my focus, and I wouldn't want to leave them, even for a long weekend. This is only talk—an escape valve for George.

We eat more and drink more. I'm on my third gin when I put my fork down. I've got a buzz and George is at least two drinks ahead of me. He is a big guy and he can hold his liquor, but the cadence of his speech is a little slower and more deliberate than before. I think he is a little drunk.

"Hey," I ask, on impulse. "Can you think of anyone who'd want me dead?"

"What?" George sets down his drink and stares at me. "Is this a joke?"

"No. Well, yeah, sort of," I say, aiming for nonchalance. "I'm just wondering if you can think of anyone."

"That's a ridiculous question. It's plain goofy," George takes another sip and sets his glass back down. "But let me think."

He stares at me as he ponders. What he is thinking? Is he trying to come up with a good answer, or is he trying to hide his anxiety that I confronted him with this? He seems calm and wears a slight smile. I wonder why I even asked him. It's the alcohol, I think. That, and the fact the question keeps popping up in my mind, no matter how much I try not to think about it. George has nearly finished the meat in front of him, while I still have a big slab left. I'm uncomfortably full. George takes his time thinking, then takes another big gulp of his drink and nods emphatically.

"I've got it!" George says confidently. "Jen has a secret lover and wants you out of the picture, right?"

My breath catches in my throat. I am flushed and dizzy.

George laughs. A big belly laugh, and I can't think of anything that is funny about this situation.

"Come on, brother," he laughs again. "That is the stupidest question I've ever heard. Who would want to hurt you? You're a good guy, a family man. You're too damned boring to make any enemies. That's why we need to get out and cut loose again. We need to go have some adventures and add a little risk to our lives." He laughs again. "God, what a question."

I try and laugh with him. I say it was an idle thought. I smile and try to act normal, but inside, I'm still shaking.

George looks at his watch and shakes his head. "Damn, I've got to get back. I've got a conference call in half an hour, and I'm doing a big presentation at the union hall in a couple of nights. Lots to do for that."

We signal the waitress over and George pays the bill, ignoring my attempts to split it or even pick up the tip. The leftovers on the table are enough to feed a starving family for a week.

At the door, we hug again.

"Thanks," I say. "This was great. Congratulations again on your deal."

"Thanks for celebrating with me, brother. And take care of that beautiful wife of yours," He laughs again. "If something were to happen to you, I know I'd be first in line to take your place."

I smile, but this isn't funny. As George walks toward his office across the parking lot, I wonder if he is only joking. I'm not buzzed anymore. The adrenaline has kicked in and I want to hit someone.

7

I leave the restaurant feeling unsettled. Jen loves me. I know she does. But everybody keeps secrets, as I know all too well. Could she be hiding something from me? I think of us as the perfect family and Jen as a model wife. I'm a good provider and an attentive husband. Perhaps she craves more. She was adventurous when we first met. Am I enough for her now? I pull onto the highway and head north, light-headed and anxious.

I try and push the thoughts of Jen from my mind. I'm questioning everything now, but the simplest answer is usually the right one. I have been avoiding thinking about it, but I know I must see Dad. He has the most opportunity and, being who he is, he doesn't need any true motive.

I head north.

In my side mirror, I spot a green Toyota a few cars back. It looks the same as the car that pulled out of the coffee shop last night. My pulse quickens. Am I being followed? I slow down and pull into the right lane. The Toyota passes me, and I see it's a middle-aged black man driving. He doesn't even glance at me as he passes. He is not the man I saw before. I shake my head. I'm getting paranoid, seeing danger everywhere. Without focus, I can't be effective. I take a deep breath and concentrate on my immediate problem. Dad is the key. He has to be.

Meadowbrook Manor is right off the expressway, across from a Public Storage facility and a Wendy's hamburger joint. The name conjures up images of an English countryside, but this is in the heart of the suburbs, and the traffic buzzes by as I park my car. The location isn't peaceful, but this is a top-rated facility and my sister, Beth and I. picked it because it specializes in patients with Alzheimer's and in need of long-term care.

Brightly colored flowers, red, yellow and purple, line the front walk. The strip of grass is a vibrant green. I recall the last time I visited and realize it has been a while. There was snow on the ground at the time, and I guess it was near Christmas. I know I'm not a good son to avoid him, but he wasn't the best father, either.

I walk through the doors, stop at the front desk, and give my name to the young girl behind the counter. She hands me a pass and buzzes me in through the facility's double security doors. The setup here reminds me of a low security prison. They aren't as worried about people coming in as having someone walk out. I take the elevator to the third floor and check in at the desk. They tell me Dad is in the common area with the other residents, so I go down the hall to find him.

The common area is made up like a big living room. There are couches and chairs around the edges of the room and a big TV against one wall. The TV is on and an old musical is playing, the sound blaring. I don't know which one this is, but the actors on the screen are dressed as cowboys and cowgirls, dancing and singing in Technicolor glory. The song sounds familiar. The chairs and couches are mostly filled. The residents—that's what they call them, not patients—are old, white haired, and most look frail. Most of them stare at the TV, blank eyed and not taking it in. One lady with short hair that looks like silver straw, is staring at me. A big smile creases her face. As my eyes connect with hers, the smile grows bigger.

"Hello, Donnie," she says. "I knew you would come."

I smile back and shake my head. I look past her. Dad is over by the window. He's not watching the TV. He's standing straight, staring outside at the street below. I walk in front of the TV, past the other residents toward the window.

"Donnie?" the lady behind me calls, but I don't stop to tell her she is mistaken.

At the window, I put my hand on Dad's shoulder. He turns with a start. Most of the other old people here look stooped and frail, but dad still has some life in him. He is old, I know. He was nearly forty when I was born, and I'm nearly that old now. His hair is thin and silver gray, but he stands straight and is still slim and wiry. Spry was the term the nurses used when I saw him last time. I squeeze his shoulder and he turns away from the window. He looks into my eyes but doesn't seem to register any connection. The lights are on, but no one is home.

"Hi, Dad. How are you today?"

He looks at me for a second without saying anything, and then turns back to the window.

One of the attendants, young and perky, dressed in a green smock, comes over from the other side, a big smile on her face.

"Hi," she says. "I'm Missy. Charles likes to look outside. He does it a lot."

I'm thankful for the interruption. He's my dad, but I don't know how to relate to him. Not now. Maybe I never have.

"Hi," I say. "I'm Charley, his son."

"I know," Missy says. "I've seen your picture. Charles is one of my favorites. He is such a sweet guy."

This throws me. I've never thought of my dad as sweet. I think of his temper when he was younger. I think of what he has done and who he was. He is different now, and he has changed since coming here. But I still can't imagine him being sweet in any way. Perhaps this is what it's like to see a bear at the zoo and think of how cute it is, but not realizing that the bear would happily rip you apart if the bars were removed.

"There's too much activity here. Maybe you'd like to visit with your dad in his room?"

I nod and agree. Missy takes Dad by the elbow and leads him from the window. "Let's go, Charles, back to your room for a nice visit. Your son Charley is here. Isn't that exciting?"

Dad looks up as he starts to walk with her and seems to see me for the first time. "Are we going home?" he asks.

"This is your home," Missy says. "You live here, Charles."

I follow as she leads him out past the other residents and down a hallway. The air smells like flowers and Clorox. The music swells in the background, and I remember the name of the musical, Oklahoma. One of mom's favorites.

We reach a door with an old picture taped to it of my dad and my mom, both young and happy, and dressed for a night on the town. This is a fantasy. I don't remember them this way at all.

Missy leads us into Dad's small room. There is a bed with a night stand, a big chair and a small TV in front of it. Dad goes toward the big chair and I sit on the edge of his bed.

"Isn't it nice that your son is visiting, Charles?" Missy helps Dad settle into the chair. She talks to him like he is a four-year-old with a hearing problem. She turns to me. "Let me know if you need anything. I'll be right down the hall."

Missy smiles and bustles from the room.

Alone with Dad, we sit in silence. I look at him and try to divine the mysteries inside his head. Is he really the blank slate he seems to be, or is something more going on below the surface? What does he remember? Is he aware of what he did in his life? Does he have any regrets?

"How are you, Dad?"

He looks away from the blank TV and stares at me. For a moment, I think I see a flicker of recognition and eyes go wide. But the flicker is just that, and his eyes glaze over again. I'd come here seeing him as a suspect, but it isn't possible. He's an empty shell. He can hardly feed himself or go to the bathroom on his own. How could I suspect him?

"You're looking good," I add, wanting to say something. "They are taking good care of you here."

Dad stares at the blank TV. Is he looking at a blank screen, or does he see something in his mind? Is he thinking of the past? I wonder if somewhere inside he remembers who I am and how we are connected? I lean forward and put my hand on his shoulder.

"Dad," I say. "I don't know if you remember me, but it's me, Charley. Your son."

He keeps his eyes on the blank screen, but he is breathing harder now, and I think he is listening to me.

"I need your help, Dad," I say. "I'm in trouble. Someone's out to get me. Do you know anything about this?"

He doesn't look at me, but his breathing is heavier still.

"Do you know anyone who'd want to kill me?" I continue. His eyes are wider, and his breath is fast, still he doesn't look at me. I know I've upset him, but I can't get through.

"The Agency, Dad," I say, urgent, but keeping my voice to a whisper. "How did you start working with them? Do you know who they really are? Back in the old days, how did you get in touch with them?"

Still nothing. My heart beats faster, I have worked myself into a state. He is upset because he is mirroring me. He felt my emotions and sensed my fear. I take my hand off his shoulder and lean back.

I take a deep breath to calm myself and look around the room. He has a couple of books on a shelf, though I never remember him reading. There are pictures from the old house on the walls, calming landscapes my mother had in their bedroom—a tie to his old life. On the bed stand, several photos are lined up in small standup frames. There is an old picture of my parents with a river in the background. They are young and happy, smiling and holding each other. Next to this is a family portrait of Beth and her family, her husband Mike, and their two young girls. It looks recent. I look closer. There's a sign in the background for a magic show. This was from a recent trip they took to the Wisconsin Dells. Another picture stands next to that. This one's of me and my family. Also, a recent picture. Beth must have brought them. I talk with my sister regularly, but I'm surprised these pictures are here. I don't know why, but I'm surprised she has seen him recently.

I'm lost in thought when Dad makes a sound. Almost a moan. I turn toward him, concerned he is in pain, that something is happening to him. His arms are shaking, and he's nodding vehemently. I stand and move in front of him. I put my hands on his shoulders and look into his eyes.

"Dad, are you okay?"

He doesn't look at me, but his whole body is tense, and he is shaking.

"Dad, should I get someone? Are you going to be alright?"

He looks up at me and, for the first time, our eyes connect, and I see him. The real him.

"They're going to get you," he mumbles. "They're going to get you."

"It's okay, Dad. I just needed to know if you knew anything about this."

"They're going to get you." He is louder now, staring into my eyes with a fierce look. A shudder vibrates up through his shoulders. It's like I've reanimated a ghost and he is back here with me.

"They're going to get you!"

He is shouting now, angry and upset. Is it really him? Or is he just parroting back what I said. I'm tense and not sure what to do.

"Dad, please—"

He shouts it again, over and over. I try to comfort him, but he is looking through me now. The life I saw was there for a moment, and now it's gone. I can't get him to stop shouting.

I hear movement behind me, and Missy breezes into the room.

"Hi Charles, it's all right." She is soothing and soft as she comes to his side. "It's been a busy day. You need a rest now, don't you?"

I move back, not sure what to do.

"Why don't you wait outside for a minute, Mr. Fieldner? This happens sometimes when he gets overstimulated."

I nod and race out of the room like I'm escaping from a crime scene. My breath catches in the back of my throat and I'm guilty for upsetting him. I wait in the hallway and listen to the sounds in the room. Dad gradually calms down as Missy keeps up a one-sided conversation in her soothing voice. I'm not sure why I came here. I get upset every time I see him. I can't deal with him the way he is, but I couldn't deal with him the way he was before, either. I clasp my hands together as I realize that I'm shaking. I can't wait to get out of this place.

Dad has stopped yelling or even talking and it's quiet inside the room. Missy finally comes back out into the hall. She smiles at me and nods down the hallway. We walk away from the room.

"He has nightmares sometimes," she says. "That's the first time he's been that way during the day."

Nightmares. Another thing we share.

"I'll mention it to Beth when she comes this week."

This surprises me too. "Beth?" I say. "She'll be here this week?"

"Yes, she comes regularly. She's here every week."

I nod, and Missy continues talking as she walks me to the elevator. She talks, but I'm not listening. What else don't I know? I want to talk with Beth, but I need to think more first. I'm suffocating in here, and I need to get out.

8

I walk out the front doors of the facility and breathe in deeply. The cars buzz by on the road next to me. I'm sucking in soot and car exhaust, but it feels like freedom. I'm glad to be outside and away from Dad. I want to talk with Beth. She's twelve years younger than me, and her relationship with Dad is different than mine. Though she is a grown woman with a family of her own, I still think of her as an innocent little girl. I've always thought of myself as her protector, keeping her from Dad's dark side. I want to find out what she really knows, but I need to see her and be with her while we talk. Not today, but soon. The buzz from my earlier drinks with George has long since dissipated. I take another deep breath and climb back in my car and drive.

I have much yet to do. It's late afternoon and I still have several hours before I need to be home for Emily's soccer practice. I head back toward Naperville and turn into my office complex along the way. I have an office here, though I don't use it much. It's a place to go to, a front, if you like. It's shared space and I fit in with the manufacturer's reps and salesmen in the nearby offices.

The receptionist, Tracy, greets me by name as I walk through the door and asks if I need anything. I thank her as I pass and turn a corner to the door marked—Global Outreach Consulting. That's me. My door is thicker than the others and I had special security locks installed, though I keep nothing of value inside.

I open the door, lock it behind me, and take in the space. The room is small, but comfortable and well lit. I have some filing cabinets stacked up by the outside window, all empty. I have my desk and leather chair, with a couple of upholstered chairs in front for clients who never show up. On the desk, I have a brass plate with my name and title engraved, and a business card holder with the cards I placed there years before. No one comes to the office and very little work gets done here. Still, I visit here at least once a week. Mostly to get out of the house, but it does have fast and secure internet. It's my safe place. I power up my laptop, sit behind the desk, and get to work.

The internet is an amazing thing. It has changed our lives in so many ways. I have research to do, and I know I could start with Google or Facebook, but this will only tell me what I already know. I navigate to the deep web, the dark side of the internet—a world most people don't know about. It's in the code below the surface web, and it's not indexed by search engines. Here, it's an open bazaar. You can buy illegal drugs, weapons, or the worst kinds of porn. You can buy fake IDs and stolen credit cards, or recruit for your terrorist organization. The Agency is here, selling my services.

There's a world of information here on the deep web. There are data bases and tools to trace down anyone. You can find most anything here, and if I had the time and patience I could find a lot here on my own. But I don't have enough of either. On the surface web you can pay for a background check and a few days later, you will receive a file showing all the known details of the person you are looking at. Their age and employment history, credit rating and public records. You can find out whether they have a criminal record. I need to go deeper. I use a proxy address, so I can't be traced, and traverse to a site I have used before—an information broker that works on a much deeper level.

We think we are safe and that our lives are private. But privacy is an illusion. Marketing and insurance companies have data on everyone. But this is the tip of a massive iceberg of information. Nearly everything we do is tracked somewhere. There is a record of where we go what we do and who we do it with. Your movements are tracked by the GPS in your car and on your phone. Your credit card activities, and the sites you visit on the internet are all monitored and recorded. So much more is visible if you know where to look and know how to piece the information together. I enter the site and enter a secure code. I key in the name of my first target, *Jen*. After entering the basic information about her, her date of birth, address, social security number, cell phone and email address, I upload an encrypted picture of her face. When I'm done, I upload the file and repeat the process with the other main suspects on my list: George, my Dad, and Beth. I pay a hefty price in Bitcoin to rush the information for a rapid delivery.

When I'm done, I sign off and shut my laptop. Although the air conditioning is blowing frigid air, I'm melting. I feel dirty and want to wash my hands. I have broken a trust here. We all need to have our own secrets, and I'm peering into the lives of the people closest to me. It's a betrayal, but someone betrayed me and I hope this will tell me who. I sit silently and think.

The truth is, I have considered quitting. Even before Silverman, but more seriously now. I have enough money saved to stop working and build a new life. I can buy a franchise yogurt shop or invest in a car wash. I can stop killing people. I can stop the lying and live an authentic life. I think this, but have a hard time believing it's truly possible. Change is hard, and I am who I am. But maybe this time it will be different. Once I find out who placed the hit and stop it, I will make a clean break and move on.

Maybe.

I gather up my things, turn off the lights, and step outside. I'm locking my office when I hear my name called.

"Charley, hey, how are you? Do you have a minute?"

It's Brent Bingham, and he is standing in the doorway of the office across the hall. I paste a smile on my face as I turn to greet him. Brent is about my age, and he sells medical records software. I run into him regularly and mostly we just smile and wave, though we have shared some conversations over coffee in our common office area. He has kids about my age and is a pleasant guy, but I know him as well as I want to know him.

"Hi, Brent," I say. "What's up?"

"The usual. If I had a clone I might be able to keep up. Very busy."

I nod and smile, not wanting to encourage him.

"Hey," he says. "There is something I've been meaning to tell you. I ran into this guy recently, and he was asking about you."

"Someone was asking about me?" My breath catches.

"Yeah, I didn't think about it at the time, but afterwards, it seemed a little strange. I was on my way into the building a week or so ago, and this guy came up to me and asked if I could help him. He was looking for an office and it wasn't listed on the directory. So, I told him there were a lot of companies working out of shared suites, and they weren't listed on the directory. That's when he mentioned your name."

"What did you say?"

"Well, nothing really. I told him that, yeah, you had an office here and you came by, but not all the time. I thought that was the end of it, but then he started asking all sorts of questions, about you and what you did, and I got to thinking. My brother, he's going through a nasty divorce, and he got served when he was at a bar, by a guy who was sitting there drinking a beer before he even got there. It was like he knew his schedule, and he was waiting for him. I don't mean to pry, but are you having some problems at home, or whatever? Not that it's any of my business. It's probably nothing, but I wanted you to know."

"Thanks, Brent," my voice is tight as I reply. "I appreciate your telling me. This guy. What did he look like?"

"God, I wasn't really paying attention. He was big, I remember that," Brent makes a face. "Maybe a little rough looking?"

I think of the coffee shop and the Gorilla.

"When did this happen, Brent?"

"I don't know, the other day, maybe two or three days ago? Do you know who it is?"

"No," I reply, adding a shrug. "It's a mystery to me. Probably nothing. Maybe a client doing a little research before they contact me?" I smile and try to keep it light.

"Well, again, I just wanted to let you know."

"Thanks," I say. "Please, let me know if you see this guy again, OK?"

"Oh yeah, of course. Anything I can do to help, let me know."

I thank him again and head for the door. Now I know I'm being watched and monitored, but in a way, I feel a sense of relief. This guy isn't a professional. A professional would stay in the background and I wouldn't have a clue he was there until it was too late. This guy might as well hang a sign around himself. I have been warned, and now I'm watchful.

I head outside and back to my car. In the parking lot, I find myself looking for green Toyotas. I try and shake this off. I can't worry about this guy. I have a bigger problem to deal with. There is a time limit on the contract, and I have much to find out and a short time to do it. Still, as I drive away, I scan the road ahead and my rearview mirror, looking for green cars.

I PICK EMILY UP at soccer practice, and Jen is putting dinner on the table as we get home. Emily goes to hang up her backpack and wash up. I walk over to Jen to give her a kiss, and she turns away. My lips brush against her cheek.

"Could you get out the milk, please?" she asks, not looking directly at me.

I pull out a gallon of two percent milk from the refrigerator, pour it into the kid's glasses, and return the bottle to the inside door. I stand back and watch Jen as she bustles around the kitchen. Does she seem tense? She's busy now, and I know she's been busy with the kids all afternoon. I try to read if there is something more. I have a flash of an image in my mind, and I see her and George together. A familiar tightness returns to my stomach. Could it be true?

A loud, tuneless humming and stomping on the stairs announces Jason's arrival. He is all energy, and he nearly runs into the room and throws his arms around me.

"Hi, Dad!"

I scoop him up and give him a big hug, twirling him around the kitchen.

"Hey, Buddy. How was your day?"

"Good! At school Robert got sick after lunch and puked all over the floor."

"Oh. That doesn't sound so good."

"Yeah, it smelled bad, but it was really funny. We had spaghetti for lunch."

I set him back down giving him an extra little squeeze.

"Let's everybody sit down, please. Dinner is ready," Jen places a big salad bowl in the middle of the table. She's still not looking at me.

Emily comes back in the room and she and Jason take their places at each side of the table. Jen sits at one end and I sit across from her at the other.

"I don't like salad," Jason declares.

"Well, it's good for you," Emily says. "You should eat at least five servings of vegetables every day. We learned that in health class."

"That is true, honey," Jen agrees. She puts a big mound of the salad on Emily's plate, and a little scoop for Jason. "Everybody has to eat some salad before they can eat anything else. At least try some, Jason."

"But I don't want any."

"Eat just a little," I say. "It's good for you. It will make you run faster. Think how fast rabbits are, and they eat nothing but salad."

"They eat grass and vegetables," Emily says. "They don't actually eat salad."

"Well, it's the same thing," I say.

I pick up the salad bowl and put a big heap on my plate. My stomach is still tight, and I can't keep my mind still. My family is my life. Everything I do is for them. I look at Jen, and she is silently eating, keeping her gaze away from me. Is this normal? Is this how she usually eats, and I don't pay attention? Is she thinking about George? Is it possible she really *does* want me dead? I can't imagine it and yet I can't think of anything else.

"Sarah Dudley just started horseback riding lessons," Emily says after swallowing a mouthful of food. "I love horses. Can I get horseback riding lessons too?"

"When would we do it?" Jen asks. "Between soccer, dance class, Kumon, and all the other things you have scheduled in, we can't fit in another thing."

"But I want to," Emily whines. "I don't even like Kumon. And I can quit soccer."

"You are not going to quit soccer," Jen declares. "Last week you told us how much you loved soccer, and Coach Reynolds says you are showing real promise."

I chew my salad and try not to think about Jen and George. How could I have missed this? I clench my fork tightly and anger rises. My own wife. My best friend. How could I have missed it? How long have they been plotting my death? Whose idea was it to have me killed? How did they find out about the Agency, and which of them made the contact?

"Charley?"

I break out of my thoughts. Jen is staring at me, speaking directly to me.

"What?" I snap, more aggressively than I mean to. Jen's face changes as she reacts to my tone.

"What do you think of Emily's horseback riding idea?" Jen asks, her tone composed. "I need a little support here."

"Right," I say. "Of course. You don't have time for this now, honey. Maybe we can do some horseback riding this summer."

"But I want to do it now!"

"I finished my salad," Jason nearly shouts. "Now give me some real food."

Jen looks over at his plate, and the small scoop of salad is still there.

"You haven't eaten anything yet." Jen says.

"No! Really, I did. I tried a piece."

"Well, you have to try some more."

I chew the salad and it tastes like sawdust. How could she risk everything we have, everything we've worked for? Our whole life together? How could she do this to me?

Jen gets up and serves the rest of the meal to us. Grilled salmon, green beans and rice.

"Fish? I hate fish!" Jason is incensed.

"You'll grow to like it," Jen says calmly. "Fish is good for you and we will have it once a week."

"Hate is a bad word," Emily says, very properly, playing her role as the good girl to the hilt. "You dislike fish. Hate is for animals, not people."

Does Jen hate me? To do something as drastic as setting a contract on my life, it must be much more than my being an inconvenience or her wanting something different. How could she hate me after everything I've done for her? I've shown her nothing but love, and she repays me like this? My hand is shaking. I release the death grip on my fork and put my hand in my lap. I take a deep breath to regain control.

"Emily, did you finish the essay for the Taylor award?" Jen asks. "I want to go over it with you before you turn it in."

"I'm almost done. I'll finish it tonight," Emily says.

"That's great, honey. We are really proud of you."

I'm still shaking. It's so hard to sit and act calm, pretending everything is okay, when my whole life has been thrown up for grabs. Maybe I'm overreacting. Maybe I misinterpreted what George said and this has nothing to do with him, or Jen. I'm jumping off the deep end into an empty pool. The hit might have nothing to do with Jen or George, but I keep thinking, why would the two people closest to me want me dead?

"You have our meeting tomorrow in your schedule, right, Charley?"

I pull out of my thoughts as she addresses me again.

"The meeting?"

"Remember? We've been talking about this for the last two weeks. Emily is up for the Taylor award. We have a meeting with the principal and her guidance counselor to go over this. It's at ten thirty tomorrow morning at the school. I sent you a calendar invitation."

"Right, right. Of course. I have it scheduled in."

"This is quite an honor," Jen says. "It's for the outstanding student in the third grade. If she wins they'll announce it at the assembly and she'll get a plaque. It goes down in her permanent record, which will look good later."

"Can I be excused, please?" Jason says. "I'm done."

"But you've hardly eaten anything."

"I don't like any of this. I don't want to eat it."

"Well, you aren't getting anything else tonight. Do you want to go to bed hungry?"

Suddenly I feel like I can't sit here anymore. I try to act natural, like everything is normal, but it's not. I push myself away from the table and stand.

"I'm sorry, babe. Dinner was great, but I had a big lunch with George." I hesitate a moment to check her reaction, but her face is blank. "I need to get some air. I'm going out for a walk."

"You've hardly touched your food," a hint of anger in her voice. "Are you okay?"

I don't respond. I'm already out of the room and heading toward the door.

9

In the morning I escape the house and leave before anyone is up. I don't want to explain myself and it's hard to act natural when I don't know who to trust. I go to my gym as I do most mornings and work myself hard. The tension converts to sweat as I push myself. When I'm done, I'm calm and focused again. Beth lives far north, close to the Wisconsin border. She stays at home with the kids. I know her life is busy, and common courtesy says I should call, but I don't want to give her any warning. I head up the tollway and reach her subdivision just after nine.

I drive slowly past the houses, all newer, mid-sized and close together, brick and aluminum, tidy green grass. This is farther away from the city than where I live, but it's a nice tidy neighborhood. This is the suburbs and it could be anyplace. It's not that different from my neighborhood and a hundred other towns around the country. I turn into a cul-de-sac and park in front of Beth's house. I walk up to the door past the toys scattered around the yard. The grass is a little long and needs a cut. I ring the bell at the front door.

A moment later Beth answers, a look of surprise on her face.

"Charley, what are you doing here?" Beth opens the door for me.

She is dressed in sweatpants and a T-shirt splattered with bits food, no makeup. But she still looks great to me.

"Sorry for the surprise visit, sis. I was in the area, so I thought I'd drop by."

She ushers me in.

"You should have called," she scolds. "I could have been gone."

"And then I would have missed you."

We hug warmly as I cross the threshold. I hug her tight and try not to think of her as my little sister but the mother she has become. The TV is going in the background playing a sing-song tune about vegetables. The song is familiar, and I know this kind of music is the background to her life now.

"Kids, say *hi* to your Uncle Charley, he's come for a visit," Beth calls.

We walk in to the room and the twins, Audrey and Bria, blonde-haired, cute as buttons, and three years old, are up close to the TV set, transfixed. They don't respond.

"Bria, Audrey, say *hi* to Uncle Charley," Beth says it loud, and stands in front of the set, breaking the spell. The kids look up and over at me. Audrey bounces up and runs over to hug my knees. Bria is shy and looks away. I hug Audrey, pick her up and give her a big kiss. I set her down and do the same with Bria. She squirms in my grip and tries to turn away, not wanting to be kissed. I hug her in tight and tell her I'm the kissing monster, kissing her all over both cheeks. She laughs, and her sister wants in on the game. I scoot onto the floor with them and we all play wrestle for a minute. I pick them both up, one in each arm, and lope around the room. They are all giggly and happy, and when I put them back down, they want more.

"Give Uncle Charley a break," Beth says.

The twins protest and grip my knees, but then the song on the TV changes, and suddenly, they are transfixed again. Beth steals me away to the kitchen while they listen to a song about fruit salad.

"Sorry for the mess. I wasn't expecting company."

I sit at the kitchen table. There are dirty dishes in the sink. Whenever I come by, her house is always immaculate, which is impossible with young kids, and I'm sorry I intruded without warning.

"Life with kids," I say. "It's a constant struggle. How are you?"

Beth pours me a cup of coffee without asking. I thank her and wait for her to sit. She has a spot with her coffee cup and a laptop in her place. She sits and closes the laptop.

"Mike's out of town," she says. "It's harder to get work done when he's gone. They really don't watch TV all the time."

"I know. They're great kids. They're growing so fast."

We talk about her kids and mine. She asks about Jen, and I ask about Mike, who seems to travel a lot. My coffee is old and stale, but I don't say a thing and sip it slowly.

"I was up at the Manor," I say casually.

"You went to see Dad?" she asks with surprise. We don't talk about why I don't visit, but she knows my reasons.

"I did. He looks good. He didn't know who I was, but he looks good."

"Sometimes he's better," Beth says. "At times he seems like he used to be."

"You visit regularly," I say. "I didn't realize you were up there every week."

Beth nods and looks directly at me. "I try to. He likes it when we come. Sometimes he remembers, mostly he doesn't. But it's good for me and I want my kids to know they have a grandfather. It was an accident, Charley. He wasn't himself when it happened."

"Sure," I say. "I know."

My mind flashes back to the day we took his car away. We were at the old house, Beth was in the kitchen, talking on the phone, I was in the back room, with Dad. It had been two years since Mom died of cancer, and dad was slipping away more and more. First there was the forgetfulness. He would get frustrated and upset when he couldn't find his keys or his reading glasses. Then after a while he would find them where he put them. Sometimes it was in the refrigerator, or the microwave. At first, we laughed off these issues, but they happened more and more frequently.

Earlier that day, I'd gotten a call from the LaGrange police department. They had Dad. He was alright, but he'd run off the road and crashed the car into a signpost, narrowly missing several pedestrians. I picked him up, and, after talking with Beth, we agreed he shouldn't be driving anymore.

I'd sat down with Dad and gave him the news that we had no choice and we were taking the car away. He didn't say anything at first, and I thought he took it as well as could be expected. I was still sitting when he stood up and walked out of the room without saying anything. I got up and looked out the window.

I remember it was a bright sunny day. I was trying to think where Dad would hide the extra sets of keys. I heard Dad's footsteps in the hall and knew he was coming back, but before I turned away from the window, there was an explosion and the window in front of me shattered. My adrenaline kicked in and I covered my head, dropped to the floor, and rolled away. Dad fired two more times, missing again, before I could get to him and take the gun away. I remember the look in his eyes, the hate and the anger. He made me what I am, and now he wanted to destroy me. That was the day he tried to kill me. The first time, at least.

"You know that was the dementia and the stress," Beth says. "Dad might have had a temper, but he was never violent."

We have different memories, my sister and me. I nod but don't say a thing. I listen to the TV in the other room. The twins are singing along with the song. I sip my coffee. What am I doing here?

"When you see Dad," I ask, "is he always the same? Is he ever fully there?"

Beth shakes her head. "Some days are better than others. Some days he recognizes me, and we talk. Mostly I talk to him and tell him about the kids and what we are doing. I always talk about you and Jen, and how your kids are doing, too. Sometimes he talks, but not that often. Mostly he just listens, but I think he is glad when I'm there."

"When he does talk, what does he talk about?"

Beth thought for a second before responding. "I don't know. He talked about Mom once, and how they first met, but it was different than the story they always told us. It was all kind of mixed up."

"Anything else he talks about?"

"Well, sure. The other week, he was really agitated. He kept telling me he had to go, he had a job to do. We sat down and talked, and he finally calmed down, but he kept talking about the job, and I asked him what he had to do, why was it so important. Finally, I got it out of him. He was convinced that he had to go somewhere to kill someone. Can you imagine?"

"Wow." My heart is pumping, and I wonder if the secret is finally out.

"It's kind of funny, but that's the thing. He can't tell what's real and what's not. This had to come from a dream or something he saw on TV. But at the time, it was real to him."

I take another sip of the stale coffee and hope my hands aren't shaking. "Does Dad still make any phone calls?"

"By himself? No. He doesn't remember anyone's numbers, and I don't think he could dial it himself if he did." Beth leans forward in her chair, close to me. "I'm glad you went to see him, Charley. I know how you feel, but he's not the same. It wasn't his fault. He's our Dad, and we don't know how much longer he'll be around."

I smile and nod sadly, but I don't believe it. His mind may be gone, but he knew what he was doing the day he tried to shoot me. That was my real Dad. The other one, the loving dad who took us out for ice cream and read us bed time stories, was a shell and a fake. I know the real man all too well. Beth doesn't.

I think back to after we put Dad in the home. I searched the house for any records and ties to his work but found nothing. Dad always taught me to not leave any records or anything that could be used to trace back to a job. He'd done everything in his head, by memory. But his memory had been fading for a long while before we even knew it. I had mostly taken over the business by then, but, as Dad's memory went, did he keep notes on anything? Was there anything he had that I might have missed, anything that would link him to the Agency? Maybe I missed something important.

"When we were cleaning out the house, did you find anything that didn't make sense?" I take another sip of my coffee and try to appear calm.

"Like what?"

"I don't know, maybe records of some kind?"

Beth thinks before answering. "Records? Like what?"

"I don't know, anything that seemed unusual."

"Are you okay, Charley? Is something wrong?" Beth leans in again and touches my arm. She knows me too well. I can try and hide my fear and stress, but she sees it.

"No, it's nothing. I'm just thinking about Dad, and what he left that we don't know about."

"Is this about money? You know we have enough for his care set aside. There should be plenty."

"No, it's not money. I'm thinking he might have kept some records, but I'm not even sure what it would be."

I'm trying to think about how I can explain what I'm looking for, without telling her the family secret. Without letting her know her father and brother are killers, and without letting her know my current predicament. At that moment, the twins come bouncing in from the other room. They come right over to Beth and hang on her, hugging her around the waist.

"I'm hungry," Bria says.

"Me too," says Audrey.

"You guys just ate. You can't be hungry." Beth pulls them both in close.

"Then I'm bored," Bria replies.

"Let me finish talking with Uncle Charley, and then we'll do something fun." Beth turns back to me. "Well," she says, "you saw everything when we moved it out of the house. If we didn't sell it or give it away, it's still in storage."

I know this, but Beth handled all the details. I was busy with something at the time, and even with younger kids, she took the lead. I'm vaguely guilty about this, too.

"I have the key to the storage if you want to go through it. At some point, we're going to have to decide what to do with all that stuff anyway. There are things I'd like to keep, but we don't have the room."

The kids are bouncing around and demanding their mother's attention. It's time to go.

"That will be great," I say. "It's probably nothing, but I'll let you know what I find."

Beth stands and gets the key, attached to a chain with the storage facility address, and passes it across. I hug her and the twins, and quickly make my exit. I hope there is something worthwhile in the storage facility.

10

As I leave Beth's house it's windy. I should have worn a thicker coat. I'm feeling better now than when I first went inside. Beth is my family and my roots, we have our shared history. I can trust her, but I wonder if she is right about Dad and his capabilities. If he can do more than she thinks, then the simplest answer still seems like the right answer to me. I get into the car with the storage key weighing heavy in my pocket.

The storage facility is in Brookfield, back near our old house, on the other side of the city. I'm anxious to go through it. Although I've seen everything before, I'm looking for different things now. I start up my car, and as I back up, I notice a man standing by a parked car a few houses down. He is staring at me. My heart booms in my chest, am I being followed? Is another contract out on me? Then he waves, and I see that he wasn't staring at me at all, but a woman walking her dog on the sidewalk. She waves back to him, and I drive away.

I'm still on edge. I need to stay calm and find a way to be the hunter again. The reports I ordered will be ready this afternoon and I'm anxious to see what they show. I drive out of the subdivision and back to the interstate, heading south. My phone rings and I see it's

Jen. I left before anyone else was up. No doubt she's calling to check in and say good morning, but as the phone rings again, a wave of anxiety washes across me. I let it ring one more time before I answer.

"Hi babe, good morning," I try and sound happy and carefree.

"Where are you?" she asks. There is tension in her voice.

"I'm driving," I say. "I'm on the expressway."

"You didn't say anything, and you left so early."

"Didn't I tell you? I had a meeting," I lie. "I didn't want to wake you."

"You didn't say anything about it last night. Is something going on?"

"No, nothing's wrong. I'm just busy. I thought I told you about it, but I guess I forgot."

"We have the meeting with Emily's teacher this morning. Remember? I reminded you about it last night!"

Damn it. I was preoccupied when she was talking last night, and hardly listening, but now I remember.

"That's right," I say, cursing to myself. "I'm on my way. The meeting took a little longer than expected, but I'll be there as soon as I can."

"I'm about to leave now. Where are you?" I don't like her tone of voice. I hear the tension and anger and I know I messed up. "Are you going to make it? I told you it was important."

"Look, I'm on my way. I might be a little late, but I will be there." I step on the gas and wish I had a time machine.

She doesn't say anything, but I can feel the chill over the line as she hangs up. I stomp on the gas and drive like a madman. The speed limit on the tollway is sixty-five, but cruising speed is about seventy-five. My speedometer passes one hundred. I look ahead for cop cars as I weave in and out of traffic. I realize how stupid this is, but I have to make up time. As it is, I'll arrive way later than I should.

I have an hour's drive to get to a meeting that starts in twenty minutes. There is no way I will make it on time. My only hope is that the meeting starts late. How I could have forgotten? Last night wasn't the first time we talked about it. Emily is up for an award, and this is part of the process. It slipped my mind, but I knew about it and agreed to the date over a week ago. I tell myself to focus and maintain control as I fly past a row of cars and edge into the far lane. I hit my brakes as I reach a stretch of road where the cars are all bunched together and there is nowhere to go.

I ride up on the bumper of the car in front of me, willing him to go faster, hoping he will give me an opening to pass, and at least feel like I'm in control. I find an opening, but within a minute brake lights flare again. The traffic comes to a standstill and I have nowhere to go. I want to hit my steering wheel. I want to be in control of the situation. But I'm stuck. I take a deep breath and try to calm down. The clock in my car console tells me there's no way I can make the meeting on time. My heart hammers, as I realize I will have to tell Jen I'm not going to make it after all.

It seems like ages as we slowly move forward, starting and stopping, inching along. I glance at the clock again. The meeting has already started. As the car in front hits the brakes again, I text Jen and tell her the bad news. As I creep forward, I wait for her reply, but it doesn't come.

This meeting is a priority for Jen and it should be for me, but I have too much on my mind. If I could tell her, she would understand, but of course I can't say a word. I have done everything to protect and provide for Jen and the kids, but she doesn't know what I do, and of course she couldn't understand. I will make it up to her, I think, and she will get over this, I hope. Then, I wonder if is she who I think she is, and can I truly trust her?

Traffic finally breaks through, but it's too late, and I head straight to the storage unit. I haven't been here for almost two years, since right after Dad moved into Meadowbrook Manor. I punch the code at the front gate, and the mechanical arm raises and lets me into the complex. I park off to the side and sign in with a guard at the front before entering the big concrete block building. This is a monstrous warehouse, climate controlled so it's always about seventy degrees and dry. There are rows and rows of connected units, all with orange pull-up doors, and security locks. I march through the maze until I find the right unit.

When I open the door, I smell dust and cedar and something I can't place that immediately reminds me of home. I switch on the light and close the big door behind me. The room is stuffed, mostly with cardboard boxes and plastic containers, but there are some other things out in the open that I notice right away. There is an old bike, its tires flat, and I'm certain it hasn't been ridden in ages. I'm not sure why we even kept it. My mother's makeup table is near the front. It's ornate and old fashioned with a Japanese design. It has no practical value. We only kept it for sentimental reasons, figuring we would throw it out later. On top of that sits a varnished wooden board with a big mounted fish attached, a muskie Dad caught on a family vacation years ago. I have a quick image of Dad's office in the old house, and how hung on the wall above his desk.

I take another deep breath, and it smells even more like home. This is everything left after we sold the old house. Dad's room in the facility is barely big enough to fit a bed and a chair. We took some family pictures and put them on his walls. We moved in his old leather chair and a few knickknacks and sold or tossed out most everything else. I'm not sure what I'm looking for. I'm grasping here, but I don't know what else to do and hope this will give me some hint at the things dad never told me. Maybe a clue into his dealings with the Agency.

I go to the first box. It's labeled on the side with magic marker: photo albums. I pull back the cardboard flaps and look inside. There are several photo albums and I pull the top one out and set it on another box. Mom was sentimental and we had pictures to mark every event in our family life when she was around. I have several albums at home, and Beth kept more than I did. I turn the big pages and glance through the images, their colors fading. One picture is of me when I was very young. I'm missing a front tooth, and I wear a big smile. I'm behind a birthday cake, candles blazing. I count and confirm it was taken on my eighth birthday.

I think back to that day and the memory is still vivid. I was having a party at home and friends from school and relatives were coming in the afternoon. Mom ordered a special cake. I was really into boats and pirates then, and the cake was shaped like a pirate ship. I went with Dad to pick it up at the bakery. I think back to how we took a side trip on the way and stopped in a neighborhood I'd never been to. My mind takes me back and I'm reliving the events. The home has a long driveway, secluded by the trees and bushes in the front. I don't know where we are, but I've been with dad on these kinds of outings so many times before.

He has a key to the front door, and we enter silently. A TV blares in the background. Dad turns to me and puts his fingers to his lips. He knows where he is going. I follow in his footsteps, making sure to creep silently. At the back of the house, there is an old man, bald and bony, in a dark room, watching TV with the sound up high. He looks up in shock as we enter the room, and it looks as if he is going to shout. Before he does, my dad walks to his chair and quickly grabs him by the neck. He hardly struggles. I hear a snap, and the man goes limp. Dad picks him up and carries the body through the old kitchen.

"Grab that door for me, will you, Charley Boy?"

He doesn't have to tell me, I open it with my hand covered by my shirt, so I won't leave any prints. The door opens to the basement, a long flight of twisting stairs lead to darkness below. Dad takes the body and sets the old man standing limp at the top of the stairs, then he lets go, and the old man tumbles forward, down the stairs. Dad flips the light switch and examines the position.

"What do you think, buddy? Looks good?"

"Sure, Dad," I say. I don't know if it looks good or not, but I do know he wants my agreement.

I blink back to the present, close the photo album and put it off to the side. Going through the family pictures will bring back more memories like that, but it won't help me get any closer to my goal. I pick up the next album from the box and see more family pictures, but this is from when I was older. I glance at it and put this off to the side, too. I might look through them later, but not now. There is one more photo album in the box, and I'm sure it's more of the same, but I take it out and open it anyway. When I open it, I see this is something entirely different. This is an older album, and the pictures here are of my dad. I'd never seen this one, and I want to see what he was like when he was a young man. I take it over to a chair we had stored, sit down and place the book on my lap as I leaf through it.

The first couple of pages are of my dad with his family. The family wasn't close, and I don't remember ever meeting my grandparents. He was the oldest of five, and when I see the picture of them all together, they are all solemn, grim-faced as they stare at the camera. Another picture is of Dad in his high school graduation cap and gown. He has the same look then as he has even now, lean and forceful, a cocky, confident look in his eyes. Again, he doesn't smile. I flip a few more pages. I see the car he owned when he was young, and a picture of him with a hunting rifle, kneeling by the deer he'd recently killed. When I was growing up, he smiled a lot, though I sometimes think the smile was a mask. Here again, he is solemn.

The next pages really catch my interest. He is in the Army now, and his face seems even more sharp and angular with his hair buzzed down to the scalp. There are pictures from training camp, with groups of lean young men with short hair and faded fatigues. Then, we are in Vietnam. The pictures aren't of him now, mostly, at least. There are pictures of motorcycles driving down hectic streets, with cryptic signs and young men drinking beer or holding even younger Asian girls around the waist. There are pictures of a building set up in the mud, with the deep green jungle as the backdrop. I flip the pages with fascination. As a kid, I remember finding Dad's old uniform and how excited I was. I asked him about his time in the war, but he wouldn't tell me a thing. It happened a long time ago, he'd say. I longed to hear war stories, and I imagined myself in a fight, running and gunning and being the hero. He never told me what he did.

I turn a page and this picture grabs me. Dad is in the shot with another man, a head shorter than him. Both men are shirtless, and Dad's wearing a big smile. This is the first picture I've seen with my dad smiling, and I look closer, trying to imagine what has happened. Dad has a rifle in one hand, and his other arm is draped across his friend's shoulder. The other man has binoculars dangling from a strap around his neck and a deep intensity in his eyes that jumps right out of the picture. I lift back the plastic sheet and take the photo out of the book. I try and imagine what is happening, but I can't even guess. I turn the picture over and see it has writing scrawled on the back. It says: *Up country with Peepers, 1965.*

I put the picture back in its place and close the album. This might give me some insight into who Dad had been, but it doesn't relate to my present problem. I put it aside to look at later. I go through the stacks and grab another box. This one is packed with my mother's Christmas plates and some Hummel figurines. Again, we saved them because Beth didn't want to toss it. Its value is only sentimental. There are boxes of books, though neither dad or mom were big readers. They looked good on the bookshelves and were mainly decorative. Most of the books are classics that were sold as a set. But one, a fat volume with a deep blue cover, looks out of place. I pull it out. The title on the spine says, *Principals and Methods of Statistical Analysis.* This seems curious, so I open the book and leaf through it. I read a paragraph and the language is so dense and ponderous I have no idea what it's saying. Now I'm sure this was bought for show, and no one has read it. I flick my thumb across the pages before putting it back, and a piece of paper falls to the floor.

I pick it up and glance at it. It's a sheet of note paper, folded in half. I open it and look at it closely. It's a list of some kind, numbered, with names and series of numbers that might be dates, followed by check marks. A surge of excitement rushes through me. The numbers run from one to ninety-seven and the names are coded, like the way I receive my targets from the Agency. Dad told me never to keep records, nothing that can be used to trace anything back, but it appears he broke his own rule. This is a clue, I think, and maybe something I can use. I turn the book upside down and fan it open, but nothing else falls out. I pull out the other books in this box and do the same with them, but the note is the only thing I find.

I go through more boxes, but don't find anything useful. There are boxes of old tax forms and financial records. I find one with my mom's medical records and a copy of her death certificate. This brings back more memories but nothing I need to dwell on now. I go through the rest of the items in the storage unit and do nothing but stir up more dust. I glance at my watch. I've been here almost two hours. I found something, but I don't know what it is or what use it might be. I take the list with me and lock up the unit before I leave.

11

I feel better after washing the dust off my hands and face and stopping for a quick lunch. It's mid-afternoon when I reach my office suite. I'm relieved that no one is out in the common area, and I can slip into my own space undisturbed. I turn on my secure laptop and, using my proxy, I enter the deep web. The background files I ordered were placed on rush, and I tap my fingers on the desk impatiently as I access the site. The reports are ready and were sent as fully encrypted files. I use the key provided, and unlock the first report, it's about my Dad.

I'm not sure what I will find here, but the file is short. He came of age before the internet, and he never felt comfortable with computers. The main breakdown shows his name and birthdate, his current and former addresses. His occupation is listed as retired, and his job history shows self-employed or unknown. It shows a list of his tax earnings by year, and an estimate of his savings. The estimate for his savings is low. He has no arrest record and doesn't currently own any real estate. It shows his military record and that he served in Vietnam where he was decorated for bravery, and honorably discharged. It has no social media history and his credit profile is nearly nonexistent, as he always paid cash for everything. He had a few parking tickets, which he promptly paid, but those were from decades ago. It shows the date of his wedding and the date of mom's death, and that he has two children and no other living relatives. The only picture is from his army induction. His driver's license expired in 1983 and he never renewed it though he drove up until I took his keys away. This profile shows a man passing through life without leaving a mark. He is nearly a ghost, and his footprint is already fading. The records only go so far, and Dad has been successful in keeping his profile low.

I open Beth's profile next. Although she is so much younger than Dad, there is much more here to see. They have her age right, and that she is married with young twins. I quickly read through the record for Mike, her husband, and the background is as bland and uninteresting as I think he is. I pass over Beth's school records and her work history. I feel like I'm prying when I look at their account balances, but I need to make sure that they haven't made any big withdrawals lately, and there aren't any financial problems that would cause distress. Thankfully, I see nothing to cause concern, and it looks like they are living well below their means. Beth's social connections show she has many friends and relationships, all well documented on social media. I scroll through pictures of her and her family—lots with the twins—and plenty of her with me and my family. There are pictures of her and Jen, and of her with girlfriends I know, and some who I don't. Mike also has a life on social media, but not nearly so robust. I look at their credit cards and scan for any evidence of gambling or porn addictions, anything showing the seedy side of an outwardly good relationship. Nothing. No arrest records, no speeding tickets and not even any outstanding parking tickets. Maybe they're too young to have gotten into serious trouble yet, but Beth and Mike are both as clean as can be.

I get up and walk around the room for a minute. I don't like to sit still for a long time, but I know this is a different kind of anxiety. I'm getting too close to home now, but I have to know. I sit back down, unable to put it off any longer. I open Jen's report. I scan through all the legal and background stuff. I know there aren't any surprises there. I want to see her secrets, the part she shields from me. I look at her social media activity first, and she is very active there. The report helpfully lists her top connections, those who she interacts with the most. It's the usual suspects, all her close friends with one exception: George. My heart beats harder.

I keep on reading. I gave the service the IP address for her computer, and I see she has an email address I don't know about. My heart skips again. I could have set something up to monitor her, but I saw no need before. Now, I wonder if I was too trusting. Is this the email she uses with George? I want to see secret messages they've passed, but the report doesn't go that far.

I take a deep breath and try to relax. Our relationship is based on love and trust. I have email addresses I use to keep from being bothered by marketers and constant spam. Maybe, she has set one up for the same reason. George is a close friend. Hers, as well as mine. They've known each other as long as I've known her. I try not to jump to conclusions and keep my pulse in check.

I look at the activity on her computer and her history for the last month. The sites she frequents most are Facebook and Instagram. She reads mommy blogs and watches YouTube painting videos and cooking demos. Nothing alarming at all. If she used her computer to access the deep web, it would have shown in her history. Unless she used a proxy, like I do. But I don't think she has the tech skills to know how to set it up.

I look through her asset accounts, and they list only the ones I know about, mostly our joint accounts. No surprises here. If she has money to spend on outside activities—like paying for a hit—the report doesn't show it. There are no significant withdrawals at any rate. I look at her credit rating, and as I'd expect, it's flawless. There's a credit card account I didn't know about, a store account for Bianco's. I don't know what this is, so I open a standard browser window and look it up. It's a high-end dress shop, and the only location in the area is on Michigan Avenue in the city. She hasn't mentioned buying any new dresses, though she can do as she pleases and doesn't need my permission. I check the date the card was used last, and the charge was for the fifteenth of this month. Last Tuesday, and the charge is

$1,800. I inhale sharply. This is more than she would ever spend without talking it through beforehand. My palms are sweaty. Is there an occasion I should be remembering? Is there a wedding coming up? Something important that I can't recall? Why would she need an expensive new dress?

Her medical records show nothing I don't already know. She had a doctor's appointment in the last month. Did she tell me about it? I can't remember. It looks like it was for a routine physical, and nothing out of the ordinary was noted. I go through the rest of the file, but there's nothing else of concern. Still, there is enough. I have my secrets, but it appears she has some of her own.

I click open George's file. I clench my hands and wait for something to jump out and confirm my suspicions. The file contains all his background info, his date of birth, birthplace and previous addresses, his school history, and though we were roommates in college I never knew he had started out as a biology major before changing to business. His family information shows no surprises and I don't even read the information on his wife Christine. I go straight for the finances. His accounts show he has done quite well for himself. There was a time after he went on his own, when he was really struggling. It was only cash flow, he'd said, but he went through a long period where he had a hard time paying the bills. I'd lent him money several times before turning him down the last time occasion he'd asked a few months back. When we'd had lunch, he told me he had reason to celebrate, and his business account confirmed it. There were several big deposits in the last month, totaling over a million dollars.

I let the numbers rumble around in my head a bit. He is flush now, but this is all recent. There is money being transferred in and out to several different accounts. It's hard to tell what'swhat. Though he clearly has a lot coming in, there is a lot of money going out. I can't tell where the money is going, but if he'd hired a hitman, he wouldn't write a memo on his check. He'd try and hide the payments.

I look at George's social media use. I don't use Facebook much, but it's the only one I use at all. I post pictures of the kids occasionally and use it to remember people's birthdays. George is highly active. He passes on a lot of jokes and keeps up with relationships from when we went to school. He even keeps in touch with kids he went to grammar school with. I scroll through the posts and look at who he is connecting with. Jen is in his top ten, too, as well as several other women in our social circle. George was always a flirt, so this isn't surprising. I don't even make the list. My stomach's, and I clench my hands tighter.

I look at his public record and I'm surprised to see he has a couple of things listed. There is a drunken driving arrest from two years earlier. George was always a drinker, and more so during the cash flow problems. He'd never said a word about this to me, even though we talk or text several times a week. The court record shows a conviction, but this was later vacated. Another listing is even more of a shock. There is a police report from last Christmas Eve, for a domestic disturbance at his home. No details are listed, but I wonder what happened.

I scroll down to his credit report and see his score is somewhere between fair and poor. He has big expenses and a history of paying things slowly. Several of his accounts are now paid off, where they showed late payments the previous month. I go to the credit account statement for his major card and look at the history for the last thirty days. There is a lot of activity, but one thing jumps out at me. A bill is listed for Emmanuel's on Tuesday the fifteenth. The bill isn't big, not compared to some of the things he is paying, but it brings the hardness in my stomach up to my throat. Emmanuel's is a trendy place in the city, a block over from where Jen bought the dress on the same day.

This isn't exactly a smoking gun, but it's not far off. There could be a reasonable explanation. It could be a coincidence, or it could be something entirely innocent. But I don't think so. I push myself away from the desk and stand. I'm sweating and breathing hard. This feels like a betrayal, and I'm not sure which hurts me the most, my wife or my best friend? My hands shake, and I want to smoke a cigarette, even though I quit years ago. What should I do now? Do I confront them? If I do, how do I explain how I know what I know? And if this is evidence, is it evidence of cheating, or does this mean I have found what I've been looking for, and they are planning my murder?

I'm about to shut the computer down when I notice a new message in my secure channel. This is the way I contact the Agency, and how they contact me. Outside of taking on new assignments, I don't have a lot of direct communication with my employer. What do they want now? My pulse quickens as I open the file.

The message is short:

Martin, please respond with progress report and expected completion time for your current project. Time is of the essence.

This throws me a little. When I took on the job they gave me two weeks—fourteen days to complete. It's only the third day now since I took on the job. I don't normally report progress unless it's a set requirement when I first agree to the job. I'm an autonomous operator. They tell me what to do and I do it, but I do it the way I think is best. All within their set time period. Why are they pushing on this?

I think for a moment before typing a response.

Target is identified, and project is moving forward. This is a delicate situation and needs to be handled as such. Completion will be within contract parameters.

I look at the message and read it out loud. I don't want to say anything that will cause concern or alert them that is any different from all the jobs I have completed for them over the years. I need to stretch this out and buy myself some time to solve this problem. I read the message through again. I'm sure it sets the right tone. I hit send.

I try not to think about the Agency. I need to keep my focus. Is this what I was looking for? Jen and George? It's possible. It could be a coincidence, but the connections need to be explained. If this is true, my whole life is a lie. I'm still not sure what I should do. Could they have placed the hit? It seems incredible, but I certainly have to consider the possibility.

I shut down my computer and leave the office feeling lost.

12

When I reach home the house is dark. Jen and the kids should be there, but it's all too quiet. I walk from room to room, switching on lights and calling their names, but it's clear no one is home. I search my brain and think if there was something going on tonight. The kids have busy schedules and Jen taxis them around from one place to another, but I don't think there was anything scheduled. I check my phone to see if she sent me a message, but the last text exchange was when I told her I wouldn't be able to make the meeting after all. She never responded after that. Is she still angry?

I walk into the kitchen and see it's clean, with no signs of meal preparation. I go back to the front hall and glance at the hooks by the door. The kids' backpacks are gone. She could have picked them straight from school and gone somewhere. I return to the kitchen and pull a beer out of the refrigerator. I don't drink often, but I've earned the right. I open it up and prowl into the living room to wait. I'm still trying to decide what to do. Do I act normal and pretend everything is OK? Do I confront her with what I know, or think I know? What will I do if she is the one, the principal? Even with what I have found, I still love her. I can't imagine living my life without her and the kids.

If something happened, it was George's fault. George is my best friend, but if he's betrayed me he'll have to pay the price.

I finish the beer and return to the kitchen for another. I can't believe they still aren't home. I take out my phone and text Jen.

Where are you?

I sit and wait for a reply. I try not to think about them together while I wait. I'm nearly done with my second beer, with no reply, when I first think something might be wrong. I call her number and the message picks up after the sixth ring.

"Hi honey, it's me," I say. "Where are you? I'm at home and no one is here, obviously. Where are you guys at? Give me a call."

As I end the call, I wonder if she is still upset about my missing the meeting? She was mad earlier, but I'm almost always there when she needs me. This was a rare oversight on my part, but it's nothing serious. It's not like cheating on me with my best friend. Maybe. I was wrong to miss the meeting, but she has to have a sense of perspective. I can't exactly tell her someone's taken out contract on me—especially since she's near the top of my suspect list. This is all wrong. I'm a great husband and father. I'm a good provider and I do my best to give her the life that she wants. Why isn't she answering?

I pick my phone up again and look at my address list. I scroll down and call her best friend, Tabitha.

"Hey, Tabby," I say as she answers. "Sorry to call around dinner time, but is Jen there by any chance?"

She tells me no, and I try to pick up any inflection in her voice that would tell me if she is lying. Jen and Tab have been friends for years. What has Jen told her? Has she confided to Tabby about her and George? How many other people know. What's being said behind my back?

"Well, thanks. I was just wondering where everyone is. I'm sure it's nothing. I'm sure I'll talk with her soon."

I hang up and call the next friend in the area, and I get the same response. She hasn't heard from her and doesn't know where Jen and the kids are. I'm starting to get concerned now. This isn't like Jen, and I don't know why she isn't getting back to me. The sudden, gut-wrenching thought hits me with the force of a bullet to the gut. Is my family safe? If someone is looking to kill me, and if it isn't my wife, maybe they are going to harm her, too. This doesn't make sense, but I'm now worried for her safety, and my kids. Where are they, and are they OK?

I ring Jen's sister, Jackie. She lives in the city and though they are tight, I can't imagine her visiting on a school night without telling me about it first. Jackie answers the phone right before I'm sure it will go to voice mail.

"Hey, Jackie," I say. "Sorry to bother you, but is Jen over there by any chance?"

There is a hesitation on the line before she answers. "Yes," she says. "She's here with the kids."

I'm relieved. They are safe.

"Great, I was worried. Can you put her on the line, please?"

The hesitation is there again, and her voice sounds funny. The tone is cold and distant. "She doesn't want to talk with you, Charley."

"What do you mean she doesn't want to talk to me? She's my wife. Please put her on."

"She doesn't want to talk. Not now," Jackie says, her voice firm. "She and the kids are staying here tonight. Maybe for a few days. Let it rest, Charley. I'm not sure what's going on with you guys, but she isn't going to talk with you. Give it a few days and I'm sure she'll calm down."

I protest, but I'm talking to a rock that won't budge. She hangs up on me while I'm still pleading.

I'm breathing heavy when she ends the call. I drink the last of my second beer in a gulp and try to make sense of this. I missed a meeting. It isn't the end of the world. Why is she so mad? She's never done anything like this before. I pick up the phone again and think to call her, but I set it back down. I think of what I have learned. Am I misreading this somehow? I should be the angry one.

I get up and start to pace again. I'm balled up and constrained. How can she be the injured party when I know she is keeping things from me? I think of her and George again. I can't believe it, but I can't get it out of my mind either. I grab another beer from the fridge, but I set it aside before opening it. The house is uncomfortable. Too quiet, too empty. I need to get out of here. Suddenly I want to go somewhere and be around other people just to get out of this damned empty house. I grab my coat and keys and head to my car.

Inside the car, I turn the music up loud and drive aimlessly. I don't know where I'm going, but I have to process this whole thing somehow. My life was so good a few days ago, and now everything has turned to shit. If Jen was really trying to kill me, why would she run away? She wouldn't alert me, she would try and act as though nothing was going on, and just wait for my death. It's what I would do. If I'd placed the hit on someone, I'd want to keep my normal routines. I would maintain the same schedule as always, so I wouldn't raise any suspicions. Before or after.

I consider calling George, but I'm not quite in control, and what would I say? There is something there, but he can't know what I now know. I don't want to tip my hand. The weather is misty, and my automatic windshield wipers turn on and off, not quite fast enough to keep the glass dry. I look out at the lights of the cars on the road and the bright signs of the businesses I pass. The lights blur, and then wipe clean. The neon beer signs on a place I have never been in before, calls to me. I turn off the road and into the parking lot of Jilly's, an old tavern that has been there as long as can I remember, though I'd never even thought to go in before.

I park at the back of the lot, away from the door, and turn up my collar as I hurry across the gravel parking lot. This stretch of road is filled with auto dealers, chain restaurants and strip malls. This is a smaller building on a big lot. I wonder how it's still here when everything else has been redeveloped.

The heat hits me as I walk in the door. It's wet and chilly outside, and inside it's warm and dry. I smell beer, grilled meat, and frying onions. The place is lined with blond wood and has black velvet paintings and fuzzy plush animals mounted like trophies on the walls. The bar is a long oval, with the liquor bottles backlit to bring out the colors, and blinking Christmas lights, though we are long past the holiday. The vibe is cozy and kitschy. It reminds me of a fishing lodge up in Wisconsin more than an old place on a busy street in the suburbs.

I cross the room and sit on a stool at the bar. There are groups and couples in the booths and tables, eating, but I'm the only one at the bar. I look up at the TV. It's tuned to an old movie. The sound is off, and an Eagles song is playing in the background. The bartender, a plump woman with short brown hair and a friendly smile, comes over and I order a draft beer. I sit and sip and try to let my mind go. I'm too tense. I should be in control, but I'm running around like a decapitated chicken, moving but not seeing a thing. The beer, my third, goes down smooth and I order another. I'm halfway through this when I remember I haven't eaten since early in the day. I feel a warm glow, and know I should eat something, but not quite yet.

A few people join me at the bar. We silently acknowledge each other as they sit. I watch the TV and try and figure out what is happening on the movie. It's black and white and I think it's comedy, but I'm not sure. The men might be gangsters in their dark suits with wide lapels, and they wave their arms around and make exaggerated faces. It might not be a comedy, but it strikes me as funny. Though it's a week night, the bar is filling up. The sounds of blended conversations make me feel warm and comfortable.

"Hey!" calls a man about my age, two seats down. "Do I know you? You look familiar."

I look at him. He is heavyset and broad shouldered, with short blond hair and a goatee. If I know him, it doesn't come to mind.

"No," I say. "I don't think so."

"No, I do know you. I'm really good with faces," he says. "You live in Ashton Meadows, right?"

I nod. I do.

"I live over on Sussex. There was a party, I think it was at the Taylor's last year? We met there."

I nod again. I vaguely remember it, a summer barbecue that went late. But I still don't remember meeting him.

"My names Joe. Joe Sanders." He reaches out to shake my hand.

"Charley. Charley Fieldner," I say as we shake.

"I've never seen you here before. You stop by much?"

"First time," I say. "My wife and kids are away. I wanted to get out of the house."

"I hear you," my new friend says. "I come here to get away from them." He laughs. "Hey, it looks like you're almost out. Let me buy you another."

I protest but he orders, and soon we are conversing like old friends. Though I don't remember him, we have friends and acquaintances in common. He has lived in the neighborhood longer than me and his kids go to the same school as mine though they are a little older. We talk easily about many things and he doesn't ask what I do for a living, so I don't have to dance around that subject. We finish our beers and I order the next round. I'm still not hungry and the drinks are going down easy. I'm enjoying this moment and the escape from the tension I have felt over the last few days.

"You know what I hate?" Joe asks.

I shake my head and hope he isn't about to go into some kind of racist or political rant.

"I hate how it always rains on the weekends. Do you notice that? The last three weekends, beautiful weather throughout the week, and then the weekend it rains."

I hadn't noticed that, I tell him. But statistically it should work itself out over the course of time, and since it's raining tonight, the weekend has a chance to be better. He toasts my logic and our conversation turns to statistics. He has all sorts of facts and trivia that I haven't heard before. We are talking about nothing, and I'm laughing and having a good time. We order another beer and I'm starting to feel it. I'm not drunk. Definitely not impaired. But I do have a nice buzz. The alcohol has helped my mood tremendously, and I'm sure my new friend would not seem quite so engaging if I was completely sober.

I announce that it's getting late, and I should probably get going. Joe agrees, but calls for one more, first. While the bartender is refilling, I get up to find the men's room. I'm surprised how busy the bar is now, as I hadn't noticed it fill up. The music and conversation is are louder, and everyone seems happy. I'm glad I happened to come here and wonder why I'd never stopped in before. In the bathroom I relieve myself and feel satisfied. I wash up and look at myself in the mirror. There are bags under my eyes. I need to get more sleep. I smile in the mirror. It's a goofy smile, and I feel like laughing. I might be a little drunk after all.

On the way back to my seat my walk is a little wobbly. I'm not swaying and I'm not out of control, but I do have to concentrate more on what I'm doing. This will be the last drink, I assure myself.

I look around as I come back into the main room. There is a mix of younger people and middle aged. There are more men drinking in small groups, but also couples and a group of women are at a long table laughing and talking loudly. Then I notice him, a big man, hunched over to appear smaller, bald and alone at a table on the far edge of the room. He looks away as soon as my gaze turns toward him, but I know it's him—the Gorilla. I keep my gaze away from him as I cross the room and reclaim my stool at the bar. My highly-tuned defense mechanism floods adrenaline through my system Now, I'm sober.

"You know what I'd like to do?" Joe asks as soon as I sit, but he doesn't wait for my reply. "I'd like to quit my job and move to Thailand."

He launches into a story of a time he visited there and how he thought he might have been one of them in a previous life, it all felt so good and natural. He is telling a funny story, but I'm not laughing.

I keep my eyes away from the man at the outside table, but my thoughts are focused on him. Who is he? What is he doing here and why is he following me? Has the Agency realized their mistake and placed a new hitman on me to finish the contract? I stare at the beer in front of me, and it doesn't tempt me at all.

"And I rode an elephant. Can you believe it? You can ride goddamned elephants there! Can you imagine commuting to work in the morning on an elephant?"

I smile, but I'm not laughing, and this throws Joe off a bit. I push away the beer and reach into my pocket for my cash. I throw money on the bar, more than I need, and announce that I need to go.

"You need to go?" Joe is heartbroken. "It's still early. Come on, you've got a full beer to finish. You can't leave now."

But I need to. I tell Joe I got a text from my wife and have to get home. He calls me a pussy and asks if she checks my balls at the door when I get home. His taunts mean nothing. I tell him I will see him again and slip on my jacket. I turn away, leaving him to drink alone. As I head for the door, I let myself sway a little more than is called for. The adrenaline in my body is canceling out the beer, but I don't want to show it. I weave a little as I go through the exit.

Outside, the cold hits me. It was so warm inside, it seems chillier now than before, and it's still raining. A miserable night to be outside, but I don't care about the weather. The parking lot is filled with cars, but no one is around. If I'm right, the big guy will follow me out, and I'll be ready for him. My car is at the back of the lot. I search for his green Toyota, but it isn't there. He could have changed cars. Or more likely, he parked in the next lot over like he did before. I duck down between two cars about halfway back in the lot.

A few seconds later, the bar door opens, and someone comes out. I'm in my hiding place between the cars and I can't see who it is, but I know it's him. I feel the kick of adrenaline and the sense of anticipation. I hear footsteps on the gravel. He's heading this way, and he's rushing. Then his pace slows, and I know he is looking around to see where I went. I stay low and try to control my breath. I feel like a spring compressed too long. My muscles are tensed and ready to fire. I clench my hands into fists. The cold isn't bothering me now. I'm warm all over and in full control.

Footsteps crunch on gravel. He is walking again, but slowly. He's confused. He sees my car, but I'm not there. I can't see him, but I expect he has his weapon out now. If I was in his shoes, I would be ready and looking for my hiding space. I tense up as I hear his footsteps come close, almost to where I am. Then he comes into view. He steps right past me. I spring up at him and catch him unawares. I hit him in the neck with full force, hitting him with the heel of my hand.

As big as he is, he goes down hard. I land on top of him and get him in a choke hold. He struggles, bucking against my weight, but I apply pressure, squeezing tight. As I look into his eyes, I see his fear.

I could kill him now. I'm in full control and it would be an easy thing to do. But I'm right outside a busy bar on a busy street. Someone could come outside, or a car could pull into the lot and I'd have another problem on my hands. My first job is to get him out of sight, so we aren't in plain view. My second job is to find out who he is, and who put him on to me. I squeeze harder and his eyes close.

He isn't dead, but he's out. I stand and reach under his arms. I'm panting with effort as I pull the Gorilla back past the cars and over to the side of a big green dumpster, out of view. We are still more public than I'd like to be, but at least we're not out in the open. I put myself in a position of control, kneeling behind him, my arm locked around his throat, ready to choke him out, and wait for him to come around. It's raining harder, but I ignore it. Within a minute, his eyes flutter open and he focuses on me. He is much bigger than me, but his eyes widen with fear.

"Who are you?" I ask. "Why are you following me?"

"You're crazy!" his voice cracks.

"Who are you?" I say again, pushing a thumb into his eye, making him squeal. "Who sent you. How did you pick up the contract?"

"Contract? You're paranoid. You've got to be insane." He spits the words out and I think he is going to struggle, but he doesn't. He knows I have the upper hand and resisting won't help.

"I'm a P.I. A private investigator."

The way he says this, I believe him. He was an amateur, too easily spotted. I ease off on my hold and let him gasp as he pulls in air.

"My name is Daryl Owens. I'm a licensed investigator with the Warwick agency. Check my front jacket pocket. My license and ID are there."

I keep my choke hold as I reach with my other hand into his pocket and take out his wallet. One handed, I open the wallet and find the ID. His picture and the information match. Faking a license is an easy thing to do. I know, because I have many sets of IDs, whatever I need for the occasion, but I don't think this one's fake. He's telling the truth. I ease up on my hold some more.

"I was hired by Jensen and Jensen. All I'm doing is monitoring where you go." His anger is winning out over his fear. "I was thinking this was all a bust, until now. You are a piece of work, buddy."

"Jensen and Jensen?" I release his neck completely. I'm in shock myself.

"Divorce attorneys, moron. Talk with your wife, she can fill you in on everything."

I move back and he gets up unsteadily. I stand, but I'm shaky and it's an effort to keep upright. I feel like I've been punched in the gut. He is wet and angry, and he backs away.

"Assault is a crime, you know!" He is bolder as he puts distance between us. "This isn't over. You'll be hearing more from me."

I don't bother to respond as he nearly runs away, toward his car in the next lot over. I stand by myself and let the rain wash over me.

13

My hangover is mild, but I feel awful in the morning. I can't wrap my head around what has happened. We have a great marriage. How could she do this to me—to us? How could I have missed the signs?

Divorce.

The word sounds so bitter and final. Like death. And in a way, it is. But I'm not ready for this to end, and I need to hear it in Jen's own words. I almost called her last night, and I consider calling her again now. But she won't pick up the phone, and even if she does, what will I say? I'm not sure I trust myself to talk with her yet. I need to process this more, to come to terms with where we are. I want to say good morning to the kids, but I can't, which makes things worse. I'm cut off not just from Jen, but my whole family. My anger rises. She has no right to do this to me. I think about driving over to her sister's house, but I know this won't help.

I roll out of bed and stare through the window. The day is sunny, but it does nothing to help my mood. I throw down three Advils and consider mu next move. The house taunts me with its silence. I shower, dress and am about to leave the house, when a thought occurs to me. Jen has secrets, that is clear. What else don't I know about her? I go back upstairs to our bedroom. Our room is divided into what is hers, and what is mine. She has her privacy, and I've never thought to intrude on it. But now it's different. I go to her bedside dresser and search it first.

This is her stuff, and I feel a tinge of guilt as I look through it and find nothing more than hand and facial lotions, lip balms and a box of Kleenex. There is a bottle of scented massage oil I bought her as a gift. A small album of the kids' pictures, and a few candles. Nothing interesting, nothing incriminating. I check the bottom drawer on the night stand, her underwear drawer. She has panties and bras, and at the bottom some lacy lingerie she has never worn. It still has the tag on it. Did she buy this, or was this a gift? I didn't buy it for her. Did George?

There are pictures on top of her big dresser in the corner. Pictures of us, together. Jen and me, the kids, and all of us together. Looking at this, we appear to be the perfect family, smiling and happy. What changed? I open the top drawer and there are more undergarments. I pull them out and pass my hands under them. I find something solid. I know what it's by feel, and a sense of dread overwhelms me as I move aside the lacy things and pick it up. It's a handgun, a small .22 caliber. I feel faint, my hands shake. Jen always hated the idea of guns and told me she would never want one in her home. I'm her protector, and I make her feel safe. So why does she have the gun? Who does she need protection from? I check and see it's unloaded. A minor relief, but it doesn't change anything. Should I take it? If I do, when she returns she'll know I looked in her things, and she'll know what I found. I don't want to alert her in any way. At least not until I decide what to do.

I place the gun back where I found it, and arrange the garments as best I can, to appear untouched. It's clear Jen has her secrets. I keep looking. I find her jewelry box, more clothes and a box filled with Greeting cards, going back years. There are birthday cards, anniversary and Valentine's Day cards, some with little notes, others just the signature. Some are from me, other's her mom, her sister, and the kids. Jen is sentimental, and I'm not surprised she kept them.

In the closet everything is divided in two, her side and mine. I'm in here every day but take it for granted that her side is hers, and mine is mine. Though we are together, we have our own things. Her side is packed with clothes. Dresses for every season on hangers, along with jeans and casual wear, some folded neatly in compartments. On the floor, there are more shoes than she can ever wear. I quickly go through all of this, looking for anything she might have hidden. I don't know what I'm looking for, and I check her pockets and move stuff around. I don't find a thing.

There are boxes and bins on the top shelf of her closet. I reach up to get them, but they are too high up to see behind. I go back into the bedroom and bring back a chair, step up and pull down the first box. Balancing it against the ledge, I remove the top. It's filled with the kids' school stuff, art projects and report cards. I replace the top and return the box back where I found it, then pull down the box next to it. It's filled with sweaters, some she wears when the weather is cold, and others I haven't seen in years. I start to put it back, but there is something behind it. It's a folding file, brown with an elastic loop holding it together. I step down and put the big box on the ground, then reach up to get the file folder.

I slip off the elastic band and open it while standing on top of the chair. I'm surprised to find it's filled with letters. In this age of emails, texts and instant conversations, letters seem absurd. Yet this file is filled with them. I pull out a clump, and they are on different kinds of paper, some on stationary, others on lined yellow paper. These all look old.

I unfold the one on top, and see it's dated from years back, from her college days. Before I even met her. I quickly read through it and see it's a love letter of a kind. I skim through and the writer is telling how much he misses her, and how he thinks of her all the time. It isn't graphic, but I can tell they were lovers, and I know I shouldn't be reading this. I skip ahead to the end and it's signed, Tony. Without meaning to, I picture him as young, dark and muscular, a gold chain around his neck. I get a feeling in my gut and I think of Jen's face when we make love, and I think of them together. This is crazy, I realize. This was from before we even knew each other. She has her history as I have mine. She is sentimental, and though it hurts me to see these, I understand why she kept them.

I scan through the letters and there are more from Tony, but there are others, too. One is from high school and there are others over the years. This is all ancient history, from before we even met. I never wrote her letters. I consider myself romantic, but the only record I have is from the notes I put in Hallmark cards. I'm caught up in this, and the tension in my gut grows. I shouldn't be reading these, they are old, and they don't matter. I'm the one who won. Up until now, at least.

I'm about to put them back, when I notice a single piece of thin paper. It's on a to do list, like the one we have stuck on our refrigerator door, the kind you list what you need from the grocery store, or to write a note to remind you to get your oil changed. I pull this sheet out and look at it closely. This isn't a love letter, it's a single line – *Thinking of you*. It has a crudely drawn smiley face, winking, and is signed simply, *G*.

My hands start to shake. The adrenaline rises and I'm suddenly lost and angry. *G*. Is it George? It could be from a Gary or a Glen or a Gabe. For all I know it could be Grandma. It could be anybody. It isn't dated, and this type of list is on our refrigerator, but we had something similar back when I lived at home, years ago. These lists are common. It could be from years ago, or it could be more recent. I look at the paper and it doesn't appear old or aged, but then it's hard to tell. Still, I feel a certainty. It has to be George.

I'm hot as I replace the letters in the file, snap back the elastic band and replace them where I found them. I put the box back, so the hiding place looks safe and undisturbed. I go through the rest of the closet and don't find anything else, but I know I have found enough.

George. My good friend George.

Downstairs I go through the kitchen and the den. I search in the little places Jen uses to store things, looking for any other evidence of infidelity. I don't find a thing. In the basement I do the same. I pull out all the boxes and junk we have stored there. I look through everything and find lots of stuff from the kids: old toys and games, clothes Jen plans to give away, and things we've saved from our old apartment, things we will never use. But I don't find anything new.

Still, I think I have found what I need. It's George. And maybe Jen, too. They are together on this. I'm still shaking as I go back upstairs. How long have they been doing this behind my back? How could I have been such a fool? I think of the gun, and I wonder if their first plan was to do this themselves? Jen calls me over when a bug is in the house, and she can't kill it herself. I can't see her pointing the gun at me and pulling the trigger herself.

Besides, this is too obvious. As much as she might want to get rid of me, and it seems she does, she isn't going to do it on her own and go to jail for it. Making an arrangement, placing a contract with an unknown third party, seems to be more her style.

I can't stay in the house anymore. I'm about to leave, but I can't get the gun out of my mind. Where did she get this? Her brother Adam is a gun enthusiast and I can easily imagine him offering her a firearm for protection. Maybe she took him up on it. It was unloaded, but there could be bullets somewhere else—she could have them in her purse. It's safer to take it.

I return to the bedroom and pull it out of her drawer. I check the firing pin and see it is filed off. I sigh with relief. The gun is useless, it won't work. But does she know this? Maybe not. I leave the gun as it is and exit the house.

I jump in my car and drive. I need to process this, I need to think about what to do. George is behind this. I feel a certainty now. He is behind Jen's anger and her leaving me. He has to be. They are together, but it's him. He's flush with money and big sums are going in and out of his accounts. He has the means to place the contract. Jen, I think, is his motive. *He wants what's mine.* I know how he's looked at her and it's clear he has poisoned her toward me.

As I drive, I think back to when I first met George, when we were both freshmen at school. I was a state away from Dad, and it was the first time he didn't control my movements. Going away to school is freedom for most kids, but it was different for me. I wasn't just getting away from curfews and rules. For the first time, I wasn't my dad's helper. For the first time in my life, I controlled who I was, and what I did. I was drunk with new ideas and experiences, and the possibilities of what I could do with my life. For the first time, I had a sense of who I really was as my own person.

George was on my dorm floor and I knew him, but we never hung out together at first. He had his friends and I had mine. We ended up having a philosophy class together my second semester. We walked back to the dorm after that class, talking for the first time, and everything sort of clicked. George grew up in a wealthy suburb north of Chicago, and his dad was a on a treadmill, chasing money, obsessed with appearances and living a lie. According to George, his dad was a phony, and George was going to live a real life.

His dad sounded a lot like mine, without the killing part. From then on, we became great friends.

I flow with the traffic and think of George, remembering the time my junior year when a group of us went out drinking and ended up at a townie bar away from the school. We were talking with some local girls, and the local guys didn't approve. A few were big, aggressive, ready to defend their turf. It ended up ugly, and our friends scattered as we went outside. George and I ended up facing down four guys on our own. George is big, and he wasn't about to back away. I looked mismatched, but I remember my anticipation as we faced them down. How I realized I'd missed the violence I'd sworn off when I left home. We walked away from that bar knowing each other better than we did before. We weren't just friends; we were brothers.

I drive on automatic pilot, my mind in the past. George and I started doing everything together. We traveled together that summer, backpacking across Eastern Europe, and spending almost a month in the Greek islands. I remember the conversations we had, the plans we made. Life was in front of us and anything was possible. I wasn't sure what I was going to do after school and was thinking of joining the Peace Corps. George was going to travel on his own for a while and see the rest of the world before he even thought about the future. He was going to do something meaningful, though. He was going to make a difference. We got stoned a lot and spent days in old monasteries, contemplating the meaning of life and our place in this vast universe.

George was with me the night I met Jen. It was New Year's Eve at a friend's house the year after we graduated. By this time, we were back home, and I was living with my parents again. He'd started an internship with his dad's wealth planning firm, bought a new car and moved into an apartment in the city. After four years of being away, only coming home for holidays, I'd returned to Dad's orbit. After years away from the family business, I'd helped him with an assignment earlier that day. Although I'd sworn not to help him anymore, stepping back in felt easy, natural.

Jen was a friend of Christine's, who George met at his dad's country club earlier that year. Jen and I hit it off that night, and we were together from then on.

We were together a lot back then, the four of us. We'd go out for long nights of drinking and dancing, and quieter nights at one of our apartments with bottles of wine and deep conversations. We traveled together, and life was good. It's funny how we fell into the conventional life. George thought Christine was pregnant when they got engaged. It was a false alarm, but they went through with the plans and had a big wedding in the spring. I was his best man, and he was mine the following year. George and I stayed close, while Jen and Christine fell away. We don't see them so much as couples now. Kids come and life changes.

George told me about the first time he cheated on his wife—at a conference when he was away for a week. This was a few years in, after his second son, Robbie was born. I'm his friend and I listen. I don't judge. He doesn't tell me about other times, but it's part of who he is. I know him that well.

I stop at a red light and notice my surroundings as I return to the present. I'm on the way to George's house. I think about him and my car points its way there, on automatic. The light turns green and I continue, turning off the main road, suddenly aware of my turns I've been this way so many times before.

George lives a couple suburbs over in an old money town where there are big homes on big lots, and big homes on small lots. There are still a few small homes left, but most have been torn down and rebuilt over the years. George's home is small compared to his neighbors' places, but it's still huge. It was a stretch when he bought it, but Christine came from money, and her father helped make it possible. Keeping up appearances is stressful, but for George, it's a necessary part of his business plan. Rich people don't want to deal with a middle-class financial planner, he says. He has followed his father's path as I have followed mine.

As I drive by his home, I ease of on the gas pedal. I don't want to stop or be noticed, in case Christine is home and looking out the window, although I know this isn't likely. An old Jeep is in the driveway, and I'm sure this is the nanny's car. I slow to a crawl as I think things through. My next move is clear.

I need to kill George.

14

I can't sit still, and I need to walk. As I enter the quaint town square, I pull in and park on an open diagonal near the Starbucks on the corner. The town is old, in a fashionable way. It's trendy and nearly reeks of money. On a weekend night, the area would be busy with couples walking around, the restaurants busy and an energy in the air. This morning it's quiet. After locking my car, I start to walk.

I've got to move. I need to walk and think this through. Killing George. It's the right decision, my only choice. Killing George will void the contract he put in, and it might be the only way I can truly get my life and my wife back. It comes down to him, or me. Although this is the right move, the tightness still grips my gut.

The day is warm and sunny, a beautiful day. I try and take it all in and accept where I am now. I keep walking, past a dress shop and a Thai takeout place. I pass a bakery and breathe in the smell of fresh baked bread. The aroma is comforting and reminds me of home. A tear comes to my eye. I wipe it away and try to ignore sense of loss. I already miss my best friend.

I keep walking and a little ways up, a man walks out of a storefront and onto the sidewalk in front of me. He doesn't look my way, and I don't know if he is even aware I'm here. I follow him, leaving almost a quarter block gap between us. As I keep walking, I start to consider, how I'll do it.

There are a thousand ways to kill a man, and I have experience with a great many of them. It could be set up as a random assault or made to look like an accident. I could do it in a way that will appear to be a home invasion, an accident or even suicide. There are countless ways to do this. But it won't be easy.

The man in front of me pauses as he looks in a barber shop window. I cut the distance between us before he starts moving again. I picture George and wonder how I will do this. The truth is that most murders are committed by people close to the victim. A spouse, a lover, a family member. Maybe a best friend. These cases are usually solved, because the police look for connections. They look for motives and opportunities. Everyone close is a suspect, and they assume the worst of everyone.

I can kill a stranger and disappear. I'm a ghost. My best friend? This will be more difficult. I drink, eat and golf with him regularly, see his family socially, and I'm in his phone and text log several times a week. When George dies, I will get a call and the investigators will look at me closely.

The man in front of me pauses again. It seems that he is out for a stroll with no set destination in mind. He turns right at the corner, and without thinking, I follow him. This will be different from my normal type of job. The people I kill are strangers. We have no connections, and the only way I can be traced to them is if I screw it up somehow, leaving physical evidence or an eye witness to connect me. It's easy to kill a stranger. It will be much harder to kill George.

The man stops again, and I nearly catch up to him before he starts moving. He sees me now and is surely aware of me. He quickens his pace, just by a little. A thought comes to me. It would be easy to kill this man, and I could get away with it. For the first time, I start to pay him conscious attention. Maybe in his late fifties or early sixties, but trim and in good shape, he's dressed well and has a full head of graying hair, and glasses, though I can't see the frames. He has a step to his walk that makes me think he is happy. I could kill him easily. How would I do it?

I'm a few steps behind him now. I know he hears my footsteps close to him, and this has to put him on edge, if just in a small way. He isn't scared or worried. It's daylight in a safe town, and I don't appear to be a threat in any way. At the same time, there is something in our DNA that makes us anxious when someone is following us. Even when we think they are not a threat. And I'm much more of a threat than he knows.

I look ahead. We are nearing the end of the downtown section and the only ones on the street now. There are no cars or traffic of any kind. I know this town well. Ahead, there is an old building that was once used for offices but is now empty and slated for renovation into luxury condos. Beyond this is a small park, and then the train station.

I glance behind me and see that the sidewalk is empty. I glance around. We are alone, he and I. This is the place to do it, right up ahead by the empty building. There are all sorts of little alcoves and entrance ways. I'd attack from behind as he gets near one, drag him in so he is out of the sight of potential witnesses, and do what I need to do. It would be over fast, and no one would see or hear us. I'm breathing fast and my adrenaline has kicked in.

I stop in the middle of the sidewalk. I'm treating this as if it were real. I'm not playing a game of *what if*—I'm truly stalking him. The man quickens his pace, and glances back at me, right before he turns the corner on to a side street. I take a deep breath. I'm not a psychopath. It was only an exercise. I wouldn't have done it.

But I could have. And I would have gotten away with it.

I turn around and head back to my car.

I HEAD BACK to my house. Jen and the kids won't be there, and I don't want to be alone, but I'm too keyed up to be out on my own. Besides, I have to plan, and I feel more secure at home.

How will I kill George?

It would be so much easier if I could put some distance between us and have someone else do it for me. But I don't know anyone like myself. Clearly, there's no such thing as a hitman directory or convention and, although I could go through the Agency myself, as a client, that would take too long and open me up to a host of other problems. Besides, it wouldn't be right. George is my friend, I love him like a brother. It's only fair I do the job myself, unpleasant as it might be.

In my office I turn on my secure computer. Every time I take on a new target, I have to find the answers to some questions. I already know the *Who*, George is my intended target. I usually don't care about the *Why*, as the targets are selected and vetted for me. In George's case the *Why* is crucial, but I know what I have to do. I need to determine the *When*, the *Where* and most importantly, the *How*.

A good start will be looking closer at George's habits and patterns. I know a lot of this already. For example, he leaves his house early every work day and spends an hour in gym before heading to his office. Typically, he leaves the office after six, because that's when he often calls me while on his way home. He sometimes stops off for a drink on the way home, but that's not a regular habit. At night, he is either at home with his family, at some kind of event with his kids, or occasionally a business meeting with a client. These are the things I know, but this is the tip of his behavioral iceberg. We all have patterns and habits of where we go and what we do. We all have secrets we don't share with others, no matter how close they might be. I need to find the things George doesn't tell me about, the little things he does regularly that have become routines.

I check his credit card purchases again, searching for patterns, but nothing jumps out. There are daily charges for lunches and incidentals, but most of these are in his building or at random places on the way to or from his office. I see charges on Amazon where he orders and gets stuff shipped to his home. The big charges are all for things I already know about, or restaurant bills on an irregular basis. If he has hidden activities he does regularly, I'm guessing he pays cash.

How will I kill George?

It must look like an accident, or something so random the investigators don't take a second look. I run through the possibilities. An accidental death at home is the best option. Falling down a flight of stairs has worked in the past. An accidental overdose on medication is always a good option, though I don't think George is taking anything appropriate.

Maybe he could have too much to drink and drown in the bathtub, or slip in the shower? That would be a freakish way to die, and probably wouldn't merit a second look if I set it up right. Or I could make it look like a suicide somehow. If he died in his garage with his car running, his system filled with scotch and carbon monoxide, it could be explained away as an accident. Or despair. When the investigators come to interview me, I will show my authentic grief and tell them about the pressure he faced at work, and how I knew he was having a hard time, but I had no idea it was this serious.

Doing this at his home would be best, but the logistics are overwhelming. There is security of course, but I can work around that. The bigger worry is that he won't be alone. Christine and the kids will be there too. It's a big house, but people are unpredictable. I don't see a way I can get in the neighborhood, break into their home, kill George and get away unseen with no evidence I was even there. It doesn't seem possible. If I had more time, I could wait until Christine went with her kids to visit her parents in Arizona, which she does several times a year. With George alone in an empty house it opens up far more opportunities, but I don't have the luxury of waiting and planning for the right time. I need to take care of this right away.

His office is another option. George has a small staff, but he is often there alone after business hours. I could wait until everyone is gone, break in and do something there. Office accidents are rare, but I could improvise. As I think this, I know it won't work. There is too much unpredictability. At Georges office, people come and go at all hours, and they have the overnight cleaning staff. And the security system. George is in an office with a guard at the front desk all night long, and video monitoring throughout. The security was a selling point when he signed the lease. It showed his clients that their money and information would be safe with him.

No, the office won't work.

This means I need to do it outside somewhere, out in the real world. A car accident, maybe? We spend so much time in our cars, and accidents happen every day. But this isn't easy either. In the movies you see people cutting someone's brake lines and this leads to a fatal accident. Or a near miss. Real life isn't as predictable and most anything could happen. Besides, tampering with the mechanics would leave clear evidence of foul play. It won't work. Driving a car, I could force him into an accident, but there are too many uncontrollable variables. that is a stupid plan too.

I'm running out of ideas on how to do this, and I think it's because he is too close to me. Our relationship is clouding my judgement and I'm not thinking clearly. I close my computer and head back upstairs. It's strange being alone in this empty house. The only sounds are the hum of the refrigerator and the furnace fan kicking in. It's too quiet. Even though I know it won't happen, I half expect one of the kids to run into the room. Jen won't even take my calls. I miss my kids. I miss my family. And it's all because of George.

Back in the living room I sink into the big chair by the TV. I need to do something, but I don't know what. I pick up the remote and switch on the TV for some background noise and for something else to focus on. The picture comes up along with the sound. It's a talk show with several women sitting around a set that looks like a living room, they're chatting. I switch channels and stop for a second to watch a news program, but I don't care what is happening in the world. I'm focused on my own issues. I flip through and land on The History Channel, pausing as the camera pans across a Civil War battlefield.

"Across the river, over eight-thousand Union forces were amassed in ..."

And it comes to me. I know how I will kill my friend George.

15

I need some supplies, and I go shopping. I want to be extra careful, so I start at a Walgreens a couple of towns over. My purchases include: duct tape, surgical gloves, a box cutter, a screwdriver, and a handful of household items. My mood has shifted, and I'm almost giddy with excitement and anticipation. I know how I will do it now, and I want to get it done. I'm extra cautious on the off chance someone tries to trace this back to me. I put on a baseball cap and wear sunglasses before going to a Walmart and buying a new pair of no-name gym shoes, the cheapest ones that fit well. While I'm there, I also buy a new pair of jeans, a size too big to give me more room for flexibility and movement, a sweatshirt and a ski mask.

Satisfied I have all I need, I want to make sure that George will be where he needs to be. As I drive toward home, I call his number and am surprised when he picks up right away.

"Charley, what's going on, my brother?"

"Hey, buddy. I wanted to say thanks again for our lunch the other day. It's been a while since I've gotten buzzed like that in the afternoon."

"I think you needed that. You seemed tense."

"Yeah? I guess I was. There's a lot going on right now, but it felt good. I'm glad I could celebrate with you, and it's awesome that you pulled the union deal together."

I say this, and I mean it. I truly am happy for George. I do love him as a friend, even if he did try to steal my wife and turn her away from me. I'm not even angry, anymore.

"Thanks, man. This is a real game changer. I mean, it feels like my life is about to explode. You know how you work and work, and you hardly see the progress, and then something happens and it's like the floodgates open up? Everything changes. That's what it feels like, man."

"I know exactly what you mean. It's like you think everything is one way, and then you find out its something else entirely."

"Right, right," George sounds distracted, and I hear someone talking to him in the background. "Hey, could you hold on a second?"

I drive in silence and wait for George to come back on the phone. I think through the details and check off how I will do this. I want it to be over fast. I don't want to cause my friend any more pain or anguish than is absolutely necessary. As much as he has hurt me now, our connection was real, and I'm truly going to miss him when he is gone.

"Sorry about that," George comes back on the line. "I'm finishing up the presentation for tonight. Livia had a couple of the slides wrong, and I wanted to make sure we got this all together the right way."

"Oh, the union presentation," I say, trying to sound surprised. "That's tonight?"

"Yeah, it starts at seven o'clock, though I probably won't go on for a while. I'll be on toward the end of the meeting, after they finish all their other business."

"That's great. I'd forgotten that was tonight. I was going to see if you wanted to stop for a drink or two on the way home."

"You know I'd love to, but not tonight. I'm going to get down there early and meet with Henderson, the president of the local for dinner and a few drinks, beforehand. Let's do a rain check. Maybe sometime later this week?"

"Yeah, of course," I say, letting disappointment edge into my voice. "This meeting, it's going to be down at the big hall off Madison, right?"

"It is. Then there's a bar not far from there, do you remember the Emerald Isle? I expect I'll be there afterwards, buying more drinks. I think this is going to be a late one."

"Well, knock them dead," I say. "You'll do great. We'll catch up later."

We say our goodbyes and I kill the connection. I now know for sure when and where George will be tonight. The union hall is just off Madison Street, not that far from the United Center where the Bulls and Blackhawks play. The area is hot now, with luxury condos and new retail developments popping up all over. But a few blocks over, the neighborhood changes. Where the developing areas are mostly white and upper middle class, the West Side is black and filled with poverty, blight and neglect. These are the areas you make sure to lock your doors when driving through. Gang signs and graffiti are everywhere and the crime rate is among the highest in the city. It fits right into my plan for tonight.

I know the Emerald Isle and can picture it clearly. It's an old Irish bar a few blocks from the union hall. George and I stopped there a couple of years back after a hockey game and stayed until closing time. Celtic music was playing, that night and the crowd—mostly white and mostly dressed in Blackhawk jerseys—

kept breaking into the Da-Da-Da-Da-Duh of the Blackhawk theme song. We sang along, drank Harp beer, and talked and talked. When we went outside at the end of the night, the streets were dark and empty, and it felt like we were in a little island separated from the rest of the city. This place and this time will work best.

I park in my driveway and enter my home. Once again, it's strange to be here without Jen and the kids, and suddenly, I'm hit by a wave of sadness that's so hard I want to cry. I feel like I've lost them. My life was so good, and now it's not. I clench my fists, breathe in deeply and wait for the moment to pass. I'm doing what I can to make this right. I can't imagine living without my family, but if I do what I need to do, I can win them back. I have to believe this.

I pack away the groceries I bought and take my other purchases upstairs to the bedroom. I lay it all out in front of me, and I have what I need. When someone finds the body and the police investigate, they'll mark it down as a random street crime. A sad case of someone being in the wrong place at the wrong time—another ugly statistic. No doubt it will be a bigger deal than normal. George is white and lives in the suburbs, which will make it different. The radio commentators and TV anchormen will ramp up the fear for the next few news cycles, but in the end, it will be another unsolved crime. They won't look any further. I doubt I'll even get an official call.

But if I do, I need to be prepared. I pack up my new purchases along with another change of clothes and pack them into an overnight bag. I lock up the house and get back in my car. Having the family gone works into my plan. But on the off chance someone does come around asking questions, I need to be able to show I was nowhere near the scene of the crime. I need a solid alibi. I drive to the expressway and head north, toward Wisconsin. Milwaukee is only ninety minutes away. I make some phone calls along the way. I call Jen again. I don't expect her to pick up, and she doesn't. I call a couple of old friends I rarely talk with and catch up and make small talk. This takes my mind off what I need to do, makes the drive feel shorter, and it establishes where I was, if it ever become necessary.

When I reach Milwaukee, I go downtown and check into a Hilton. I pay with my credit card. After dropping my stuff off in the room, I stroll around the neighborhood, buy lunch and a new pair of sunglasses at a local store, again charging everything. Then, I return to my room to take a nap. It's going to be a long night and I need to be ready and well rested.

After being woken from a deep sleep when the alarm goes off at 4:30 p.m., I drink a glass of water, brush my teeth and review my plan. It all works, I think. I don't see any obvious holes. Killing George will be hard in one way, but easy in another. Most of this is routine, something I've done many times before. I need to remember not to focus on who he is, but what he has done. I need to think of this as a job, just like any other.

I go downstairs to the lobby and ask the concierge where a good place will be for dinner. He suggests a well-known theme restaurant within walking distance of the hotel. I tip him generously and wander down the block. Once I'm there, I sit at my table, order a drink, an appetizer and the special of the day. It's early, but the room is busy with families and there are a lot of kids in the room. A baby is crying a few tables over. I wait patiently, running everything through in my mind once again. When the drink arrives, I leave it untouched and tell the waitress that I changed my mind and want my food to go. On the way out, I drop everything in a trash can. I'm not hungry and the food would slow me down. I have a record of where I'm, and that's enough.

I enter the hotel by the side door and take the elevator up to my room. I change into my new clothes and put the items I need for tonight in a plastic bag. I turn on my TV and order up a movie, the longest one I can find. I'm about to walk out, when I remember to take out my cell phone, turn it off, and leave it on the dresser. I don't want the phone tracking me going to Chicago and back.

Wearing my cap, I leave my car in the garage and hail a taxi, telling him to take me to the airport. I look out the window and don't look ahead the whole drive. I pay with cash, leaving him a standard tip. I march down the long corridor and out of the airport, taking the shuttle to long-term parking. The sun is going down as I walk along the aisles of cars, chosing the one I want to take. There are a few other people in the lot, but it's not crowded, and no one will notice me. I look inside the cars until I find what I'm looking for. It's an older model Chevy sedan, and the parking stub is sticking out of the visor, which is exactly what I need.

I mentally mark the location, and take a look around at the surrounding cars. A row over, I find a car with Illinois plates. I take out the screwdriver from my bag, and quickly remove the plates. I look around again to make sure no one is close, and take the plates off the Chevy, and switch them with my new plates. It doesn't take long to break into the car and hotwire it. I haven't done this in a while, but it's like riding a bike. Within a few minutes I'm out of the lot and back on the expressway, heading south.

By the time I reach the city, it's almost eight-thirty. I drive over to the union hall and find the parking lot is full. I don't want to be conspicuous, but I want to make sure George is here. There are security cameras trained on the parking lot, but I have to risk it. I drive up and down the aisles looking for his silver BMW, but I don't see it. My heart races and I wonder if something happened. He should be here by now. I'm starting to dream up reasons why he wouldn't be here when I see the shiny new, teal green Tahoe SUV. It's got the license plate holder of the biggest GM dealer in the suburbs. It's Christine's car. She bought it a few months back. George has enough smarts to know it wouldn't make sense to drive an expensive foreign car to a union meeting.

I park on a side street across from the building, in a spot where I can see what is going on and can watch for the cars when they leave. I settle in to wait. Sitting by yourself with your own thoughts is hard for most people, but I have found that patience truly is a virtue. It's part of my job, and I've learned over the years to just let go. I quiet my mind and zone out. I'm not sure how much time passes before I notice activity across the street. People are coming out the door, first a few, and then in streams. I look for George, but with the dim yellow light from the overhead street lamps I can't tell if he is out or not. I'm guessing that he isn't. He will hang back with the leadership until they close the hall down, and then the stragglers will make their way down the road to the Emerald Isle.

The noise gets louder as people leave. Doors slam shut, engines rev and someone honks their horn. A stream of cars, their headlights bright, pull out of the parking lot and on to the street. It takes about ten minutes for the lot to empty, and when it does there are only about eight cars left, and one is the teal green Tahoe. With most of the members gone, the area grows quiet again. The hall is in an industrial area and at this time of night, the only activity is an occasional truck driving through. It's dark and quiet. Almost peaceful. I settle in to wait again and it's another half hour before anyone else comes out.

Two uniformed security guards walk out along with a handful of men. I hear loud talking and laughing. A big guy puts his arm over one man's shoulder and I know it's George. Someone calls something out to the others, and there's more laughter. The security guards lock up as the others head out to their cars. The engines fire up and the area is flooded by bright headlights. They pull out, form a line, and all turn right.

I hang back. I know where they are going, and I don't want to call attention to myself by following too closely. When they are all on the road, and some distance is between us, I pull out and follow. The line of cars turns on Madison, one after the other, and I am relieved. I almost brought along a tracking device to put on George's car, but it seemed too risky. Now I see they are going to the bar as planned and I needn't have worried.

I bypass the bar and find a spot down the block where I can watch the entrance. I roll down my windows and wait for them to park and go in. They all walk in from the side street close to the bar. They are loud and boisterous as they walk, but once they go inside, the neighborhood falls quiet. Traffic flows by intermittently. The faint sound of the El train a couple of blocks away breaks the stillness. There are no pedestrians out and other than the bar, the area seems deserted. I pick up the things I need, putting the ski mask and the box cutter in my pockets. I get out of the car and softly close the door behind me.

I walk down the sidewalk with my head down. Outside the bar, I pull my hoodie up and take a quick glance inside the windows. The place is crowded. Irish music plays along with the hum of conversations and someone singing, as I pass. I don't search for George or his new friends. I doubt if he would see me or realize it was me if he did, but it isn't worth the risk. I stroll past the building and around the corner on to the side street. The surrounding area is nothing but commercial buildings and vacant lots. The street is dark, and the only light is from a single street lamp half way up the block. I keep walking, past the other cars, until I reach the big Tahoe near the end of the dead-end street. The light of the street lamp reflects off metal giving it an almost luminous glow. If I were a car thief, this is the one I would choose.

George's car is parked by a vacant lot. It's too dark to see but I know this is covered with trash and not a place where most people would want to hang out. I find a good place to wait and settle in. After a while the darkness is comforting. The bar is a bright island in a dark sea. It's quiet back here. The wave-like sounds of the cars passing out on the main road, and the whistle and rustle of the wind blowing trash around the vacant lot makes the place peaceful.

I try not to think about what I will do to George. When they are done, maybe in an hour, maybe when the bar is closing, they'll all come back at once. They will be happy with drink, tired, and ready to go home. George is the salesman and he will be the last to leave. He'll say his goodbyes and linger and won't go to his car until the rest are on their way out. And then, alone in the dark, I'll slit his throat with the box cutter.

It sounds gruesome, but it will be a quick death. I don't want him to suffer. I'll look into his eyes and he will know it's me. I owe him that. Then, when he is gone, I'll take his keys and drive his car over a few blocks and leave it in front of an all-night fried fish stand, with the keys in the ignition. It will be gone before morning—before Christine calls to report him missing and before anyone finds his body. It hurts me to think about it, but it must be done.

I try not to think about it.

I'm starting to settle in, when I smell smoke. I get up and sniff the air. It could be a trash fire somewhere. I sniff again, and it seems more dense, closer. That's when I hear the siren, at a distance but coming closer. I walk out of the vacant lot and into the street. People stream out of the bar. There's loud talk and laughter as the people cross the street to gather on the other side. The sirens wail is louder now. I walk a little closer, still in the darkness, to see what is going on. A big crowd has gathered by the time the first fire engine arrives. So many people. Were they all in the bar, or did they magically appear from the surrounding neighborhoods? Someone yells something about marshmallows and the crowd laughs. They're having a party. They have no intention of moving. They couldn't if they wanted to as the firetruck blocks the street. I clench my fists, kick the dirt and swear silently. This isn't what I planned for.

Within a few minutes the whole street is bathed in the flashing lights of fire trucks and police cars. The blare of the sirens is loud and abrasive. I don't see a fire, but the pungent odor of burning plastic and wood fills the air. There is too much noise and traffic and commotion. My quiet place is gone. Too many people, too much light. My plan shot. I turn and start walking across the vacant lot and away from the bar and all the excitement.

This won't work now, but I will come up with another plan and try again, maybe tomorrow.

16

I hardly sleep at all that night. I have to go all the way back to Milwaukee to retrieve my car and belongings. I'm frustrated and angry and can't believe I missed out on killing George. The fire wasted a full day and I don't have the time to spare. I need to do the job tonight, but I have no idea where George will be or who he will be with. Things are much more complicated now.

I check online. The Agency has sent another message. It's almost the same as the previous one:

Urgent. We need progress report and expected completion time for your current project.

This is concerning. They are monitoring this contract much too closely. I need to send something to ease the pressure. I think for a moment, and write back:

Project will be successfully completed on schedule. Delivery imminent. I will send a full report upon completion.

I close the computer and try to put the Agency out of my mind.

It's days since Jen left, and she's still not answering my calls. Her sister is no help, and it's painful not being able to talk with my kids. Jen and I have fought before, but never like this. It seems out of character for her. Then again, it's clear there are many things about my wife I didn't know before. But I do know she is a good mother, and she will make sure the kids are well taken care of, which means she will keep them on their normal schedules. I call their school attendance office, identify myself, and say there were some mix-ups at home this morning. I want to make sure the kids got to school on time, and I'm assured they did.

I'm at their school well before the afternoon bell. I know where Jen will pick them up. I park my car in the visitor's lot and wait on a bench on the sidewalk near the front door, around the corner from the pickup area. I sit and try to appear relaxed. A mom walks up the sidewalk pushing a stroller, and sits down on the other side of the bench. I nod to her and smile. Some other moms walk up and stand in a clutch by the big flagpole, talking while we all wait. A flow of cars drives up the street and fall in line for the pickup. The big yellow school buses start streaming in and positioning themselves in the roundabout by the front doors. More moms walk up, and some glance at their watches, or check their phones. I smile and act like I belong here. I see one mom I recognize, and I give her a nod and a smile. I pretend that the world is normal, and I'm just a dad picking up his kids.

My stomach tenses as the bell rings inside. I stand up and turn toward the door. The ringing stops and there is a long pause. It's a minute, maybe more before the door opens. A teacher steps out and stands alongside the door like a sentinel. And then it's chaos. Kids rush out of the building. Some are running, though the teacher at the side calls for them to slow down, no running is allowed.

I monitor the doorway for Emily and Jason. The kids are all dressed nearly alike, and though there are different ethnicities, most are white. I don't want to miss them as they run past me. Then I see Emily. She is walking and talking with another girl. I wave to her. She sees me and there's excitement on her face. She leaves her friend and runs to meet me. She throws her arms around me as I bend down to greet her.

"Daddy! What are you doing here?"

My heart melts as I pull her close. I blink back a tear. I've been away from my kids for days at a time before, but this feels different. This wasn't a business trip I'm coming back from. I have been kept from them, and I'm now being reunited.

"It's great to see you, honey," I say. "I've missed you."

Jason comes out the door and he sees us right away. He runs over and jumps at me. I pull him in close, hugging them both. It's only been a few days, but it seems so much longer.

"Are we going home again?" Jason asks. "I'm tired of Aunt Jackie's house."

"What's going on?' Emily asks. "What's going on with you and Mom?"

"Can we go out to dinner? I want pizza." Jason declares.

"Are you and Mom getting a divorce?" Emily asks, her voice so serious. "Kayla's dad moved out and now they're getting a divorce. I don't want that to happen to me."

"We'll see about the pizza," I say. "And no, we're not getting a divorce. Everything is going to be fine."

They flank me, one on each side, and I put my arms around their shoulders. We are talking and laughing as we turn the corner to where all the parents are lined up in their cars. Jen is standing beside her car, and she sees me at the same time. Her face turns blank and she stiffens. As we get closer, she opens the doors and ushers the kids in.

"Come on Emily, Jason. Get in now. Put on your seat belts."

"Are we going for pizza?" Jason asks.

"Are we going back home? Is Daddy coming with us?" Emily knows something is up.

"Get in the car, we'll talk about this later."

"But I want Daddy to—"

"Get in the car, now!" It's a command and they both comply.

I give them both a squeeze and promise them everything will be all right. They climb in and Jen shuts the door behind them. It's just her, me, and all the other kids and parents streaming by us.

"What's going on, Jen? Why won't you take my calls?"

Her face is stone, but there is something in her eyes. Anger, I think, but also fear.

"Stay away from me," she says. Her voice has a tremble. "Stay away from my kids!"

"Your kids? They're our kids."

"Just stay away. I don't want you around. I don't want to even see you again." Her voice is low, but it hits me as though she is shouting.

Emily and Jason's faces are at the window. They are staring at us, and I hope they can't hear what Jen's saying. I'm aware of mothers passing by, staring at us. We are a spectacle. I want to raise my voice too. I want to tell her I know about her and George, but I forgive her. I know it was all his fault. He poisoned her against me. I want to let her know I'm the injured party, not her. I take a deep breath and keep a calm demeanor.

"You're being extreme. Tell me what I did wrong, and we can work this out."

"Work this out? Who are you? I don't even know you." Her voice is louder now, and I sense the anger is pushing back her fear.

"Come on, honey. You know I love you, and you know I love the kids. Let's just talk. I don't know what the misunderstanding is, but we can work this out."

"What do you do?" Her eyes flash, and her face is hard. "I know it's something bad, something illegal."

"What?" I don't know where this came from, and I'm in shock. "What are you talking about?"

"What are you?' she hisses, barely in control. "A murderer? A spy of some kind? Are you with the mob?"

People are staring and mothers move their kids to get away from us. My heart is thumping. This is hitting too close to home.

"Honey, you know me. I'm what I've always been. I take care—"

"Stop lying!" This is nearly a shout. "Everything you say is a lie!"

I take a step toward her. I want to hold on to her, pull her close and make her stop. She puts her hands up like a shield.

"Don't!"

I stop and give her space, but it feels so raw. "Where're you getting this?" I ask.

"I've always known something was off, I never really understood what you do. You come and go and never tell me anything." She's talking fast now, spitting it out at me with her hands clenched. "You're so mysterious, and I accepted that, I was naïve. But now I find this proof! Fake IDs—"

"Wait! You're getting ... Where'd you see this?" My whole body is shaking.

"I found it on the floor by the desk in your office, a different driver's license with a different name. You're not who you say you are. You're—"

"This must be a mistake! It's a practical joke of some kind! What do you have?" I'm in a panic. My life has always been in control, with my two lives neatly separated. Now, my worlds are colliding.

"Enough! I have enough to know this has all been a lie. Stay away from me, Charley!"

She starts to back away and moves in front of the car to reach the driver's side. I've been exposed, but I don't know how it happened. I've also been betrayed, and she is part of it.

"I know about you!" I say. "I know about you and George. But I forgive you. We can work this out."

"What?" This stops her in her tracks. Her expression changes, and it is true surprise. "You think me and George are—? Wow!"

I plow on. "I know this was George's fault. We can get through this."

She shakes her head and marches around to the driver's side. She has the car between us. "There is nothing going on with me and George. I've talked with him about you, and he knows as little as I do about who you really are."

She could be lying, but I don't think so. I know her too well. I know her expressions and her mannerisms and it hits me. This is the truth.

"Stay away from us, Charley," she starts to open her door. "My lawyer told me about what you did to the investigator. You must be insane. You could have killed him! I'm getting a restraining order, and I'll be filing the papers for the divorce."

"Look, Jen," I'm pleading now. "Let's talk about this."

"Stay away from us!" She steps into the car. The engine is already running, and I'm still standing in shocked silence as my family pulls away.

I look around. Several mothers and their kids are staring at me. Their expressions speak clearly. I'm the villain.

I turn toward the parking lot and head back to my car, battling the tears and the sense of desperation.

17

I sit in the cocoon of my car and catch my breath. I'm numb. My whole world is upside down. Everything I've learned over the last few days is false. She wasn't having an affair with George. Jen was telling the truth. I know this with a cold certainty now. My hands shake, and I grip the steering wheel to make them stop. As bad as I feel, this is a relief. She hasn't been unfaithful to me. This also means my case against George is no longer so clear. He's still my best friend, and I'm relieved I didn't kill him. I think of how close I came and bile rises to my throat, and I'm glad that I wasn't able to do it last night like I'd planned. I don't think I could face myself if I'd gone through with it. Killing George would have been a step too far, a betrayal for which I could never forgive myself. I'm not a religious person, but I silently offer thanks for the fire in the bar last night.

The cars on both sides of me pull away, but I stay in place. I concentrate on my breathing. I try to refocus, calm down and let it go. I take another deep breath, but I can't stop shaking. I think of what she said, and it's clear Jen knows at least some of what I do and what I am. How can she know this? Did I really leave one of my false IDs on the floor? That is much too careless, and I can't imagine I made such a mistake. Who else knows about this side of me?

Dad. He's the only one who knows what I do and how I do it. My hands still shake as I start the car and head out of the near-empty parking lot. I drive slowly and keep both hands on the wheel as I drive out of the neighborhood and toward the expressway.

Is Dad putting on an act? Is he playing some elaborate game, faking his incompetence while he acts out his grudge against me? It doesn't seem possible, but I can't think of a better answer.

By the time I reach Meadowbrook Manor, I've just about stopped shaking. I sign in at the front desk and take the elevator up to the third floor. The group is all in front of the TV again, and this time Dad is with them, sitting in a wheelchair, watching. As I step up to the group, several of the old people focus on me. A lady with stooped shoulders and an oxygen line hooked to her nose, smiles up at me expectantly, her eyes bright, her mouth wide open like a baby bird waiting for a worm. I look toward Dad, and he turns away from the TV and toward me. A light comes to his eyes, and it looks like recognition.

"Charley Boy?" he says. "Is that you?"

I start shaking again. I can't help it. A tear comes to my eye. He recognizes me.

"Hi Dad," I say. "How are you?"

"I'd be better if they got me out of this goddamned thing. They think I'm a damned baby! I can't even walk by myself."

I step over to him and grip his shoulder. It seems like I've found my old dad. I wipe tears from my eyes as I smile.

Missy, the young nurse I met before comes over from the side of the room to greet me.

"Hi, Mr. Fieldner. It's nice to see you again. Charles is having a very good day today."

"Get me out of this thing, honey," Dad says. "Let me get up and walk with my boy."

"We can't do that, dear," Missy says as she bends down and releases the brakes on the wheel-chair. Dad has a belt across his lap and shoulders, constraining him in the chair. "You almost fell yesterday, remember? We need to be careful."

Dad grumbles and I don't say a thing. It feels like I'm witnessing a miracle. I have my dad back, at least for now.

"You can take your dad for a walk," Missy says. "He likes to look out the windows in the back lounge. You can have a nice visit back there."

I thank her and go behind him. I grip the handles and carefully wheel him away from the group. A couple of the old folks turn to stare at me as I move in front of the TV. I can't believe my good luck. I have my Dad back.

We walk down the hallway past the open doors of the small apartments. "It's good to see you, Dad. You're looking good today."

"Are you here to take me home? I'm ready to go home now."

"This is your home, Dad. This is where you live now."

"Is it?" Dad seems surprised. "Have you seen your mother lately? She's supposed to come back to get me."

"Mom's gone," I say. "Mom died, remember?"

"She did?" Dad seems surprised, but not emotional. "When did that happen?"

"A long time ago, Dad. It's been years."

He ponders this as we go to the back lounge, a sofa and a couple of chairs by a big window. We're alone here. This spot overlooks a parking lot, and behind that a patch of green space that might be a small park. Sun is streaming through the window and it's warm and cozy. I set the brakes on the wheelchair and sink into a chair beside him.

"Dad, I need to ask you some questions," I say. "About the business."

"The business? What business?"

"Your business, Dad. Our business."

"Oh. Okay."

"Something is happening, Dad. I need to know. Who else knows about the business besides you?"

"Someone knows? I don't even know."

"You do, Dad. You remember what you did for a living, right?"

"I think so, but I can't quite remember. What did I do again?"

I look behind me to make sure no one else is around. "You killed people, Dad," I say this softly, my lips close to his ears. "You killed people for money. And you trained me to do it too."

"Really? Are you sure? I thought that was a movie I saw."

"Have you talked about any of this, Dad? Does anyone else know about what you did?"

"Talked about what?"

It feels like we're doing an Abbott and Costello routine. We are talking nonsense and not connecting. I'm frustrated, but I press on.

"This is important, Dad. Someone is trying to kill me. Someone knows what I do, and they are sending out information that nobody should have."

"Who's doing that?"

"I don't know, Dad. That's what I'm trying to find out."

"I'm getting cold. I need a blanket."

It's warm back here. Almost too warm. I stand up and walk to the nearby couch. A blanket is neatly folded over one arm. I pick it up and drape it over my father's lap, covering his legs.

I sit back down and return to my interrogation. "Someone else has to know about this, Dad. They are sending things out. Things about me, and our business. Who else would know this?"

"No one knows," he says firmly. "No one!"

I'm not sure if this is true or not. "No one?" I ask again. "You never told anyone else?"

"No one. Who would believe me anyhow?"

This seems like clarity, and he's right. Who would believe him?

"How about the Agency, Dad. Is it possible they know who I am?"

"The Agency," he snorts a laugh. "He doesn't know a damned thing."

"How did you start up with the Agency, Dad. Is there any way I can contact them?"

"That was a long time ago. I don't know." Dad pulls the blanket up and clutches it in his hands.

"This is important. I need to know!"

Dad looks away and stares out the window. I wait for an answer, but he doesn't say a thing. What's going on inside his head? I want to shake his shoulders and make him say something. Instead, I stand and get in front of him, staring into his eyes.

"Dad, please. I need to know!" My voice is loud. "How did you contact the Agency?"

"You're not supposed to contact them. That was the whole point!"

I've broken through. This is a real answer. "There's got to be some way!"

"Don't yell at me!" He snaps back. His face is red and his breath is hard. He may be mirroring me again, but he is worked up. He swallows hard and his hands shake. I think he is going to start yelling again. I pushed him too hard. But then his shoulders sag, and he slumps back into his seat. His eyes had an intensity for a moment, but now they seem blank again. We connected for a moment, but the moment is gone.

"I don't know. I don't know anything anymore. I'm just an old man."

I try again, asking the same thing in different ways, softer now. But I don't get any response. Still, he was there for a moment, I'm sure of it.

"When is your mom coming to take me home?"

He's slipped back into his fog. I release the brakes on the wheelchair. We're done here. I don't expect any more conversation today. I'm not sure what I expected. I'm asking him questions I know he can't answer. He's back in his own world. Dad coughs.

"Are you okay, Dad?" I ask.

"I don't feel so well," He coughs again. "I'm not feeling good at all."

He's not looking good either. His face is pale. His eyes looked so clear before, but now they're fogged and distant. His hands are shaking, and I think I've got him too worked up again.

"Let me take you back," I say. "Maybe you need to rest."

I get behind him and wheel him back through the halls, back toward the common area. Dad coughs again. It's a hard cough. He keeps coughing, over and over, a coughing jag he can't stop. I wheel him faster. I want to turn him back over to the nurses and let them handle him again.

"I..." he coughs. "I can't breathe!"

Something's wrong. I run along the hallway, pushing his chair. I'm not sure what it is, but it seems serious.

"Help!" I call. "I think something's wrong with my dad!"

My call gets attention. Missy runs over, and so does a solid looking black woman in blue scrubs.

I step around in front to look at Dad. He's grimacing now, and his eyes are wide.

"Are you okay, Charles?" Missy bends over him. Her voice is tentative.

"Call the ambulance," the other woman commands. "He's having a heart attack!"

18

The ambulance arrives within minutes. The paramedics are fast and efficient. I stand aside as they strap Dad to the gurney and minister to him. He loses consciousness and they move with a steadied urgency. They ask questions, and the nurses answer. I'm not sure what I feel. Is this my fault? Did my questions get him worked up? Did I do this to him?

All at once I realize, I'm not ready to lose my dad. Within moments they take him away. I follow them into the elevator, keeping out of their way. Dad's face is pale, his eyes closed, his skin glistens with sweat. The ventilator mask covers his mouth and nose, but his chest still quivers as he labors for breath. The elevator doors open, and I move sideways to be as small and out of the way as I can. I follow again as the paramedics rush him out of the doors of the lobby and outside to the waiting vehicle.

They slide him into the ambulance and one of the paramedic steps in and closes the door behind him, as the other gets up front.

"Sorry," he says. "We can't take you along. We're going to St. Vincent's, go to the emergency room."

I head back to my car as the sirens wail. They pull out of the parking lot and speed out onto the street. The siren is off in the distance by the time I reach my car and get it started. I drive to the hospital, following the speed limit and obeying all the traffic rules. I wonder if he will still be alive by the time I get to the hospital? My heartbeat is up, and my shoulders are tense. How will it hit me if he really does die?

I camp out in the emergency waiting room as time crawls by. I want to know what's going on, but the girl at the front desk tells me he is under a doctor's care, and someone will come out to talk with me as soon as they can. I call Jen to let her know what happened, but she doesn't pick up and the call doesn't go to her voice mail. Is she blocking my calls? There's nothing I can do about it now. I try and put it out of my mind. I glance through the old magazines and pace around. I feel like I should be doing something, but there is nothing to do but wait. My stomach rumbles and I think about going to the cafeteria to get some dinner, but I don't want to be gone when the doctor comes out.

It's already late when Beth arrives. I see her as she stops by the front desk and I get up to greet her. We hug, and she holds me tight.

"How is he? Have you seen him yet?"

"No," I say. "I'm still waiting for the doctor."

"They called and told me he collapsed, and that you were there. I tried calling but I couldn't get through."

"Oh," I pull out my phone and see I have missed calls. "I'm glad they got a hold of you. I meant to call."

"I'm just glad you were there. I'm glad you're seeing him again."

I nod. She thinks I'm seeing him because I want a relationship with my dad again. I don't tell her why I was really there. I don't tell her it was me who got him worked up, and the heart attack was all my fault.

"He seemed so much better today," I say. "He recognized me and called me by my name. He almost seemed like his old self."

"He's like that sometimes," Her eyes glaze over and she blinks back a tear. "Sometimes he seems so normal. I try not to get my hopes up, but every time I see him, I'm hoping to see Dad the way he used to be."

I drape my arm around her shoulders.

"I really miss him," Beth says. "I miss him now and he isn't even gone yet."

I'm not sure what to say, so I don't say anything.

How will I feel if he does die? Our relationship is complicated. I've been angry with him for so long. I blame him for what's wrong in my life, even as I follow his same path. My gut clenches. We shared a secret. I am who I am because he was who he was. My chest tightens. I take a deep breath and try and keep myself calm. How will I feel if he dies? And then another thought pushes through. How will my kids feel if I die?

I pull Beth in closer still, and she dabs at her eyes with a tissue.

"It's okay," I say. "It's going to be okay."

A dark-haired woman in a blue uniform comes out from behind the admissions counter and walks toward us.

"Mr. Fieldner?" She looks at me with questioning eyes.

"Yes, and this is my sister Beth."

"Dr. Hedoni is the attending physician. He will be out to speak with you in a few moments. Can you follow me?"

"How is my father?" Beth asks. "Is he going to be okay?"

"The doctor will be able to tell you everything," she says. Her voice is matter of fact, not cold, but not warm and reassuring either. "Follow me, please."

I look at Beth. She is composed but I feel her tension. We follow the nurse back through two big swinging doors, and she leads us to a small room. There is an examination table in the center of the room. We sit in the hard, plastic chairs lined against the wall.

"It won't be long," the woman says, before leaving the room and closing the door behind her.

Is he dead already? Is the doctor coming to give us the bad news? I'm breathing hard, as is Beth. I look at Beth and try and reassure her, but I don't know how. We sit in silence waiting for the word.

It's not long before the doors swing open and the doctor marches in. He is in green scrubs and carries a clipboard. He is young, no more than thirty, dark complexioned, with a two-day beard and dark circles under his eyes.

"Hello," he reaches his hand out to greet us. "I'm Dr. Hedoni, the attending physician for your father tonight."

"Is he all right?" Beth asks, her voice wavering.

"Your dad suffered a heart attack," the Doctor says. "We removed a blockage and he is in stable condition. However, there are some concerns. There may be some blood clots and the risk of another incident is elevated with his age and sedentary life style. We're running more tests, and we still don't know how much long-term damage there is. Again, he is stable for now, and we'll know more later."

I nod. I'm glad he's not gone. I'm glad I'm not alone.

"When can we see him?" Beth asks.

"Not now. He's been through a lot. When we're done with the tests he's going to need to sleep. Hopefully you can see him tomorrow."

The doctor stays for another minute, giving us details and answering questions. Dad's situation is serious and he still isn't in the clear, but it could be worse. It feels like a weight has lifted. I'm surprised at how relieved I feel. When he leaves the room, Beth and I hug again. She is shaking with emotion.

"I just hope ... That sounds so serious," Beth says.

"It seems like a relief to me. He's alive, and that's the good thing. It looks like this will be a while," I say. "Why don't I take the first shift? I'll stay here tonight, and you can go back to Mike and the kids and see him tomorrow."

"I don't know. I'd be worrying about him anyways. I don't think I can leave."

"You've got to. This might take a while. There's no sense both of us being here. Go home, try and relax and get some sleep and come back in the morning."

"Are you sure? I'm sure Jen will be worried too."

"She's visiting with her sister. There's no sense both of us staying up."

"Okay, call me as soon as you know any more. Promise?"

I walk her back through the lobby and we say goodbye. There are things I want to ask her, but they can wait.

19

In the morning I grab a big cup of coffee before heading home. It was a long night and I slept fitfully in the waiting room chair, waiting for news. They let me in to see him in the morning. He was sleeping, but his color was back. It will take a few more days of observation to make sure he is in the clear, but it seems the worst has passed. I yawn as I leave the hospital and head for home. For some reason I feel good. I'm happy. Occupied with dad and whether he would make it, I hardly thought about my own situation.

But now I grip the wheel hard and think it through. I want to call Jen again, to let her know what happened, but I know it's better to wait. Does she really want a divorce? The whole thing seems so surreal, I still can't accept it. Does she really want me out of her life? With a little more time, I know I can win her back. Although she found one of my IDs, she should give me the benefit of the doubt. How can she possibly think the worst of me?

As I pull into my subdivision, I remember it's garbage day. The street is lined on both sides with big, blue plastic trash bins. Being away last night, mine are still in my garage. The garbage truck usually doesn't come until later in the morning, so I still have time to get the trash out to the curb. I pull into my driveway and punch the button on my remote to open my garage door.

The garage door slowly rolls all the way up. Jen's car isn't there. This is another reminder that my life is out of control. I park to the far-right side, keeping her space open, just in case she changes her mind and decides to come back. A wave of emotion hits and a tear comes to my eye. I blink it away. I've lost so much. I can't imagine living my life without Jen and the kids. Without meaning to, I let out a sob. I'm a mess. I can't control my thoughts or my emotions, and I don't know what to do. I take a deep breath. I need to win her back. I rub my eyes, take another deep breath and the moment passes. I need to keep it under control. If I can't control myself, all is lost. If I can keep focused, I can still work this out.

I turn off the car, open the door and step out. The big garbage containers are on the far side of the garage, right by the big open door. I walk over and grip onto the handle of the first bin. I'm tilting it on to the back wheels to roll it out in to the street when I sense movement behind me. Before I can turn or react, he is on me. A rope slips around my neck. He is up against my back, using his force, his leverage. The rope tightens. I can't breathe.

My heart is thumping so hard I think it's going to rip through my chest. I'm gasping for breath. Panic surges. I lower my chin to my chest and grab at the cord around my neck, but it's too tight. There is no slack and nothing to grip onto. I kick back, but the man has a wide stance and I'm kicking air. He's anticipating my moves and I have no place to kick. I strike back at him with my elbows, connecting hard with his ribs. He squeezes harder. My mind is racing. I don't have much time before I pass out. I'm already feeling lightheaded this will be over in less than a minute. I don't want to die.

My body quivers as adrenaline floods my system. I push against my instincts and start to give. I let go and my body slumps. The man behind me adjusts his position to maintain his leverage and keep his pressure steady.

As he moves, I dip my shoulder and quick step in the other direction. There is a brief opening as he reacts. It turns my body enough to slam my fist down into his groin. My hand hurts with the impact. He's wearing a protective cup. It doesn't drop him, but he loosens his grip. It gives me an opening. I dip my shoulder low, and twist further, throwing my arm under his armpit, and then over his shoulder. He releases the cord as I come all the way up. The leverage is mine now, and I twist fully, explosively, the other way. His body tilts and I throw him over my shoulder. He hits the concrete of the garage floor hard, but he's back on his feet again before I can attack.

I gasp for breath and drop into a defensive posture. I see him for the first time. Younger than me with close-cropped hair, he wears loose, dark clothes. He's about my size, and clearly a professional. His eyes are hard and focused. There's barely a pause before he attacks again. He feints with his fist and, as I move to counter, he kicks me in the ribs. There's a sharp sting of pain, but I block his next attack and back away. I counter with a series of kicks and punches, a fast, aggressive combination, but he blocks and parries each attack. I've been a martial artist since I was young, and I know what I'm doing. But he is at least as good as I am.

His attacks are aggressive and confident. This isn't someone who learned his skills in a dojo, this is a military style. He's not worried about form or looking good. It's all about efficiency and finding the quickest way to kill. But we are on equal footing now. It's been a long time since I was in serious hand to hand combat, but I know I can take him.

He's coming at me again, but as he kicks out, he keeps his right arm low. Steel glints in the sunlight. There's a knife in his hand. The kicks are a diversion and the hand will do the damage as he closes. It's not a fair fight anymore.

I skip back enough to keep him from getting in close. I move to the side, aware of where I am, not wanting to be cornered, and scanning the garage for a weapon or a shield. The garden tools are at the back wall, near the corner. I raise my hand to block him, and he cuts me. Blood soaks onto my shirt sleeve.

He comes at me hard. He is kicking and punching and as he gets close, he slashes out with the knife again. I turn my body just in time.

He's using the lack of space to his advantage. He's forced me back and I'm nearly up against the wall, near the back corner of the garage. There's nowhere to move. His eyes shine with confidence, He thinks he has me, and I think he does too. He is ready for the kill. Without looking, without even thinking, I reach down to grab the long-handled shovel Jen uses in the garden. I bring it up, using it as a shield. The knife scrapes dirt from the shovel's blade.

Now it's my turn.

I grip the shovel by the middle of the handle, using both hands. I strike out with both ends, the handle and the spade, twisting and lunging, short quick strikes to drive him backwards. He takes a couple of steps back, then he tries a roundhouse kick, going for my head. He hits a glancing blow and my head rings like a bell, but he lands off balance. I swing down with the shovel and catch him hard on his leg. He yelps, staggers back. I swing the shovel blade back up and hit the side of his head. He staggers against my car. I jam the shovel into him, spade point into his stomach. Air explodes out of him and he doubles over. I send my knee into his chin, and he's down, his body smacking as it connects with the concrete.

I raise the shovel and I mean to finish him off. I'm about to smack his head, bludgeoning him, but he's stunned, hardly moving. I set down the shovel and grab his discarded cord before dropping a knee into his lower back. I slip the cord around his neck and use my leverage to pull it tight. He struggles some, but not much. He shudders and trembles as his life drains away. I keep on squeezing for a long time before checking his neck for a pulse. He's gone.

Finally, satisfied that it's over, I stand, and slump against the wall. I'm breathing hard, shaken. I've stopped counting the number of men I've killed, but this is different. I was the one who was supposed to die. I curse myself for not being prepared. I knew the Agency was getting impatient. I knew it was only a matter of time before they would pull the contract and send someone else after me. I should have prepared. I should have been ready for this.

I lurch over to the open garage door and look out on the street. It's mid-morning and the neighborhood is quiet. There's a mom further down the block pushing a stroller. Some kids down the other side are playing basketball in their driveway. I try and catch my breath listening to the ball slapping against the hard asphalt. Directly across the street my neighbor's blinds are lowered. It doesn't look like anyone is home. This is a quiet street in a quiet neighborhood. The whole fight didn't last long. No one saw this, I'm sure. And no one would believe it if they did. I walk back inside the garage and push the button. The big door slowly rolls closed.

I'm still keyed up and surging with adrenaline as I assess the damage. There's blood on the floor and it takes me a moment to remember that this is mine. My sleeve is soaked through. I roll back my cuff. The gash isn't deep. I'm lucky. I strip down to my t-shirt and throw my dress shirt on the floor by the garbage bins. There is a box of rags I use for cleaning the car. I grab a clean rag and use my teeth and my free hand to bind my wound tight.

That problem solved, I turn to my bigger problem. He is sprawled out on the floor next to my car. I was lucky to survive his attack, but there will be more to come. This is the Agency's work. They hired someone else to do the job. I get down on my hands and knees and stare closely at the man. Like me, he's an average guy, someone you would pass on the street without a second glance. I go through his pockets looking for ID, but he has none. He has no driver's license, credit cards or anything with his name on it. I check his clothes and the labels have been removed. This man is a ghost and there is no way for me to know who he is or how he got here. Questions run through my head. Where did the Agency find him? Who will miss him now that he's gone? Most of all, what I can do with him now?

Getting rid of a body is a problem I don't deal with often. Most of the jobs I take on don't require disposing of a body. If possible, I usually try to make my hits look like an accident. This is faster, easier and less messy all the way around. Accidents are always investigated, but they are routine. The investigator is just looking for a way to fill out the form and file the report in its proper spot. A murder is different. Murders shake things up and get people excited. Murders get the police asking too many questions and looking at things too closely. By the time the authorities arrive I am long gone, and I don't leave clues to connect me in any way. But it's still not a good habit to make things too obvious. If a death looks like a murder, it's bad for business.

So, I don't have a lot of experience in disposing of dead bodies. I glance around the garage. There's an unopened pack of heavy-duty, jumbo sized trash bags in a cabinet at the back of the garage. I have a chain saw, too. In theory, I could lay down plastic sheets, fire up the chain saw and cut the body into little pieces, but the thought turns my stomach. It would also leave an incredible mess, which means evidence. I could pick up the body, put it in my trunk and dump it someplace far away, but that's risky, too. I don't want the body around any longer than I have to, and the way my luck is going, I don't want to worry about a freak accident or being stopped at random and having a body in my trunk.

The simplest way is usually the best way. I slip on a pair of garden gloves before I open the new pack of trash bags. I take two and put one inside the other. Double bagging is always the best bet. I slide the bags up over the man's legs. He is all dead weight, but he hasn't gotten stiff yet and I can move him around. I push his legs in, bending him in as low and small as I can. I put another pair of trash bags over his top half, and, with some effort, I get him scrunched up enough to fit. I tie the bags together with their red pull tabs. It's a cool day but I'm already sweating through my T-shirt.

I wheel over the garbage bin and take a moment to plan how to do this. I need to get the man inside, but he is much too heavy to lift by myself. I take the full garbage bags out of the bin and set them aside. I tilt the big bin on its side and lower it down to the ground. It will be easier to slide him in than to lift him.

With effort, lifting and pushing a little at a time, I slide him all the way in. But getting the bin back up is another challenge. The container is top heavy and uneven. It's a real chore to tilt it upright again, but I'm persistent and motivated, and I finally get the job done. By the time I'm done, I hear the garbage truck rumbling down the street. I raise the garage door and wheel the container out to the curb just as the truck is finishing up with my neighbors.

They used to have a team of garbage men on each truck, but with technology and cost cuts, now one man runs the whole operation. He drives up to the head of my driveway, stops the truck and gets out. I'm waiting at the curb, and I smile as he arrives. He is in his thirties, with a bushy beard and a dark blue uniform with the company's name stitched above his pocket. He nods to me, then hooks the can into the lift. The pneumatic lift whines as it raises the container and then dumps it in. My heart is breakdancing inside my chest. What will I do if the bag breaks? The garbageman lowers the lift and tosses the empty container back before he hits another button, activating the mechanism that pushes all the new bags further into the truck. I stare inside, but all I see is trash bags. I can't tell which one holds my assailant. I'm glad Jen buys the quality brand, and they are as tough as the ads claim.

The garbageman hustles back up front and climbs in his cab, while I wheel my empty bin away. As I walk back towards my garage, I can't help thinking, that could have been me.

20

I clean myself up and use superglue and an Ace bandage to hold my cut together. It stops bleeding and seems to do the trick. I pull a beer out of the refrigerator and take a long chug. My heart is still racing. I take another long draw on my beer and it tastes good. It's satisfying. Much more satisfying than normal. And I know this is because I just won a battle. I fought for my life and I survived. I'm still alive. The beer tastes good. The air filling my lungs feels good. Even the throb of pain from the cut on my arm feels good. I'm happy to be alive. I won this time, but there will be other battles. I got lucky, but this could have easily gone the other way. The Agency won't stop. They've been contracted for a hit and they will deliver on it.

I finish my beer, crush the empty can in my hand and toss it in the recycling bin under the sink. What now? Even if I take precautions, even if I'm vigilant and prepared, odds are it will go down differently the next time. I'm the target now. I consider what this means. I still have some time, I think. The Agency won't know how this went down right away. The man who tried to kill me had to have taken on the job in the last few days. Before that, the Agency was counting on me. So, the Agency will have given him at least a few days to plan the hit and carry it out. It should be at least a day or two before they check in for a progress report. When they do, and find their man has gone silent, they'll put someone else on the case.

So again, what do I do now? It's clear I can't stay here. If I stay at home and follow my normal routines, I'm a duck, sitting in an open pond. I'll be watching and restless, growing more paranoid and anxious, waiting for someone to attack. I need to leave.

I lay my big suitcase on my bed and consider what I need. Hopefully this will all blow over in a few days, but I need to be prepared. I pack as though I'm going on a business trip, but I need to be ready for any occasion. I pack casual clothes and pull out a few suits. A gray business suit, complete with a white shirt and red and blue striped tie is presentable but not expensive. Bland, I think. I bought it off the rack at Men's Warehouse and it looks like any other suit a middle management office worker would wear. I take another suit, a dark expensive one I only wear for special occasions. I roll that up and lay it in my bag. I'm not sure what I'm going to do or where I'm going to go, but I need to be ready for any situation that arises. For shoes, I wear my New Balance trainers, but the key is to blend in, so I bring dress shoes too.

As I pack, I think of Jen. Maybe this all worked out for a reason? She is angry at me, but this is all for the best. At least she and the kids are out of the house. They are safer where they are. Anyone who comes after me will watch and wait before initiating their hit, and an empty house is no longer a target. This is a good thing. I should call her. Warn her not to come back to the house. I will tell her about Dad and let her know I will be away, for a few days at least. But telling her this will only raise her suspicions. She won't pick up my call anyway.

I think again about where I will go and what I will do. I need to leave, but running away won't solve my problem. All it will do is delay things. I need to think this through and, all at once, it comes to me. The Agency. The Agency is the key. If I can turn the tables and find them somehow, I'm going right to the source. I can stop the hit, find out who placed it, and do what I need to do to get my life back.

This is a stroke of insight and my mood brightens considerably. I walk down stairs to see what else I need to take with me, now I'm on the hunt again. In my office I sit at my desk and pull out the bottom desk drawer. It's filled with junk, knickknacks and things I have collected over the years. Things that I have no use for but haven't gotten around to throwing out. I pick up an unopened, factory-sealed box, a cable for a computer I no longer have. I look at it closely and it seems dusty. I'm satisfied it hasn't been touched recently. I take it out and place it on the floor. I do the same with all the other things in the drawer. When it's empty, I take a small screwdriver from the pen holder I keep on the top my desk. I push on one corner of the bottom drawer, and then the opposite. The bottom tilts up slightly and I use the screwdriver to pry up the false bottom.

The Agency has been part of my life since I was young, but I never really knew much about them then. For a long time, I went with Dad on his outings, and I thought of him like a superhero. His job was to take care of the bad guys, and I was his sidekick, his super helper. I didn't know how he knew the people were bad, but he told me they were, so I figured they had to be.

I turn my attention back to the contents of the drawer. In my line of work, I need to cover my tracks and make sure there is no way anything can be traced back to me. I maintain a handful of other identities I use as needed. I pull out a big manila envelope and shake the contents onto my desk top. I have five white, business-sized envelopes, each marked with initials. I pick up the one marked RH. I haven't used this in a while and it will serve my needs for now. I open it and look inside. There is an Indiana driver's license, completely legitimate down to the hologram seal. The name is listed to Robert Chambers. I like to use common names. First, they are easier to remember when I'm in character. Second, they are so generic no one thinks twice when hearing them. They are bland and forgettable, just like I want to be.

The address listed on the license is an apartment in the north side of Indianapolis. It's routed to a maildrop and forwarded to another P.O. box I maintain under a separate identity. The picture is me, but my hair is a different color and styled slightly different. I wear black-rimmed glasses. Not much of a disguise, but I'm so average-looking I usually don't need much. I pull out two credit cards, real cards I have maintained for years. This has taken some work and planning, and I need to spend a little time each month keeping my identities in good order, but it's a necessary precaution. I slip my new credentials into my pocket and return the rest to the manila envelope. I'll take these with me, too. I don't know how long I'll be gone and I may need more than one identity. I replace the false shelf and put everything back in the bottom drawer, leaving it the way it was before.

I try to think back to the first time I became aware of the Agency. I'd been Dad's helper for a while by then but, at the time, I thought that was just what he did. I never really considered how he chose the people he targeted. I remembered the day I first found out. We were out walking in the city, near a park. Dad had a pocketful of coins and I remember going to a pay phone. He dialed a number, hung up, and then we sat down to wait. I wanted to go into the park, to the playground to play with other kids, but Dad told me to stay close by. He was waiting for a call back. After a few minutes, he got the call, and we set off and Dad did his job. Up until that moment I thought Dad was in control. That's when I realized there was someone else involved. Someone on the other end of the line who lined things up and pulled his strings. He was a puppet, and the voice on the other end of the line made him dance.

I take out my wallet with my real IDs, along with my credit cards and all the other things linked to me, and put them into the top drawer of my desk. I won't be needing these for now, and in case the worst happens, I don't want anything linked back to me or my family. It pains me, but I take out my cell phone and leave that in the drawer too. I take the manila folder and walk back upstairs.

Listening to Dad on the phone that day and so many other days after that, I knew he was familiar with his contact. It was someone he knew personally. When I came into my own, and started accepting my own contracts, Dad was my contact. He gave me the names and told me how to do it. He told me where I should be and how it should all go down. At the beginning, I was an extension of my father. A guided weapon. He planned it all out and sent me out to do his work.

It wasn't until later, after I had been back home from college a while and I was already engaged to Jen, that I began to take jobs on my own, dealing directly with the Agency. By then it was all computerized. There was never any voice contact. It was all anonymous. But I know there is someone, a group of people behind it all.

Upstairs, I put the envelope in a pouch at the back of the suitcase. I think for a moment about what else I will need. If I'm taking on new identities, I will need to look the part. I go back into my closet and move my clothes organizer out of the way, exposing the open floor. It's a hardwood floor, and everything matches. But when I push down on one section in a specific sequence, a spring activates, and a small section of the floor rises up. I had the secret compartment installed right after we bought the house, before we moved in. I reach in and take out a box. The first item I remove is a disguise kit. This has makeup, fake hair and prosthetic ears and noses. I have trained in this and, if I need to, I can make myself look very different without much effort. I have extra cash here, and I take out a stack of bills. Enough to keep me going, even if this takes longer than I hope. The last item I remove is a gun. This is untraceable and has never been used. I don't like guns. They are loud and messy, and I've never seen the value in them, at least not for work. But I'm in a different position now than I have been before. I put the box back, replace the flooring and set everything back to look undisturbed.

I consider my problem again as I finish packing. How do you find something that is invisible by design? I'd always gotten my orders online by encrypted messages. I never wanted to know who was giving the order or how the job came to them. This was for my protection as well as theirs, and ignorance was an asset. But things have changed. My life now depends on finding the hand that pulls my strings.

I finish packing and lug my suitcase downstairs. I do another check to make sure I have everything I will need. I grab my laptop and an extra battery, and my satellite phone from my car's trunk.

Back in the kitchen, I look around one more time. Being here now feels so strange. I'm not sure how long it will be before I will be back. My home isn't the sanctuary I always thought it was. It seems cold and empty without my family inside.

I grab my bags, leave my car keys on the counter and lock up the house. I set the alarm on the way out, though I know it won't do any good against a trained operator.

It's still early evening and the sun has set. The sky is lit up in shades of pink, gold and orange and it's a beautiful night. I wave to a neighbor as she backs out of her driveway, and she waves back. I pull my suitcase along as I walk toward the train station. An idea is beginning to form.

The Agency is the key, but it's a locked box. A mystery. There is nothing online that will lead me to them, that's clear. But there may be another way to approach this. Every job I've done, someone, somewhere, paid money to make it happen. Someone benefited by the person's death. If I can find one person who placed a contract, I can find out how they contacted the Agency. Using one piece of information I can push a little more, and find my way in through a backdoor. It isn't much to start with, but all I need is an opening and I can leverage it, expand it, and find a way in.

And I know where I need to start. I need to start with my last job. Silverman.

21

I check into a hotel on the north side that believes more in discretion than in protocol. They take a hefty cash deposit in place of my ID and credit card. A thin, nervous man gets off the elevator as I step on. He looks away from me, careful to avoid eye contact. I'm not the only one with secrets here.

In my room I unpack, hang up my clothes and put my valuables in the safe in the closet. The low sound of a TV in one of the adjoining rooms vibrates through the thin walls, but otherwise it's quiet. The room is smaller than most of the name brand hotels, but it's clean and comfortable. Good enough.

I sit at the desk, turn on my secure computer and wait impatiently while it boots up. If I can reverse engineer Silverman to find out who targeted him, and how they found the Agency, maybe I can trace it back to the source. Did I delete the dossier? I usually do once a job is completed. Though my computer is secure, and the file is stored on the deep web, it makes no sense to hold on to incriminating evidence. No matter how hard it is to access. But the Silverman job was different. I botched it. I connect to my storage site on the deep web and fidget as I wait for it to load. I'm still keyed up from the attack. My mind goes to Jen again, and my Dad, but these are problems I can't fix now. When the screen finally comes up I enter my password and I'm in luck. The file is still active. I click on the link, thankful that I broke my own rule and left it up.

I know a lot about Silverman already. I researched his habits and schedules to find the best way to do the job. I know a great deal about him on a surface level, but not the things I need to know now. To find the Agency I need to do something I have never done before. I need to find out who placed the contract on him in the first place. To do this, I need to think like a detective. The file opens, and I scan through it.

On TV detective shows it all comes down to motive. Find the person with the biggest motive, the most to gain, and you've most likely solved the case. That's what I was looking at to see who targeted me, and that makes me think of Jen. I wonder again if I can get her back. I'm raw and on the edge of losing control. I screwed it up. I had a great life, and I want it back. But I can't let my emotions control me. I wipe a tear from my eye and try to push the thought away and refocus on my task. Motive alone isn't enough, I know that now, but I need to start someplace. I read through the file trying to look at this in a new way.

Silverman was a successful lawyer, a partner in a prestigious firm and listed in *Who's Who* in the legal profession. As a litigator representing big business no doubt he made enemies along the way. But the file is broader than it's deep. It doesn't tell me who he fought for or who he fought against. I make a note to explore this further. I get back to the file. He wasn't married and had no children. He was never married, which strikes me as odd. He was in his mid-fifties, he had to have had some romantic relationships along the way. Did he have a mistress or girlfriend? Was he gay? My file doesn't say. Another avenue to explore.

I read on.

Silverman owned a home in Wilmette, and a condo downtown within walking distance of his office. I'd researched this before and knew he usually went back to Wilmette each evening. He was an observant Jew, active in his North Shore synagogue. I knew this before and now note it as one more thing to look in to. He belonged to a socially prominent health and social club, but it's clear health wasn't his focus. I continue to scan. He was a prominent benefactor to a number of local charities, and on the board of several small to medium sized corporations. Nothing jumps out at me.

I look through the pictures in the Agency's file, and many seem like they've been copied from trade magazines or publicity photos. There is one of him standing with the other partners of his firm. He is at the edge of the picture, looking like a human bowling bowl in his dark suit. He leans away from the others and his expression tells me he doesn't want to be there. Or maybe he doesn't want his picture taken. Another picture shows him seated behind his desk, a serious look on his face. There are pictures of him receiving awards, and other pictures with him at charity events. There are no candid photos. No pictures of him on vacation or hanging out with friends. He wears a dark suit and tie in every picture in the file.

I sit back and take this in. Does that mean he doesn't have anyone close to him? That he is so focused on his work to be nearly one-dimensional? When I took on this assignment, I didn't give this a second thought. I was focused on his patterns and habits. I was looking for weak links or associations I could exploit. Now, I think this is significant. Does this mean that he was truly a closed off person with no close social ties? Or does it mean that whoever put the contract on him wasn't someone socially close? I write this down as another place to dig deeper.

I look through the rest of the file and I don't see anything of interest. When I look at most Agency dossiers I get a sense of who my target is as a real person. It shows them in different facets of their lives, their work, their family, and relationships. I get a sense of them as fully-rounded human beings. I'm not getting this with Silverman. I see his roles, but I don't see who he is. I close the file and click out of the site. I think better of it, and log back in to the site. This time, I delete the file.

I sit back in my chair and review what I know, and what I don't. I have an outline, a shadow, of who Silverman was, but the dossier reads more like a resume than a description of a real, living, breathing person. He was single, but I don't know if he was alone. He had to have a sizable fortune, but I don't know who the beneficiary of his estate is. His profession couldn't be his whole life. Could it? There had to be more. He had to have passions and interests outside his job. He had to be more than he appeared. Who did he spend his time with? What did he do when he was away from his office? Was there someone who loved him, or someone who hated him? There had to be more. Maybe Silverman really was as bland as he seemed.

On the other hand, someone cared enough to want him dead.

I turn back to my computer screen. Using the information from his dossier, I visit the deep investigation site and place an order for a full background check. I doubt I will learn anything helpful, but I must check everything. I mark the order as a rush for delivery tomorrow. I go through all the normal sources and run a quick investigation of Silverman for myself. I did this before when I first took on the assignment, and I do it again now to see what is new. I read his obituary. His death earned a write-up in the Tribune with an old picture attached. It focuses on his business success, some legal victories and his prominent clients. It says he was a lover of the arts, but that might be reaching as no other personal details are listed. The only surviving relatives are a brother who lives in Washington, and a couple of nieces and nephews. I don't know how much money he had, but if its split between these few, that could be a motive.

There aren't any stories about his death in the local papers, but I find a write-up in the *Chicago Law Review* of his professional life and his standing in the local legal community. It makes no mention of how he died, only saying it was accidental. I find a press release from his firm, saying how much he will be missed. This is signed by the firm's managing partner, David Shapiro. I put this in my notebook. Pat Griffin from Silverman's firm is quoted in two of the articles, so I add his name to the list. The name Jerry Calhoun appears in another article and this name sounds familiar, so I write it on my pad as another person to talk with. Nothing else comes up in my searches. Silverman didn't use Facebook or have any social media accounts that I can find. Not even LinkedIn. He is mentioned in Facebook posts from charity events and such, but other than that, I can find no trace of a social life.

I try different searches in different ways, anything that will give me another angle to look at Silverman, but there's not much to see. I lean back in my chair and try to think this through. If I want to find out more about Silverman, I'm going to have to talk with people who knew him. I think of how I can do this. It looks so easy on the movies and TV shows. It always struck me as funny that an amateur sleuth, some busybody from the neighborhood or a visiting aunt of the deceased would go around asking questions, and everyone would talk with her. They would tell all their long-held secrets, and she'd gather up the clues and solve the case easily. It doesn't happen like that in real life. People aren't that open. People are naturally suspicious and they only talk if they are forced to talk.

Showing authority might be the answer. If I showed a badge and presented myself as a detective, that could work. People would make time for me and think that they had to answer my questions. But the downside is big. It's been weeks since Silverman died, and his death has already been ruled an accident. If I came around now, showing a badge, it's going to look like there is a problem. Anyone involved will keep their mouth shut. And someone might make a call to check on my name and badge number. Impersonating a policeman is not just a serious charge, they take it personally. That would put me in much too risky a position. Being a detective won't work.

I consider posing as a reporter. Although it could get me access, everyone who talked with me would filter their answer to what they felt comfortable reading about. I might get information, but I wouldn't necessarily find the truth. I need a different way in. I open my curtains and peek out the window. I'm up on the eighth floor and the lights on the street below are warm and inviting. The hotel is on a busy street, across from an old theatre, and the marquee lights seem festive and alive. The street is lined with bars, restaurants and businesses of all sorts. It's late evening and there are people walking and a steady flow of cars along the street, but it's quiet in my room and the activity seems far away. I close the drapes again.

A thought comes to me, and I sit back at the desk. I take a few more minutes to use a program on my computer to design a business card. I've done often before and I have skills. Within a few minutes I have a business card for Robert Chambers with the title Senior Investigator, and the logo for Cleveland Life Insurance. The phone number is an extension routed to my own voice drop. I'll head over to an all-night Kinkos later and print them on hard business card stock. When I'm done they will look professional and authentic.

I want to check in on Dad, but I can't do anything that could trace back to me or even let anyone know I'm still alive. I'm the hunter now, and I'll continue my investigation in the morning.

22

In the morning I go to Silverman's office. I'm dressed for my role in my gray suit and a red and blue striped tie. My hair is grayer and parted differently, and the black frame glasses give me a more studious look. It's not an elaborate disguise, but it's enough. When I look in the mirror I see a different person.

The firm takes up the full floor on the twenty-third story of a building on Lasalle Street. The reception area is an appealing mix of grays and forest green. The furniture in the waiting area is sleek and modern, and a big raised platinum sign on the wall proudly displays the firm's name: SHAPIRO WARREN AND SILVERMAN. I walk toward the big curved front desk. The receptionist, a perky, young Hispanic girl gives me an oversized smile as I approach. I return her smile and hand her one of my spiffy new business cards.

"Good morning," I say. "Robert Chambers, with Cleveland Life Insurance. I'm here to see Mr. Shapiro."

"I'm sorry, sir. Mr. Shapiro isn't in today."

"No?" I say, feigning confusion. "But we had an appointment for this morning."

"You did? I'm so sorry, there must have been some sort of mix up.

Mr. Shapiro has been out of the office all week. Let me call back to his office."

I wait patiently as she makes the call. I have no appointment and I picked Shapiro because he is the managing partner and his name is included in the dossier. I'm grasping here, and not sure what I intend to find. The receptionist looks down at my business card as she softly talks into her headset. Then she pauses and turns back to me.

"I'm sorry, Mr. Chambers. They have no record of any appointments today."

"Well, my office called, and they confirmed it yesterday. I flew in specifically to talk with Mr. Shapiro."

"I'm sorry, but there is nothing in his calendar, and Mr. Shapiro has been out all week." She holds the big smile, but her eyes have narrowed. "I'm afraid you'll have to make a new appointment with his office."

"Is there someone else I can talk with?" I ask. "This is regarding Alan Silverman. We are handling the details for his policy and need to firm up on a few points."

At the mention of Silverman, her smile falters, before the mask returns.

"One moment," she says. She turns away and speaks softly into her headset once again.

I try and act calm, though my gut is tight. I don't like being here. Silverman's death was marked as an accident and a closed case. By asking around I'm muddying the waters. But I need to learn more to get to the Agency. I have no choice.

The receptionist faces me once more. "Could you have a seat, please, Mr. Chambers? Mr. Shapiro's personal assistant will be out to see you shortly."

I take a seat on a couch in the lobby and pretend to relax. I look around the office and search for hidden cameras. I don't see anything obvious, but I would think security would be an issue. If so, they have pictures of me. The more I think about it, the more I regret coming here. My arm is starting to throb, and my muscles are sore. I'm feeling the effects of yesterday's battle and regret not taking some Advil earlier. This is another reminder that I'm getting old. If I get out of this, I really need to quit. I pick up a *Chicago* magazine from the table in front of me and scan through it. I'm not sure what I can gain by being here.

After a few minutes, a tall, slim, black woman in a navy-blue business suit comes around the corner. She doesn't smile as she approaches. I stand to greet her.

"Mr. Chambers?" She reaches out her hand, and her shake is firm. "I'm so sorry if there has been some confusion. I'm Lucinda Baker, Mr. Shapiro's assistant. I understand you have some questions about Mr. Silverman?"

She sits tall in a chair close to mine and motions for me to sit.

"Yes," I say. "We are handling Mr. Silverman's policy and with any cover of this size, it's customary for us to do a preliminary investigation before we can disburse any funds. This is all quite routine."

She nods.

"This is our normal procedure any time there is an unusual death. We just need to verify the details and make sure there is nothing more to it."

"Wait," Lucinda holds her hand up to stop me. "I'm sorry, are you saying that this wasn't an accident?"

"No," I say. "Not at all. We want to make sure we do our due diligence and cover our bases. We don't expect to find anything, we just need to ask the questions. This is all completely routine."

She nods again, but her defenses are up.

"Did you know Mr. Silverman well?"

"I knew him of course, but I can't say I knew him well at all."

I nod studiously. "You work with Mr. Shapiro. Would you say that he and Mr. Silverman were close?"

"Of course, they were. They were partners."

"Yes," I say. "But outside of business, did they socialize?"

"Well, I really couldn't say."

"You ran Mr. Shapiro's calendar, didn't you?"

"His work calendar, yes. His wife handles his social calendar, I'm sure." She glances at her watch. "They didn't socialize together much as far as I know, if that's what you are asking. For the most part, Mr. Silverman ran his own group, and was independent from the rest of the firm. His interaction with Mr. Shapiro was mostly through partners' meetings and such."

I note this down in my book.

"How was Mr. Silverman regarded by the staff here?" I ask. I'm blundering down an unlit hallway looking for something to light my way.

"I really couldn't say." Her speech is precise, her spine ruler straight ,and she has a military air about her. She glances at her watch again. "I'm sorry Mr. Chambers, but I really don't have much time and I don't see how I can help you with these questions. I only knew Mr. Silverman through the office. He and his staff mostly kept to themselves. I can tell you that he was a full partner and obviously very important to our firm. He had an excellent reputation in the legal community and I know that he is missed here."

"Miss. Baker," I put my pad down. "Do you mind if I call you Lucinda?"

She nods, but her expression is like she bit into a lemon.

"Can I be frank, Lucinda?"

She nods again.

"I really don't want to spend any more time here than I have to, and I know you are busy and have other things you should be doing. But I need to file a report by tomorrow night. If I don't have at least a minimal amount of access and some verifiable information, the company will escalate this and send down another team to dig in deeper. We are talking about a great deal of money, and my company does not take these investigations lightly."

I finally have her full attention.

"If they broaden the investigation, this will be more intrusive. It will involve Mr. Shapiro personally, and possibly bring more attention to the firm. I have a family. I just want to get this over, file my report and go back home. I'd rather just do enough to put this together and get it done. I would really appreciate your help and candor, Lucinda."

She nods again, but her eyes are a little softer now.

"Can you tell me," I ask again. "What did people say about Mr. Silverman?"

Lucinda glances at the receptionist, who is once again talking into her headset. She looks at me again and seems to decide. She leans in closer.

"This is fully confidential, right? I trust that my name will not be mentioned in this report?"

My heartrate spikes. "Of course. This is all background and I promise not to use your name or title. This report is only for our internal use."

"Okay." She speaks softly to make sure I'm the only one who will hear her. "The truth is he was not very popular with the staff. He was very demanding, and not known for his people skills."

"So, he was a hard person to get along with?" I whisper conspiratorially.

"Well, he'd never win any popularity contests around here, I can tell you that." There is a break in her façade and she speaks with a bit of sass.

"Was there anything specific?"

She glances around again, making sure the receptionist is still occupied.

"Look Mr. Chambers, I've already said more than I should have. As I told you, I didn't have much contact with him. You really should be talking to someone closer to him. The person you should really be talking with is Pat Griffin."

"Pat Griffin?" I know the name. I'd seen it quoted in some of the articles after his death. "Then I really need to talk with him. Is Mr. Griffin available?"

She covers her mouth as she smiles. "It's not Mr. Griffin. Pat is a *Ms*. Pat is short for Patricia."

"Oh, I'm sorry. I assumed he was a man."

"I'm sure everyone does," Lucinda gives me a scolding look. "There are a lot of women attorneys here you know. Almost half of our newer associates are women. Ms. Griffin has taken over Mr. Silverman's division and she is about to be made a full partner," She says this with pride in her voice.

"I'm sorry. I shouldn't have assumed."

She nods, agreeing with me.

"Would it be possible for me to get in to see her? It won't take long, and it sounds as though she is the one I should be talking with."

Lucinda considers this and takes a while make a decision. She walks to a phone on a table nearby, picks up the receiver, and speaks to the receptionist, a tone of command in her voice. "Tanya, please patch me in to Ms. Griffin's office."

She turns her back to me. I try to listen in as she is connected, but it's difficult to make out a word. After a minute she hangs up the receiver and turns back to me.

"It's all set. I spoke with her assistant and she will fit you in. She has a busy morning, of course, but if you hang tight you won't have to make another trip."

I thank her for her help and shake her hand again. She gives me a tight smile as she leaves.

I sit back to wait. I page through the Chicago magazine and occupy myself with the articles about food and real estate. I'm usually good at waiting. It's part of what I do, and when I'm on a job, waiting for my target to appear, I can get into a zone, an almost mindless state where I'm alert and rested at the same time. When I'm in my hunter mode I can stay that way for hours and not even be aware of the time. But this feels more like hanging around for a dental appointment. It's a chore. A bother. I can't trick my mind into relaxing. I'm bored, impatient and time creeps by.

Two men in dark suits arrive, see the receptionist, and are shown back into the office. More people come in and are shown through. I alone am a fixture in the office. I feel like a potted plant or another piece of furniture. After a while I stand, take the key from the receptionist and go out in the hall to find the men's room. While there I take some deep breaths, practice my stretching and do some quick calisthenics to keep my blood flowing. My arm still hurts, but it is bearable. Back in the reception area, I wait some more.

It's over two hours later before Griffin's secretary comes and leads me back to her office. I'm hungry and a little pissed I had to wait so long. I try and shake this off as I step into Pat Griffin's office. She's writing something down on a legal pad as I enter. She looks up for a moment, then looks right back down, continuing with what she is doing. I guess Griffin to be in her late thirties or early forties. She has red hair, and it looks natural, not the flaming red that comes out of a bottle. Her features are sharp, and she is wearing a sleeveless top. Her arms have tone and definition. My initial impression tells me she is an athlete. As I glance around the office, my impression is confirmed. There are several newspaper articles, framed, with headlines about the top finishers for the Chicago Marathon. A credenza behind her is filled with law books, but there are several small trophies there too, and above it, next to her framed law school diploma, in a bigger frame, is a T-shirt for the Boston Marathon. It's obvious she is a serious runner and a proud competitor. She glances up at me again and impatiently waves me to a seat.

"Sit down please," she says. "I'm not sure how you got on my schedule, but I can only spare a few minutes."

"Thank you, Ms. Griffin. That's all I need. I just have a few questions, and I was told you are the person to talk with. As you know, I'm conducting the investigation for my company into Mr. Silverman's death. This is part of our process before we can pay out any claim."

She doesn't say anything, so I continue.

"I understand you worked closely with Mr. Silverman, and you have now taken over his position here at the firm?"

She nods but doesn't volunteer anything further.

"As someone who knew him well and knew what he was involved with in the firm, I was hoping you could give me some insight into how he was viewed professionally."

"Alan was a great lawyer, and a great man." The look on her face reveals impatience, but her voice is sincere. "I learned everything I know from him. He was my mentor and I wouldn't be where I'm now if not for him. It goes without saying I miss him."

"That's interesting," I say. "I've heard that Mr. Silverman was a hard person to get to know. It sounds as though he was more feared than liked."

"Sure," she shrugs. "A lot of people felt that way. Allan wasn't an easy man to be around. He was demanding and competitive, but he was also one of the kindest, most generous people I've ever met. Is there anything specific you need to know, Mr. Chambers? As I told you, I don't have much time to spare."

"Yes, of course. I guess the big question is if you know of anyone who would want to cause harm to Mr. Silverman?"

"This is all routine?" Griffin leans forward and looks at me quizzically. "This seems to be a rather loaded question for something that was by all accounts an accident."

"I just need to make sure we are looking at all the angles. Covering all the bases." I recite this like I have memorized it. I'm fully in character with my role now.

"The answer is no." Griffin says with conviction. "Alan ruffled a lot of feathers, that's true. But that's what you do when you practice law at this level. I know people who wouldn't want to share a meal with him, but no one who would want to harm him in any way. This is just a ridiculous idea."

She glances at her watch again and stands. She is lean and trim and has an assured presence.

"That's all the time I can spare, Mr. Chambers. You'll have to excuse me, but I have work to do."

"Thank you. I appreciate you're making time for me on such short notice." I stand with her and make my way toward the door, but I hesitate before leaving her office. My stomach grumbles with hunger and I'm pissed that I waited over two hours and I'm being shown out after just a couple of minutes. "I do have one more question. You've taken over Mr. Silverman's position at the firm, and I understand you are about to be made partner. I assume this has meant a big increase in your income?"

Her expression stiffens. "We're done here. I can see you have some kind of agenda. If you want anything further, put it in writing and send it through your legal department."

She nearly slams the door behind me.

23

I grab a late lunch at a cafeteria on the ground floor. I stepped too far with Griffin, and it bothers me. If she is the one—and she clearly gained a lot from Silverman's death—I've alerted her to my interest and put her on the defensive. I shouldn't have approached it that way, but her attitude set me off. That and the stress of the last few days. I should have grabbed some breakfast before heading in. These are excuses, and the truth is I messed up. I should have maintained control, but I didn't. I let her get to me and I showed my hand. I won't let I t happen again.

The next name on my list is Jerry Calhoun. The file lists him only as a long-time client and a big part of Silverman's practice. He is one of the top developers in the city, and his name has been in the news lately. With the announcement that the Obama Presidential Library will be built in Washington Park, near the lakefront on the far South Side, the surrounding area has suddenly become a target for development. It was recently revealed that Calhoun and some other big developers had bought up most of land well before the announcement when the prices were low. They'd now locked in big profits, before the first hole was even dug. The political commentators have been calling this corruption, and proof that word was leaked about the location well before any announcement was made.

Calhoun's office is only a few blocks away so I slam down the last few bites of my sandwich as I walk over. The man is private and busy and avoids the press. I doubt I can get in to see him without an appointment, but I need to try. At his building I sign in with the security guard and take the elevator up. The name on the gold sign by the door reads, Calhoun and Associates.

As I step into his office, the first thing I notice is the model. In the center of the room between the couches at the corner and the reception area raised on a wooden platform, lighted and boxed in glass, stands a three-dimensional scale model of a development. The buildings are all white in a setting surrounded by green, with tiny trees and landscaping. It's framed at the side by the blue of Lake Michigan. This is a shining depiction of the New City Plaza. I walk over and gaze at it. It shows two gleaming towers, with a large low building at its base. The tags on the side identify this as a mix of office, hotel and residential, and an expected opening date two years from now. I glance at the walls and see big photos of completed developments, shining examples of the company's success.

"Good morning, sir," the cute, blonde receptionist smiles at me as I move past the big display. "Can I help you?"

"Yes, please." I hand her another of my new business cards. "I need to talk with Mr. Calhoun."

"Do you have an appointment?"

"No, but this is an important matter, and I just need a few minutes of his time."

"I'm sorry, sir. Mr. Calhoun never sees anyone without an appointment. Perhaps someone else can help you?"

"No, this is a personal matter. I'm investigating the death of his attorney, and I understand they were very close."

The receptionist's eyes widen slightly and I know I've peaked her interest. But she shakes her head again.

"I'm sorry, sir. But Mr. Calhoun has a firm policy. He never takes unscheduled meetings."

"I understand." I nod. "But this isn't about business, it's personal. Could you please call and let him know that I'm here about the unexplained death of Alan Silverman? I only need a few minutes of his time."

The receptionist wavers. This sets me apart from all the salesman and others who try and get in to see him. I'm hoping it's enough.

"Let me call back," she says. "Please take a seat. This might take a while."

I settle on one of the green couches and prepare to wait. My arm throbs and my body is sore. It's been a long time since I've been in a battle like that and I'm feeling my age. The receptionist talks into her headset, but I can't hear what she is saying. I sit back and wait. I will my mind to let go. A couple of people enter the reception area and go right back into the main office. The phones continue to ring, and the receptionist is kept busy. A man with a big, flat portfolio case arrives, walks up to the desk, and then comes back to sit on the adjacent sofa. We nod to acknowledge each other. He takes out his phone and types something with his thumbs. A few minutes later, someone comes out to fetch him and he passes back into the inner office.

I think about calling Jen again. I have a new number, so it won't be blocked, and I might get through to talk with her. But as soon as I think this, I know it's a bad idea. I can't contact her. The Agency is probably monitoring her calls. This would make it more dangerous for her and the kids. Besides, I don't have anything to say and I know she will hang up on me. I need to get to the Agency, fix the mess I'm in, and then I can reach out and try to make things right. More people come and go. I sit silently, and the receptionist doesn't even look at me. After a while, I'm sure this is a waste of my time. I'm about ready to give it up, when a tall, dark-haired lady in a floral dress comes in and calls my name.

"Mr. Chambers? Mr. Calhoun will see you now, but he only has a few minutes."

I follow her into the inner sanctum. We pass windowed conference rooms filled with people. We cross an open area filled with cubicles, and head to the far corner of the space. She stops and turns to face me.

"This is Mr. Calhoun's office, but you only have a few minutes," she scolds. "He runs on a very tight schedule."

She knocks on the door and opens it without waiting for a reply.

I'm in the doorway and Calhoun is on the phone. He waves me in and motions me to a seat. The office is not as big as I would expect, but it has tall windows on two sides, facing the Chicago skyline. I sit in a chair across from his massive desk, clear except for a telephone and a computer screen.

Calhoun leans back in his posh leather chair and stares at me as he talks into the phone. "As long as we hit the dates, I don't really give a damn. Do what you have to do."

He is slim and old, with a full head of white hair, combed back from a high forehead. He has a short, neat, gray-white beard and is wearing a white long-sleeved shirt, with no tie. He looks familiar, but I can't place him. Probably from the news or a feature on TV. As he stares straight at me, I can't help but focus on his eyes. They are cool green, and they drill into me. I'm guessing he is in his late sixties, maybe older, but he is intense and energetic.

"Okay. Yeah, I can live with that," he speaks into his phone, "but no fucking around. Let me know when you get it done." He hangs up without saying goodbye.

"Thank you, Mr. Calhoun," I start to say, but he points his finger at me and I stop.

"You've got five minutes," his voice is stern. "What's this about Alan Silverman? An unexplained death?"

"I'm an investigator for Cleveland Life, and any time we have a policy of this size, it's normal practice to do an investigation to make—"

"You told my girl it was unexplained. I heard it was an accident. Which is it?"

"To be honest, sir, this is a routine investigation, for now. It's marked as an accident, but I needed to see you and I did want to get your attention."

Calhoun glares at me with his intense eyes, and I'm sure he is going to yell, or throw me out of his office. But instead, he suddenly laughs.

"You've got stones, son. I should kick your ass out on general principal, but I gotta' say I appreciate your gumption." He looks at his watch. "You've got four minutes left. Go!"

"I know you and Mr. Silverman were close—"

"No," he interrupts me again. "We weren't close. Whoever told you that was wrong. I couldn't stand being around the bastard."

"But I understand you worked together for years, and—"

"Right. We worked together. We weren't close. We were never close. It irritated me just being around the guy. But he was damned good at what he did."

"How often did you see Mr. Silverman?"

"Actually see him? Not that often," Calhoun leans closer. "I'd bring him in for meetings when I had to. Settlement meetings, he was always there for those, but I didn't see him all that often. He was a tool, you understand? A weapon for me."

"Sure." I nod.

"I didn't care much for him as a person, but that's part of what made him so effective. He didn't care if you liked him. He was relentless. A goddamned man-eating Rottweiler. And he was my goddamned dog."

"When you say he was an attack dog, you mean he was aggressive in court?"

"In court, in the office, at the breakfast table. Wherever. He had a nose for blood. Whenever I had a problem, I'd put Silverman on it, and he'd go after his target like a heat-seeking missile. A good lawyer is worth everything they charge, and he charged a hell of a lot. But, like I said, he was a damned good at what he did. I hate to say it, but I already miss the bastard."

"So, you didn't see him that often? Most of your contact—was it by phone?"

"Sure, phone, email. A lot of it was handled by my team. They'd deal with the day to day issues with him or someone on his team. I'd get a hold of him when I needed something."

"You mean like a new development or something like—"

"What the hell do you really want to ask me, son?" Calhoun glances at his watch. "Your time is ticking away, and you haven't asked me anything that's going to help you with that report you say you need to write."

"You're right, Mr. Calhoun," I say. "What I really want to know is, was there anyone you know of who would benefit by his death?"

Calhoun raises his eyebrows, as he stares straight at me. His gaze makes me uncomfortable and I'm sure this is another weapon in his arsenal. Another way to intimidate and gain advantage from his adversaries. After a pause, he answers.

"Lots of people, I'd imagine." Calhoun pushes away from the desk, stands and turns toward the window. Standing, I see he is shorter than I thought he was. As intimidating and forceful as he seems, he is thin and looks physically frail. "That new gal that took his place on my team, Pat Griffin. I imagine she's sitting pretty well now. Good gal. She's almost as ruthless as he was. Who else? Whoever was in his will, I'm sure. That insurance policy you have, whoever is on that is likely to benefit, I'd guess. I don't know if he had much in the way of family, or anyone close. He never talked about it and I never asked. But, yes, I'm sure there were quite a few people who were glad to see him go."

"Miss Griffin—do you know her well?"

"She's my new attack dog, so yeah I know her. She's been on his team for a long time and we dealt with her as much as him."

"Did she and Mr. Silverman appear to get along well?"

"They were thick as the thieves they were." He smiles at his joke.

"Right," I say. "As aggressive as he was, did he have any enemies that you know of? Anyone who would want to harm him, possibly?"

"Enemies?" Calhoun turns back to face me. He arches his eyebrows again. "Is this just part of a report or are you really going somewhere with this?"

"I'm just exploring the possibilities, sir. I need to make sure we aren't missing anything."

"I was told he got hit by a taxi. That sounds pretty damned accidental to me."

"It does. But again, this is our standard procedure with policies of this size."

"Enemies? It depends on what you mean by 'enemies'." Calhoun goes back behind his desk and sits back down. "He made a lot of people angry, I know that. Hell, he pissed me off and he worked for me. He pissed everyone off, that's just how he was. Whether that makes someone an enemy? I can't really say."

"Anyone in particular?" I ask.

"Look, he had a reputation." He shakes his head. "That worked to my advantage. Sometimes all we needed to do was have him send a letter or make a phone call threatening to do something, and they'd fold. People, other lawyers, didn't want to face him. He'd go after everything, and he made them look bad." He stops and stokes his goatee, apparently deep in thought. "There might be one guy though."

I lean forward. "Yes, sir?"

"Yeah, now that I think of it, there was this one guy recently. A big-name guy. He's kind of a big shooter, they had a run-in lately and I heard it was ugly."

"Can you tell me who that was, and what happened?"

Calhoun strokes his beard and turns away from me. It's good not having to take in his withering stare.

"God, that bothers me," he shakes his head. "I can't think of his name, but we won a case against him a couple of months back. It was big news. I'm sure you can find it."

I wait for him to go on, and the anticipation builds.

"What the hell was that guy's name? It'll come to me. Anyways, Alan knew the guy. I mean he knew him well. They ran in the same circles and I reckon there was something there. I got the impression there was more to the story, but the guy didn't take it well when he lost. I wasn't there, but I heard he pretty much exploded outside the court. A big temper tantrum. Silverman told me all about it and you could tell he just loved it. If there was an enemy, I'd put my money on that guy."

Calhoun looks at his watch. "I told you five minutes, but I gave you more." He stands again and the meeting is over.

"Thank you, Mr. Calhoun. I appreciate your time." I stand. "This has been very helpful."

He walks around the desk and touches my elbow, moving me toward the door.

"Glad I could help. Let me know if you find something. I know Alan's death was an accident, but God, that would be crazy if it wasn't."

"If I have any other questions, would it be okay if I called you?" I ask.

"If you can get a hold of me, I'll talk with you. I'll call you if anything else comes to mind. You know, it's funny. I always thought the guy would die from a heart attack. He wasn't a healthy person."

He guides me out. I'm outside the door and about to leave the office when Calhoun calls out something.

"Leach," he says.

"I'm sorry, what?"

"I remember his name now. The other lawyer. His name was Samuel Leach."

On the way out, I make a note to add a request for two more background reports, for Pat Griffin and Samuel Leach.

24

In the morning I rent a car and head up to Silverman's home in the North Shore. Does the Agency know the hit was a bust? Do they know I'm still alive? They have to by now, and I'm sure someone else has been assigned and is on the job. Although I've disappeared, I'm still not safe. I'm not doing anything under my own identity, so they can't trace me for now, but I'm certain they're watching my family and waiting to see if I contact them. It's what I would do.

I can't stop thinking about my family, and how much my life has changed in the last few days. Jen doesn't want me in her life anymore. The look in her eyes showed hate and fear. She sees me as a monster now. How can I undo that? I can't even talk with my kids. What will they think of me? I grip the steering wheel like I want to choke it. I'm breathing hard and can feel my blood pressure rise. I want my life back, but I'm not sure this is even possible. Too much has changed. I breathe in deeply, trying to calm myself and keep control. I loosen my grip on the wheel and shake out my hands, but it doesn't help. My mind is too active.

Jen and I have been through a lot, and we've survived and stayed together. I've got to believe we can get through this, too. I can bring her around, maybe convince her she is mistaken and jumping to the wrong conclusions. For the sake of our family she needs to forgive me. This won't be easy, and it might take time, but I know I can win her back. But first, I need to stop the hit and find out who was behind it. Someone has tried to ruin my life, and I will make them pay. I need to stop feeling sorry for myself and take control. Once I get through to the Agency, everything will work out.

I drive on automatic pilot, lost in my thoughts and hardly aware of what I'm doing. It's a shock when I realize I'm nearly there. I pull off the expressway and head east, toward the lake, toward Silverman's home. I'm still not sure what I'm doing. I have no plan and it feels as though I'm floating aimlessly. But Silverman is the key. There's no doubt in my mind.

I pass a sign welcoming me to the village of Wilmette. I was here a few weeks ago and know my way around. I drive past a strip mall that looks like a European village and another that looks like a small town in New England. The signs are understated and sedate. Trees are everywhere, and the cars parked along the street are BMWs, Mercedes, and Range Rovers. The golden dome of the Bahai temple is straight ahead and I use it as a landmark. As I get closer to the lake, I turn off the main road and drive down a tree-lined street of big houses. Colonials, Georgians, traditional, and modern. All types, but all large and pristinely maintained. I slow down as I reach Silverman's house. No one is about, so I stop in the street, shift into park and take in the view.

Silverman's place is a white brick Manor home with blue shutters and a gray roof, two stories high with plenty of oversized windows. It's beautiful and fits in with the neighborhood. Expensive-looking without being flashy. Old, but well kept. The windows are all dark, but it's still day time. Everything here looks the same is it did the last time I came through, when I was still planning his hit. This surprises me in a way. I expected something to be different. Maybe a 'For Sale' sign in the yard, though it's clearly too recent for that. I expect to see something that shows how things have changed, but nothing's changed. I look at the house and try to see what it says about its owner. Was he the only one living there? This place is way too large for one man. He probably bought it to fit in with his image and maybe as an investment for the resale value.

I sense movement and glance at my rearview mirror. A car has turned onto the street and is coming up behind me. I shift into gear and drive on. It feels strange being back here. With all the jobs I've done over the years, I never looked back. From time to time I've wondered how the world changed after I completed the hit. One minute my target was a part of the world, the next minute he was gone. The person would have had a family or people he was close to. There had to be people he loved and people who loved him. My rationale was always that the target was picked for a reason. They had done something bad enough to be marked for death, and that was always enough for me. I did what I was contracted to do, and I moved on. It's healthier not to think too much about it. Now, I'm not sure. It feels different with the shoe on my own foot and I'm a marked man.

I drive up another street and turn toward the lake. It's clear I need to learn more about Silverman to find who placed the contract, but I don't even know where to start. In the detective shows one thing leads on to another until they have a clear suspect. But they have the badge and the authority to talk with anyone they want to. All I have are some brand new business cards.

But I'm not restricted by the law. I don't have to make a case that stands up in court. If I find the suspect, the source, I can be the judge and jury. I can use any means I need to make them talk and tell me how they placed the hit with the Agency.

If I can just find a suspect.

I head back to the main road. People here in town knew Silverman, and they can tell me what they know. At least I have my start.

I FIND the Congregation Beth Shalom and park near the entrance, alongside the only two other cars in the big lot. I take the leather notebook with me as I slide out of my car. It's a prop, to make my visit seem more official.

The building is red brick with stone accents, big, stately, and modern. The cross is missing, but otherwise it looks like it could be any one of the big-box protestant churches that have popped up all over the suburbs. Impressive and successful-looking, without showing any sign of character or history. The parking lot is newly paved, and the spaces painted with crisp, yellow lines. The whole building looks new. I wonder if it has been renovated, or if they tore the old one down and started from scratch. I walk through the front door and look around in the big entranceway. Torn down and rebuilt, I decide. Everything is new, and I breathe in the sharp scent of fresh paint.

A sign points to the office and I head toward it. My footsteps are loud in the empty hall. The office door is halfway open. I knock and poke my head in. There are two empty desks in the front of the room and a hallway leading back further in the building. I don't see anyone inside.

"Hello," I call out. "Anyone here?"

A noise comes from further back. I step all the way into the room and wait.

After a moment a dark-haired lady, middle-aged and plump, steps out of a side room, and into the hallway. She is carrying a box and is surprised to see me.

"Oh, hello," she says. "I didn't hear you come in."

"The door was open, and I knew someone had to be here. I did call out."

She enters the room and sets the box on one of the desks. She is breathing slightly heavy.

"Can I help you?" she asks. She isn't smiling, but her tone is friendly.

"Yes. At least, I hope so. My name is Robert Chambers and I'm with Cleveland Mutual Life Insurance." I say this smoothly and convincingly. "Can I ask you a few questions?"

"I'm afraid there is no soliciting here," she says, her tone still pleasant, but now carries a slight edge.

"Of course. I completely understand. I'm here regarding one of your parishioners. Or, he was until recently."

"Oh! I'm sorry. We get a lot of salesman here. Of course. Please sit down." She waves me to a seat across from her desk and I smile and thank her as I sit.

"I should have called ahead, but I was in the area and thought I'd stop by." I wait as she plops into the chair across from me. "I'm here about Alan Silverman. He was a member here, I believe? Did you know him?"

Her face changes, but I can't read what she is thinking. "Oh, Mr. Silverman. Yes, of course. It was quite a shock when he died."

"Yes, I'm sure it was. The reason I'm here, Miss...?" I pause and wait. I want to build trust and knowing her name will help.

"It's Courtney. Gail Courtney."

"Thank you, Ms. Courtney," I say, and add her name to my notebook. "The reason I'm here, Ms. Courtney, is that Mr. Silverman had rather a large policy with us. And this congregation was one of the beneficiaries." I say that without thinking or planning ahead. It's the first thing that comes to mind. Her eyes widen in surprise, and I know my improvisation is working. "Did you know him well?"

"No, I knew him, but I can't say I knew him well at all. Mr. Silverman tended to keep to himself." She seems excited to hear of the congregation's good fortune.

I make a show of writing this down too.

"Maybe you can tell me a little about Mr. Silverman," I say. "How was he viewed by the members of this community?"

"You know," Gail says suddenly. "You really should be talking with Rabbi Posner. He's back in his office now. He is very busy, but I'm sure he will want to talk with you about this. Could you wait here for a moment, please?"

"Of course, I can wait."

She hurries off and I try to think of what I should say and what I expect to gain here. The lie about the windfall is enough to get them talking. I sit quietly. After a couple of minutes, footsteps echo in the hallway outside, and I know there are two people. I sit up straighter and try to appear as official as possible.

"Mr. Chambers? How are you? Thank you for coming." Rabbi Posner comes around the corner wearing a big smile.

I stand to greet him.

He is nearly bald with a dark goatee, and though he is not tall, he is a big man. An orange golf shirt is stretched to the limit over his thick body. He looks more like a competitive weightlifter or wrestler than a holy man. He grabs my hand and gives it a tight squeeze. "Come. Come on back and let's talk."

I follow him along the hallway and into his office. The office is large and filled with sun from a big, south-facing window overlooking the parking lot. The Rabbi leads me away from the desk and we sit in two comfortable chairs, side by side, close enough to touch.

"So, Mr. Chambers, thank you for coming. Gail tells me this is about Alan? Alan Silverman?"

"Yes, Rabbi," I say. "He had a policy with us and I need to check some things out before we can authorize any dispersions. It's a standard procedure."

"And we are the beneficiary? This is quite a surprise."

"Well, you are *a* beneficiary. I'm not at liberty to tell you how much or if you are the only one, but yes, the congregation is listed as a beneficiary to his policy. And with the size of the policy, we of course need to complete due diligence before the funds can be released."

"Yes, of course. I completely understand." The rabbi's eyes are bright, and I imagine he's already thinking of ways to spend the money.

"I wonder if you could tell me what kind of man Mr. Silverman was?"

The rabbi sits back and wrinkles his brow in thought. He takes a minute to speak, clearly considering his words.

"Alan was a good man. A devoted Jew and a very generous donor to our community."

"Yes," I nod and write this on my pad. "Did you know him well, Rabbi?"

"I think so. He was quite active, and we talked regularly. So, yes. I considered him a friend."

"Can you tell me anything about his personal life? I know he wasn't married, but did he have any close relationships, maybe romantic involvements that you knew of? We need to be aware of anyone else who might file a claim."

"Alan was a very private person. He never shared that side of his life with me, and always came to services alone."

"Yes," I say, writing this all in my notebook "On a personal level, what was he like as an person?"

The rabbi pauses. He seems to consider what he wants to say.

"Alan was a man of strong opinions. He would do his best to persuade you to seeing things his way. He could be stubborn, not intentionally, I think. But he didn't try to make friends. If he thought he was right about something, he would push you on it. He could be ... well, he was a little difficult at times." The rabbi scratches his chin. "Of course, this was a great attribute in his profession. It was part of why he was so good at what he did."

I nod again. "Being the way that he was, was there anyone he had particular friction with? Anyone you can think of who might have wanted to harm him?"

The rabbi sits straight up. "Why are you asking? That's a strange question to ask."

"We're just being thorough," I reply smoothly, adding what I hope is a disarming smile. "This is standard procedure whenever we are finalizing distributions for such a large policy."

"Yes, but my understanding is that his death was accidental. He fell into traffic, I understand. It was some kind of freak accident, am I right?"

"That's my understanding too. Again, we are just covering all the bases."

"His passing was quite a shock to us all. I was saddened to see him go. We all were. I worked closely with him at times. He was a generous supporter of our building fund, and I spoke to several people who said how surprised and sad they were that he passed in this way, so tragically."

"Yes," I say. "But you said he could be difficult. Was there anyone in particular who he had run-ins with? Anyone who he may have had personal issues with?"

The rabbi locks into me with his deep eyes, and it unnerves me. Is he on to me? Does he know I'm not who I say I am? My pulse quickens as I hold his gaze. Then he nods as if he has made an important decision.

"Are you a religious man, Mr. Chambers?"

"Well, I'm a believer," I say, although I have the urge to look away as I say it. His staring at me has made me uncomfortable, and I don't like the question—or my answer.

"Then, as a believer you understand," Rabbi Posner touches my arm and leans in. "I would like to help you, but you understand that one of our guiding laws is to not bear false witness." He grips onto my forearm and holds me tight. "I hear things. I know there are disagreements, differences of opinion and personality clashes at times. This happens within any group of people, and our congregation is no different. I have heard things, of course, but that's all it is. Second-hand rumors and gossip. There is nothing I can say to help you with this question."

"I understand," I say. I look down at my forearm, and he releases his grip. I'm not sure why I feel so uncomfortable, but I do. "I was hoping you knew something, just so we could finish up the report. We can't distribute the funds until we clear everything up, and this is just part of our process."

"Of course." The rabbi shrugs. "I wish I could do more to help."

We talk for a few more minutes. I ask more questions and he gives more vague answers. I know precious little more now than I did when I first entered his office. He is friendly and sincere and doesn't seem threatening in any way, but I'm uncomfortable being with him. It's the way he looked me in the eyes. He stared deep and I think I'm afraid of what he can see in me.

"Thank you, Rabbi." I say as I stand. "I appreciate your taking the time to talk."

"Yes, of course." The rabbi stands with me. "So, how long does it usually take to get this all sorted out? Will we be getting something official regarding his policy?"

"Yes," I nod and move toward the door. "I'm not sure how long it will take, but I will expedite the policy as soon as possible. You should get something in the mail soon."

I have my hand on the door knob and feel like I'm trying to escape, when he lightly touches my shoulder from behind.

"One other thing, Mr. Chambers. Can I get your business card? In case we need to get a hold of you?"

"Yes, of course." I hand him a card and smile my thanks. I open the door and do my best not to run out. As I look down the hallway, I see Ms. Courtney rounding the corner into the open office. Is it a coincidence or had she been at the door, listening?

I walk fast, happy to be leaving. I pass into the outer office and thank Ms. Courtney for her help without stopping to chat. I hardly look at her and keep walking past the reception area, out the front door and in to the sunshine of the outside world.

I'm at my car with my keys out when footsteps shuffle up from behind me. I spin around. Ms. Courtney rushes toward me, red-faced and breathing fast.

She thrusts a piece of paper into my hand, glances back toward the door for a moment, then turns to face me.

"Call me after eleven and I'll tell you what you're looking for," she pants. "Mr. Silverman had an enemy!"

She turns and hurries back toward the door. I look down at the paper in my hand. It has her name and phone number. Below this is another name: Samuel Leach.

25

I drive to a shopping mall and park at the back edge of the parking lot. I'm still a little unnerved by my talk with the rabbi. I wasn't raised in a religious family, clearly, and I try not to think of God or religion. If what they believe is real and there is an afterlife, I'm not in for a good time. Jen goes to a local Methodist church occasionally and I've gone with her and the kids to the Christmas and Easter services. But I'm playing a role. Something I do to fit in. I listen to the sermons as they talk about love and sacrifice, and another life beyond our own. But they are only words. Rituals and superstitions. They mean nothing to me.

The way the rabbi looked at me felt different. I think it is a technique. Part of his bag of tricks for building trust and rapport. He stared into my eyes, but he didn't see a thing. He is just a man like any other man, and his role and title don't give him any special powers. He wasn't judging me. But it still feels as though he was seeing who I really am, and learning that my whole life is a lie. My hands are unsteady, and it seems like a sign of some kind. No matter what happens, if I get out of this, I need to quit my business.

I glance at my watch. I have nearly an hour before I can call Gail Courtney, which gives me time for more research. I get my laptop out of the trunk and connect to a satellite server. This is the second or third time I have heard Samuel Leach's name, which strikes me as important. I start with a basic Google search by entering his name and the town, assuming he lives nearby. The first listing that comes up is a company website, which Leach as the operating partner for a law firm in Chicago: Leach, Hawes and Stratford. Like Silverman, he's a lawyer. I find this interesting.

I click on the site's *About Us* link. The firm specializes in corporate and government law. They work for the city of Chicago and some of the top corporations in the state. This page is full of company PR and propaganda, but they are clearly a big and impressive firm. I click on Leach's name and title and it takes me to his page. It shows a picture of him seated behind a desk. I don't know how tall he is, but he looks lean, fit and handsome. He has a full head of salt and pepper hair, and has the air of someone who would inspire trust. I read on. There is a summary of his history and accomplishments. The one thing that jumps out is that he graduated from the University of Chicago Law School in 1985. I try and remember from the dossier, but I think this was the same school and the same year that Silverman graduated.

I broaden my search, looking for mentions of Leach in the news. There are plenty. Mostly social and society mentions, charities he is involved with and events he attended. The press pictures confirm my suspicions—he is tall. He also has a beautiful wife who appears with him in most of the pictures. I search for his name and Silverman's together to see if I can get any connections. A few things come up. Mentions of them being at the same events, an article in *Crain's Chicago Business* where they are both quoted, and an article in the *Chicago Law Review* about a pending settlement. I click on the link but it's hidden behind a paywall. I'd need to subscribe in order to read it. I can investigate this more later if I need to.

I glance at my watch and realize it's been an hour. I take out my phone, mask my number, and call Ms. Courtney. I'm a little excited. There are some connections here. Have I stumbled onto the right person? Leach and Silverman ran in the same circles and, successful lawyers are competitive people. But this is just quick research. I'm only guessing and don't see a clear motive. Ms. Courtney picks up on the second ring.

"Hello?"

"Hello, Ms. Courtney. "This is Robert Chambers from Cleveland Life Insurance. Is this a good time?"

"Yes, Mr. Chambers, it is. I'm in my car, I just left. And please, call me Gail." Her voice sounds excited. Even now she is breathing fast.

"Yes, Gail. Thank you." I try and sound official. "You have some information about Mr. Silverman?"

"I do. But I want to make sure this is all confidential, okay? I don't want Rabbi Posner to know I talked with you about this. He is a very cautious man, and I wanted to make sure you knew the truth."

"Of course," I answer. "This is entirely confidential. No one will ever know we spoke."

"Good. And this will help the money get released earlier? Because you can finish your report, right?"

"Absolutely. The sooner I can finish my report the quicker we can distribute the proceeds."

"That's what I thought. I just wanted to make sure. Hold on a minute, please. I'm driving, and I need to pull over. My hands are shaking. I need to tell somebody about this."

I wait as she finds a spot to stop. My pulse quickens, too.

"Okay. Are you still there?"

"Yes, I am," I assure her. "You said that Mr. Silverman and Mr. Leach were enemies? How so?"

"Well, everybody knew. It was common knowledge. They competed on everything. When Mr. Leach gave to the mission fund, Mr. Silverman gave more. When Sam, that's Mr. Leach, contributed to the building fund, Mr. Silverman gave a bigger donation. This has been going on for years."

"So, it's about who gives more for your congregation?" I tried not to reveal my disappointment. It seemed thin. It also sounded like Silverman was the one trying to get the upper hand. He was the one doing all the competing.

"Well, yes. But it's much more than that. I talk with a lot of people, you know. I hear things."

"Like what?"

"Well, they are both attorneys, you know? And I understand they were very competitive at work as well. I've been told this has been going on for years too."

"Yes," I say. "But is there anything specific? How do they relate with each other when they are together?"

"Oh, they don't talk to each other. Not at all. They sit on opposite sides of the hall and don't ever say anything. Though I sat behind Mr. Silverman's normal spot, and I noticed he did look over at Sam quite a lot."

"It sounds like the competition was more on Mr. Silverman's side. Is that right?"

"Well, yes. I think Sam mostly found it amusing. Or he seemed to anyway."

This was looking more and more like a dead end.

"My question, Gail, was if there was anyone who might want to harm Mr. Silverman. It sounds like Samuel—Mr. Leach—wasn't that concerned with Mr. Silverman. It was the other way around."

"Well, that's what I'm getting to." Gail is breathless, and excited to tell me more. "It was maybe a month and a half ago, before Mr. Silverman had his tragic accident, there was an incident in the parking lot."

"An incident?"

"Yes! They were in the parking lot after the service and they got into a big fight."

"A fight? Do you mean a physical fight, or an argument?"

"Well, it was an argument, they were yelling at each other and absolutely out of control. But Sam was very angry. He poked Mr. Silverman in the chest. He got in real close and actually poked him! His wife had to pull Sam away, or who knows what could have happened."

"You saw all this yourself?"

"Well, no. But I heard it from several people, all very reliable. So, I know it's true."

"Do you have any idea what the argument was about?"

"My understanding is it was something related to their work, a case they were both involved with. I'm not sure what it was, but Sam is a very calm and dignified man. Alan must have done something awful to make him react like that."

"Thank you, Gail. This has been very helpful. Did anything happen after that?"

"Yes. Apparently, Mr. Silverman called the police and pressed charges. He filed a complaint with the bar association, at least that's what I was told. My friend Betty is very close friends with Sam's wife Gloria, so I know it's true. It was looking like things were going to get very ugly. Then Mr. Silverman had his accident, of course."

I can't believe my good luck. This seems like a clear motive, and I may have found my man.

"Thank you, Gail. you have been very helpful."

"So, we should be getting this money soon, right?"

"That's right," I lie. "You should expect it very soon."

I cut off the connection. I'm smiling. This is a big break. The motive feels right. It's both business and personal, the kind of thing someone would kill for. Silverman's death is a way to save Leach's reputation and get rid of a rival. An enemy. This feels right. I might have my man. I still have a lot of work to do. I have to investigate more so I'm not jumping to conclusions—as I did with George. I shudder as I consider how close I came to killing my best friend. And I still have to trace Leach back and find out how he got access to the Agency. But I can do this. I know I can.

I see a way to get my life back.

26

Back at my hotel, I boot up my laptop. Using my proxy account, I enter the deep web again. I'm excited about my discovery of Leach and anxious to learn more. He has the motive. Those with enough money and power live by their own rules. As connected and powerful as Leach is, he may have the contacts to place a hit on Silverman. But it seems too easy. Maybe Leach is just one of Silverman's enemies. There could be others with just as much or more of a motive. Although I need to dig in deeper on Leach, I can't have tunnel vision and focus only on him. I need to stick with my plan and find out more about Silverman.

Down in the deep web I see a message in my secure portal. It's from the Agency. My breath catches in my throat as I click on the link to open it.

Last project has been terminated. Take no more actions toward this goal. You will be paid for your time and efforts, but again, no further action is necessary.

I read the message through again. Is this a joke? They are cancelling the hit on myself after they have already re-assigned the case to someone else. I think this through. They are saying that the case is canceled, though I know it's been reassigned. Do they know they've made a mistake and that I was both the target and the operator? Or is it some kind of bureaucratic mix-up and they still don't have a clue? I delete the message and don't respond. As far as I know, the target is still on my back and this doesn't change anything.

I placed orders for reports on Silverman, Leach, and Griffin. I check the information broker site to see if they are ready, and both the Leach and Silverman reports are available. I savor the anticipation. I choose Silverman's first and click the link.

The report is different from the others. It not only gives his date of birth, but also the date of his death. I pause for a second to take this in. This is my connection to the man. His mother birthed him, and I killed him. Normally, I try not to think much about my jobs after they are completed, and I'm really uncomfortable diving into the man's life. But it's my only ticket in to find the Agency. Everything I've learned so far has confirmed what I originally thought. Most of the people I'd spoken with, when they talked about Silverman, mentioned his success and said how skilled of an attorney he was. They had to search hard to find anything good to say about him personally.

I skim through the introductory paragraph. It summarizes who he was, an attorney and the partner of a prestigious law firm. I know so much about him already and this is telling me things I already know. He was single and never married. He had no children and few living relatives. Son to an accountant and a housewife, he grew up in the middle-class suburb of Skokie. He had an older brother, who lives out of state. I skim through his school history and see he was a National Merit Scholar, on the debate club for all four years and the valedictorian for his class. He graduated from the University of Michigan and earned his law degree from the University of Chicago. I know all this already.

I skip past this and look at his social media profile. His biggest profile is on LinkedIn and he has thousands of connections. But he didn't post anything and hadn't checked his account for well over a year before his death. This was probably something his secretary or someone at the firm set up as part of their corporate media strategy. I'm surprised to see he has a Facebook account, under the name Al Silverman, and he was active on it until the day he died. This is strange. He seemed like such an unsocial person, but he maintained plenty of connections online. He had a small friend list, and, although he was active, most of the activity was likes, hearts, and thumbs-up icons. He wrote precious few comments or posts of what he was doing. The list shows most of the friends are in their mid-fifties, like Silverman, and they all went to Skokie High School. This might be something to look into.

His credit report is spotless. He has no balances on his cards, and his mortgage is paid off. I look through the trade lines, search for anything unusual, but it's what I'd expect from someone in his position. He had accounts with high limits at Nordstrom's, Hickey Freeman, and other luxury retailers. What's more, he has the highest credit limit I have seen on an American Express card.

I keep skimming through. The report gives a breakdown of his recent tax returns and an accounting of his assets. I had assumed, and now I know, that Silverman was a wealthy man. He owned several commercial properties, all through trusts and partnerships. He had accounts at two major wealth management firms and the range of his total holdings was more than ten million dollars. The size of this estate alone could be motivation enough for someone to want him dead. I continue to scroll down.

The news file is much more extensive than I found on my own, and this is where I find what I'm looking for. There's a front-page article in the *Chicago Law Review* about a law suit Silverman placed against Leach. The date is March third, less than a month before I accepted Silverman's contract. It's rare, the article states, for one attorney to sue another, and even more so among such prominent members of the local bar. The article reads more like something from a gossip magazine than a trade publication. This is big news and they treat it as such. The article explains that the lawsuit was placed after a public alteration between the two men, and the details are similar to what Gail told me.

It goes on to give all the background details. Both Silverman and Leach went to the University of Chicago Law School at the same time, and both graduated with top honors. The reporter interviewed people who knew them back then and who knew them now, and though no source was named, they maintained there had been a long-term rivalry between the two.

The physical altercation was preceded, the article continues, by the two attorneys facing each other in a recent court case. Silverman was representing Calhoun and associates, and Leach was representing another development group, Pelicano LLC. It sounds as though it was a routine case, something that associates would normally handle, not partners. Silverman won the case, and Leach immediately registered his intent to appeal. Unnamed witnesses recount a verbal altercation in the hallway, and the fight at the synagogue happened the following weekend. The article ends by stating that both parties were contacted before publication. Leach declined to comment. Silverman said that the record speaks for itself and he was looking forward to the court date and had reported the incident to the local bar for censure, as well.

I slump against the back of my seat. This is it. This is motive, and clear enough reason for Leach to place the hit. He'd been beaten in court and embarrassed in public. This would affect earnings for his firm, and if the bar association took action, it would have caused even more damage.

I know it for a fact now. Leach is the guy. I keep reading, but I'm only skimming. I've found what I need.

I read on and see that Silverman's will has been filed. I read the summary and see he has given a nominal share of his estate to his brother and a nephew and niece, just a few thousand each. He also willed a respectable sum to his synagogue, but the bulk of his estate goes to the Humane Society, a charity that takes in stray cats and dogs. I wonder if this is because he truly is a passionate supporter of abandoned pets, or if it's one last flash of his middle finger. A message to everyone showing how he feels about them. I wonder if he let his brother know beforehand, or if it will come as a surprise to them that he was mostly left out.

I read down and there is more in the file. I skim through and see people he is closely connected to, and I recognize several names on the list, including Pat Griffin, Calhoun, and Rabbi Posner. But this is all window dressing. I have what I need.

I exit the Silverman file and click on the link for Leach. I race through it. I already know what to expect, and I'm certain he is my man. The summary confirms what I already know. He is the managing partner of a large law firm, very successful in his field and well connected with the major political and business forces in the town. He's an officer and major benefactor to a number of charities, and along with his wife, Rachel, he is active on the social scene. It shows he has three kids—two boys and a girl—and has recently become a grandfather. His medical records show he takes a statin for cholesterol, medication for high blood pressure, and he has ongoing issues with his prostate. The report on his finances shows as a range, but he is even richer than Silverman. I skip down to the news articles and find the same things that I read in the Silverman file. The only new information is an arrest record, filed with the Wilmette Police Department. It's the same day as the incident, but instead of assault, a felony, the charge listed is disorderly conduct, which seems like a win for him.

I pay attention to his close associates, those he spends time with, and the places he frequents, searching for clues to his behavior and patterns. I see he is on the board for the Juvenile Diabetes Foundation, and that they have a fundraiser tomorrow night. This is helpful. I start thinking through what I need to do to connect with him and find out what he knows. I go through the rest of the file and it doesn't tell me anything new, except that Leach is well respected, generous with his time and money, and acclaimed in his industry. It seems like he is probably a good guy at heart. Was this the final straw, the breaking point, that caused him to make the phone call that would lead to my taking on the job? How did he find the Agency? Was it through one of his business buddies, or a referral from someone in the criminal law division at his firm?

I don't know how Leach connected to the Agency, but I will find out.

I check the time. It's still early evening. I ponder my next moves. I still need to find out more about Griffin, Silverman's associate, just to be sure. But I'm excited about my discovery of Leach. He has the motive and the means to make it happen.

But finding him is only the first step. If he's the one, I still need to make him talk. And then I need to use what I learn to approach the Agency. My head starts to pound as I think of all the things I still need to do, and all the things that could still go wrong.

I need to find Leach, ask him questions, and make him give me answers. I can't show up at his office; he will never see me. And I don't want to be seen, either. If I get in to see him somehow, this will raise his defenses and put him on notice that someone knows what he did. No. This has to be a different way.

I pace the small room trying to decide what to do next. Talking this out with someone would be good, but there is no one I can talk to. I start to think of Jen again. Has she tried calling me? She could have changed her mind. She's had time to think about things and time to calm down. I left my phone back at home. If she calls, I won't even know it. If she decides this has gone on long enough and goes back home, she'll be putting herself and the kids in danger. A tightness ripples my stomach, and acid rises into my throat. I pick up the phone and start to dial her number, but stop. Someone is monitoring her phone. If they are looking at me, they will be looking for me to contact her and trace me back that way.

Still, I need to know if she has called. I can't go back home and check my phone, but I can check my voicemail. I dial in and punch in my passcode. The digital voice tells me I have five voice messages. I punch the play button and listen to the first message. It's Beth.

"Hey Charley, it's me. Where are you? Call me as soon as you get this. Dad's taken a turn for the worse. I'm really worried. Call me."

I want to call her, but I can't. If Dad dies now, I know it's my fault. I delete the message. I'll call her later, but I need to stay focused now. I hit the button and the next message plays.

"Hello Mr. Fieldner, this is Jessica from Dr. Sanduski's office—"

This is my dentist, calling to remind me of an appointment. I delete the message. I click the next and it's Beth again.

"Hi Charley, it's me. Where are you? I really need to talk with you. I tried calling Jen and she's not answering either. Are you okay? This is serious. Call me!"

I don't want to dwell on this any more than I have to. I can't call her now. My hand trembles as I erase the message and play the next. This message is from George.

"Hey Dude, what's up? Did you get my texts? Wondering if your phone isn't working or if something happened? Let's get together this week if you have some time. I got a great story for you about what happened the other night. Oh, also, what's the deal with crime in Naperville?" George laughs. "Man, that is absolutely crazy. Your neighborhood is in the news! Can you believe that? Somebody tried to throw a body away in the trash, and they say it came from somewhere down your way. You gotta wonder what happened there, man. Call me."

My heart pounds. Blood rushes to my head and I am dizzy. Have I been discovered? George's message leaves me unnerved. My hand shakes more as I punch the button for the next message.

"Hello, Mr. Fieldner, this is Detective Jorgensen with the Naperville police department. An incident has occurred in your neighborhood and we need to ask you some questions. Please call as soon as you get this message, so we can arrange a time to talk. My direct line is..."

I listen to the rest of the message, write down the name and number. My heart is racing as I hang up the phone. They found the body! And the police are calling me!

I go back online and check the website for a local news station. The body is the number one story, and they spin it out as a mystery. I play a video of the story and then search for more details on other news sites. I learn that an unidentified man's body was recovered from the garbage dump after a worker noticed his leg sticking out. There is no word on the man's identity. They released a picture, but he had no identification and no identifying marks. There is also no information on how he died or how he came to be in the trash. The police are still investigating, but they have narrowed it down to having come from a garbage truck that picked up central Naperville garbage. Police are continuing to investigate.

Blood pounds in my head.

Why are the police calling me? Is this part of a routine investigation, or have they already narrowed it down and see me as a suspect? They don't know exactly where the body came from, so that is good. But the police will search through the trash looking for clues, trying to find garbage with names and addresses to narrow it down to as close as they can to the source. All the garbage bags had to be mixed in, and they might not find an exact location, but they will get close. I didn't mix any of our other garbage in with the corpse, and I'm pretty sure I sent the body off on its own. I look down at my arm and my cut is healing nicely. But a wave of anxiety hits as I remember my shirt. Did I throw it away? No, I don't think so, but if I did, it has my blood on it, a sure link to me. Did I leave fingerprints on the garbage bags? The box of garbage bags is a clue in itself. Fingerprints shouldn't be an issue. I wore gloves. Besides, I have never been arrested, never joined the military and my fingerprints aren't on file. But I left home with two full bags of garbage sitting on the garage floor, along with a bloody shirt and more blood on the floor. If the police canvass door-to-door and someone lets them into the garage this will be a problem.

I shudder as I think this through. I mask my phone to call the Peterson's landline. They live two doors down and have kids about the same age as ours. The phone rings a few times before Peg Peterson picks up.

"Hello?"

"Hi, Peg. How are you? This is Charley, Charley Fieldner."

"Oh, hi Charley. I'm great. How are you? Are you guys gone for spring break? Jen didn't say anything, but we haven't seen you around."

"No," I say. "I got called out on an unexpected trip. Jen and the kids are visiting her sister."

"Oh, well I have to say, we miss you." Kids' voices fill the background, it sounds like they are arguing. "The kids are off school this week, and Alex keeps saying he wants to play with Jason. It's been fun trying to keep them busy. So many people are gone this week."

"I know. We talked about getting away, but something came up."

"Oh, did you hear about the excitement in the neighborhood? Can you believe it?"

"Right," I say. "I saw it on the news. What happened?"

"I don't know. It's a real mystery. I asked the detective when he came by yesterday, and he wouldn't say anything, but it sounds like they think it came from over in the Parson Farms area, but it could be either here or in the Meadows, too. I talked with my friend Barbara over there, and the police stopped by her house too. Her cousin works at the station, and he says they have no idea where it came from."

"So, detectives are going door to door? They're talking with everyone?"

"Well, sure. Everyone who is home, anyway. Can you believe there's a murderer in our area? This area is so safe it's hard to believe." She doesn't sound scared. Maybe a little excited. "I told the man they should look at Henry Klingman over on Osage. You know, the one with that broken-down car in his driveway? He's always seemed a little off to me, I could see him doing something like this."

I talk with her for another few minutes, thank her and hang up. It sounds like the police are going through their paces, but they haven't narrowed it down and have a lot of ground to cover. That makes me think they aren't looking for me. Yet. But that could change.

I swallow hard and dial the number for Officer Jorgensen. The phone rings, and my tension rises. I've never had to kill someone in my own area before, and this was a big mistake leaving the body where it could be so easily found. I wasn't thinking clearly.

Voicemail picks up on the fifth ring. I listen to the message and I'm glad I don't have to talk with a real person. Not now.

"Hi, Detective. This is Charley Fieldner from over on Poplar Way. I got your message and I'm returning your call. My dad just fell ill, and I will be unavailable for the next few days, but I will try calling again later. My number again is..."

I finish my message and hang up. This is a problem, but I'll deal with it later. I have more pressing issues now.

27

In the morning I head downtown and reach Silverman's building before six. I station myself in the lobby with a good view of the elevator bank going to Silverman's office. The lobby is peaceful at this time of morning. Not at all as busy and hectic as it was when I visited the other day. The air is quiet. Some service workers come through carrying boxes. The two uniformed guards sit behind their big granite desk, and hardly pay me any mind. I stand off to the side, as relaxed and casual as I can be, taking in the sculptures and the full-grown acacia trees that make the lobby look like a Zen forest.

I'm not here more than five minutes before Pat Griffin arrives, the staccato strike of her high heels echoing against the hard marble floor. Her long, red hair is pulled back. She walks with a quick stride, her posture straight and confident. She doesn't see me at first as I make a beeline toward her, catching her by the elevator banks.

"Ms. Griffin," I call out. "Excuse me, may I have a moment?"

She doesn't respond at first, and it's not until I'm directly in her view that I see why. She has earbuds in and is listening to something. As she sees me, a look of distaste crosses her face. She takes out one of the buds and faces me full on, her hands on her hips in an aggressive posture.

"I told you before, if you have anything else you want to ask me, do it through your attorneys."

"I'm sorry, Ms. Griffin. I was out of line the other day. That was completely unprofessional to speak with you that way. I'm not sure what came over me."

She turns away from me and hits the button for the elevators. She doesn't respond, and she doesn't look back at me.

"If I could take another moment of your time, please? I'm trying to finish my report and I need your help to get a couple of details straight. It will be much easier if we do this now. It won't take more than a minute."

The monitor on the wall shows the elevators are all stopped at upper floors and descending slowly. She sighs loudly before turning to face me once more.

"What do you want?"

"Thank you," I say. "I understand you were with Mr. Silverman on the final hearing for the Pellicano case."

"That again?" The tone of her voice is exasperated and a little angry.

"Yes, ma'am. I understand there was an altercation between Mr. Silverman and Mr. Leach in the hallway after the decision, and I wanted to ask you about that."

Griffin shakes her head. "That has been blown way out of proportion. They've known each other for a long time, both personally and professionally. Alan spoke very highly of Mr. Leach, he respected him greatly. I'm sure the feeling was mutual. If you're trying to make something of this, you're running in the wrong direction."

"Yes, and I'm not trying to make this into anything more than it is. But I do need to be thorough. Can you please tell me what happened, from your point of view?"

Griffin looks at the monitor on the wall, and one of the elevators is moving now, it's on the third floor and dropping lower.

"There isn't much to tell. The decision didn't go Mr. Leach's way, and he took it personally. It happens sometimes. No one likes to lose, and he showed his emotions after a difficult defeat."

"Did he make any threats at the time?"

"Threats? No. He was angry, and he blew off a little bit of steam. It happens all the time. It happens in locker rooms and on the golf course. This time it just happened to occur in the court hallway. That's all there is."

The elevator lands on the ground floor, and the doors slide open with a ding. Griffin steps inside.

"You'll have to excuse me, Mr. Chambers. I have work to do."

She hits the button and the doors start to slide shut, but I reach my arm in, and the doors part again.

"Just one last question, please. Do you think it's possible that Mr. Leach would do anything to harm Silverman?"

"No," she says this firmly and dismissively. "Anything else you need, get it to me in writing."

The doors close again, and this time I don't try and stop them. Right before the doors completely shut, I see that Griffin is smiling. I stay rooted where I am for a minute, my eyes on the monitor, watching the car climb higher.

THE DOWNTOWN STREETS are filling up and there are people everywhere. Crowds don't normally bother me, but now I'm nervous and exposed. I've lived in this area all my life. What if I run into someone who knows me? The odds are against it, but it could happen. I duck into a drugstore to get off the street and look around me as I walk through the aisles. I look in the big curved mirror in the corner to see if anyone has followed me. I don't think anyone has, and it bothers me that I'm thinking this way. I'm usually calm and in control. Now I'm a nervous rabbit. I breathe in slowly and let it go. I cross to the magazine rack and pretend to flip though some magazines. I'm being hunted, and I think I can live with that. I know how hunters think. I'm aware and vigilant. I'll react when I need to. It's the things I can't control that bother me more.

I think of the detective again, and what I will say to him. I've followed the story and the reports all sound like the cops are grasping for a direction. I'm one of hundreds of people they are calling. It's routine, but that could change in an instant. Someone could say something. Whoever placed the hit will soon discover I'm still alive. An anonymous phone call could put me deep in the mix. If they ask where I was, I have no alibi. I disappeared right after the man was killed and there is no record of where I have been since.

And then there is the hard evidence. I cleaned up the garage before leaving, but I know there is evidence there. I know there was the bloody shirt and I wiped up after me, but there will still be traces of blood on the floor. It's my own blood, and I could explain it away as an accident where I cut myself while working on a project. That might fly, but it's more likely to arouse suspicion. If they get a search warrant, who knows what evidence they'll find? It could be fingerprints, fibers, hairs—anything. The man was in my garage, and the cops will find forensic evidence to prove it. I suddenly have the urge to drop everything and go back home to deep clean everything. A few years ago, I bought a steam pressure washer for the cars, but it'll work great on blood stains. But I can't go home yet. I have things to do.. Killing the man in my home was not a good thing. Not that I had any other choice.

Again, I think of Jen. Whenever I have a problem she's my safety valve. I can't tell her what I do, and I can't give her specifics, but just talking with her calms me down and helps me find the right way to go. What is she thinking now? Is she still angry and blaming me? Does she hate me? Is she afraid of me? She must have heard about the body by now. Has she connected this to me? Does she think I killed the guy and wheeled him out to the curb? I sink lower and a wave of sadness hits me again. I don't know how I can win her back. How can she ever trust me now? Will she give in to her suspicions and turn me in?

I replace the magazine in the rack and walk away, down the aisle and out the front door. Back on the street I find a secluded place to watch the flow of traffic without being noticed. It all comes down to the Agency. I have other problems, but I can't solve these until I know the hit is off, I'm in the clear and I know who placed it. Moping around and feeling sorry for myself won't help anything. I need to act. I need to take the fight back to them. Is Leach my way in? The evidence points that way, but it could be Griffin. She seems so sure of herself. She is ambitious and focused. The only way for her to rise higher was to get Silverman out of her way. She had a lot to gain. It could be Griffin. Or Leach. I have to do something, and I have to regain control of my life.

I walk into a nearby hotel and find a quiet place off the lobby. It's a lounge area with comfortable chairs and couches, and I'm the only one here. I choose a chair with a good view of the surrounding area and take out my burner phone. I mask the number and make a call. Someone answers on the first ring.

"Hello," I say. "Gerald Calhoun, please. This is Robert Chambers calling."

"Please hold," the voice says.

I sit back and wait. It's less than a minute before Calhoun answers.

"Mr. Chambers? This is a surprise. What can I do for you?" Calhoun says, and I'm shocked he answered.

"Thank you, sir. I have a few more questions regarding Mr. Silverman's death. It will just take a minute or two."

"Hell, son. I've been thinking about you since you stopped by the other day. Do you really think it could have been something more than an accident?"

"I can't say for sure, but I think it's possible."

"It's hard to get that out of my mind, that someone would do something like that. Ask away. What do you want to know?"

"When I stopped by, you mentioned that Mr. Silverman told you about the argument he had with Samuel Leach after court. You said Mr. Silverman was excited to tell you about it and there seemed to be something personal there?"

"Right, it was absolutely personal."

"How could you tell this?"

"Well, Alan didn't get excited much, not like this. He usually gave me the details and the bottom line. He let me know how something would affect me, and if there was anything I needed to be aware of. This time it was different. It felt like he was telling me a war story of some kind. He called the guy an arrogant asshole. Seemed damned personal to me."

"He didn't normally talk that way?"

"No, I mean he'd badmouth other lawyers all the time. Said his world was filled with morons and idiots, but this was different. The way he said it. It meant something to him."

"Did he say how?"

"I'm a pretty good judge of people, Mr. Chambers. To be as successful as I am, you need to be able to read people, and see what makes them tick. I knew Alan, and he was never like that. He put Leach on a high shelf, he wanted to be like him. He was excited that he knocked him down a little and even more excited to get him angry about it."

"Yes, and about—"

"Hold on." I hear voices in the background, Calhoun is talking with someone else. I try and pick up what they are saying, but the voices are muffled. I hold for nearly a minute before he comes back on the phone. "Listen, I got an issue here and I've got to go. If you have more questions, stop by. I'll make sure I fit you in."

He hangs up the phone before I can respond. I wanted to ask more about Silverman and what he said about Leach. I want to ask about Griffin, too. But it doesn't matter. I need to act, and I know what I have to do.

28

The Juvenile Diabetes fundraiser is tonight, this strikes me as the perfect opportunity to find my target in a vulnerable position. I spend the rest of the day preparing. It's a public event at the Skyline Hotel. There will be a lot of people in attendance, many Leach is close with. Chicago police will guard the outside, and private security will take the inside. They'll also have security cameras placed at strategic locations throughout. This will make it more difficult, but it's simply another issue to deal with. I run a search for the location and the best ways to get there. I look for public transportation, walkways, and access to cabs and taxis. This is a major public venue, so it's easy to get around. Once out of the building, I'll be able to leave the area quickly and easily. I pull up pictures of the venue, both inside and out. I look for anything that will help me tonight, and I familiarize myself with the layout. The map shows me where the fire exits are and how I can get out to the street from different parts of the building.

In my head, I run through the logistics of how this will happen. I can't allow any surprises, so I do some extra homework. I read up on the organization and skim through their major donor list. I look at pictures from previous events and look for clues of how this will be tonight. I click through pictures of men in tuxedos and woman in their evening gowns. Most of the pictures are of white, well dressed, middle-aged and older people. But I also notice people I've seen before, or who look familiar. There are politicians, sports stars and a few minor local celebrities. These are the people you see on TV or read about in the newspaper, along with the moneyed class, the people who are behind the scenes, making the rules, the true power players. These are the movers and the shakers on the local scene. These are the people who normally separate themselves from the public. And I can be one of them tonight. All I need to do is buy a ticket. I visit the charity's website, register and pay with a card linked to an untraceable crypto account.

The final detail I attend to is my appearance. The way I look doesn't normally call attention to itself. I'm average looking and easily get lost in a crowd, but with so many people, potential witnesses, as well as the inevitable paparazzi, I'm putting myself in a risky situation. Extra precautions are warranted. I take out my disguise kit and choose who I want to be.

The goal is to blend in and not call attention to myself. I pick a well-trimmed grayish-brown goatee and apply it with spirit gum. I choose a hairpiece to match, in a short, combed back style. I could change my eye color with contacts, but it's not worth the effort. I slip on and apply a nose that is a little bigger and more pronounced than my own and apply a little cover makeup to smooth it all out. To add a studious look, I select a pair of black-rimmed glasses and dress in my dark suit with a cobalt blue tie. Finally, I add an expensive-looking fake watch to complete the outfit.

When I'm done, I study myself in the mirror. I smile, raise my eyebrows and try on some different facial expressions. I look about ten years older than I really am. Still average, still forgettable, but different. I can't imagine anyone looking at this face and seeing me as I really am. I look natural. If someone were to stare at me and look closely, they might be able to tell I am wearing makeup. But I'm sure I won't be the only one. Besides, if someone is looking at me that closely, I have bigger problems. I need a weapon, and I'm not sure if they will have metal detectors or body checks before we are admitted. My belt has a hidden acrylic knife at the back loop. That should be enough.

Satisfied, I head out. I stroll through the hotel entrance to the parking lot and no one gives me a second glance. I drive toward the venue and park in a parking garage a couple of miles away from the fundraiser. I take the ticket and walk out to the street. I stand for a moment on the sidewalk, watching the mass of humanity walk by. It's right after quitting time at the offices and this is transition time. People are heading for their buses, trains, or subways on their way home, or changing into their nighttime personas, heading out for drinks and dinner and taking in the night life of the city. The air is cool and comfortable with no hint of rain. It's a beautiful spring evening and it's perfect to be outside. The sun is down, but it's still light. I inhale and hold the air in my lungs and hope this is a sign of better days to come. I still have time before the event starts, and the keyed-up anticipation I always feel before a job strikes hard. I decide to walk.

I run through the details as I walk, trying to imagine what the room will be like, where the people will be, exactly how I will do it and how I will get away. I see it clearly, flowing like a movie, exactly how it will happen, and I imagine a perfect outcome. Confidence is the key, and I am in my element again.

When I finally reach the ballroom it's six-thirty, half an hour before the event will start. I go past the valet stand, in through the main doorway, finding a place where I can watch inconspicuously. Nothing happens at first. A few couples arrive, go to the coat check and then follow the signs, around the corner to the event. As the time gets closer, the traffic picks up. More and more people pass through the doors. Most of the men are dressed in full tuxedos, but I still fit in dressed the way I am. The women, many far younger than their escorts, are dressed in long, shimmering gowns and have sparkling necklaces and prominent handbags. The buzz of conversation grows as more people enter. I don't see him yet, and I try to push the doubt from my mind. Maybe something came up. Maybe he changed his mind.

It's about ten after seven when I sneak back outside to take in the night air and see the scene from a different point of view. Two patrol cars are parked nearby their top lights flashing in red and blue, keeping the traffic at bay. The officers stand by their cars, casually talking. I move back into the shadows to watch and wait. I'm off to the side of the valet stand when a blue Jaguar pulls up. An attendant hurries over and helps the woman out of the passenger side. She has dark hair, long, but gathered up tight in the back. She is an older woman, but her green dress clings in all the right spots, and she has the air of someone who knows her place at the top of the social order. When the driver's side door opens, and the man steps out, my heart speeds up a little. The Leaches are here.

I wait while they hand their keys to the valet, and I wait a few moments more before following them through the main door. I hang back and make myself invisible. Others are still coming in, and I blend in as we make our way down the hallway to the main ballroom. Photographers are there, snapping pictures. I lower my head and walk past. There is a table set up outside the door with three young women behind it. As I expected, there is security here. A couple of uniformed guards stand by the table, another dressed in a tight suit is outside the door. There will be more security inside, but they aren't doing body scans or searches. I stand in a line right behind my target. Leach holds his wife's elbow as they move forward. I register with one of the young girls, giving the name I bought the ticket under and, in turn, she gives me a nametag and a program, and explains how the auction will work.

The Leaches are near the entrance to the ballroom, talking with another older couple. I walk past them and enter the big room. It's filled with people and the hum of conversation and soft music fills the space. The room is decorated with banners and streamers in turquoise and gold. Clusters of helium-filled balloons are festooned around, all in the same color scheme. There is a bar set up near the entrance and another off to the side and people are lined up to get their drinks. I consider getting a drink, even if it's only as a prop, but I think better of it. I walk along the side wall, staying close to the entrance, looking at all the items listed for auction.

It's another minute before the Leaches enter, and when they do, they quickly go their separate ways. Mrs. Leach hurries over to talk with a cluster of women, while Leach heads for the bar. I again consider heading over, getting behind him and staying close, but my time will come. I stay on the perimeter of the room and pretend to be interested in the gift baskets, sports paraphernalia and trip descriptions of the items up for auction. A couple of women, much younger than me and clearly out of my league, are chatting nearby and smile at me as I walk past. No one knows who I am or why I'm here, but my mere presence suggests I'm a member of the club, someone possibly wealthy or important. This is the best disguise I can wear.

Leach picks up his drink and walks a few yards out to an open area. He is only by himself for a moment before other men are drawn in. I watch as several men sidle up, shake his hand and talk. He seems to be holding court. There is now a small group gathered around him, but he is the center, the nucleus. He introduces two people and they shake hands. He says something and the men all laugh. Leach has a smile plastered on his face and his posture tells me he is comfortable and in control.

After a few minutes, Leach excuses himself and walks a little deeper into the crowded room. He smiles and greets people as he moves across the floor. I walk around to a closer vantage point, making sure not to stare or show any obvious interest. I set up near a food station with trays of cheeses, fruits and cut vegetables. Leach walks over to two people standing close together talking. One is middle aged and fat in a tight tuxedo. The other is a red-haired woman in a black dress. Her hair is long, and she looks trim. Before she even turns to greet him, I recognize her as Patricia 'Pat' Griffin.

Interesting.

Leach touches Griffin's shoulder and leans in. They greet each other warmly and talk intently. I edge closer, walking behind Leach trying to get within hearing range. She was at the hearing when the incident with Silverman went down. I'm curious to see them together here now.

Leach says something, and Griffin nods. They look intent, but not at all confrontational. They are standing close and talking low, and I'm desperate to hear what they are saying. I take a chance and move in close enough to hear them without being obvious. But as I move in closer, they break apart.

"Let's talk tomorrow. We can go over the details then," Leach says.

I can't hear Griffin's response, but their meeting is clearly over.

Leach is on the move again. This time he heads back toward the doorway, and I walk slowly behind him, mixing in with the crowd as I go. His wife motions him over as he closes on to her circle. She steps away from her group and they have a quick conversation. She glances at her watch and motions up toward the stage. He's due to talk in front of the crowd in a few minutes. He nods and motions with his head toward the doorway, and I know where he is going.

I hang back a moment before following him out of the room and into the hallway. I stand and check my watch by the door, noting which direction he turned. The tuxedoed guards are still in position, and the girls at the reception still man their table, but the hallway is mostly clear now. Except for a few stragglers, everyone is in the big room waiting for the program to start. I turn down the hallway, tracing Leach's footsteps. He is going to the bathroom I'm sure. He has a prostate condition and I guess he wants to be ready before he starts to talk. I've already seen the map of this hotel and there is a closer men's room in the other direction. This way is around a corner, in back of the stage, away from the activity. As I turn the corner, he enters the men's room, as I knew he would. I'm hoping there aren't many people around, but I have to make sure.

There is a janitor's cart in the hallway, and I push it up close so it's blocking the bathroom entrance. I check the area. There's no one else around.

I move into the bathroom, past the black granite sinks and the big mirror. Leach is at one of the three floor-length urinals, his feet spread wide, his hand down by his open fly holding himself. I bend down low and look under the stalls. No one else is here. Leach hears my footsteps and he can sense my presence, but he is otherwise preoccupied. He stays where he is, facing forward, breathing audibly. I reach back and remove my acrylic knife from its sheath at the back of my belt. Without pausing, I step right up behind Leach, push my body in hard against him and smack his head against the gray tile on the wall, hard enough to hurt, not hard enough to do any lasting damage.

Leach cries out loud in pain and shock.

I press myself in hard against him, so he is pinned against the urinal and can't move. I reach around and grab his chin with one hand and put the knife tip against his throat with the other. His body shakes and I know he wants to struggle, but he has no room to move.

"Don't make a sound," my mouth is right by his ear and I speak softly. "Make any kind of move and I will kill you."

His resistance gives way and his body shakes.

"What do you want?" Leach's voice is calmer than I expect it to be. His body is trembling, but his voice is still steady.

"I know your secret," I say. "I know your secret because I'm the man you hired to make it happen."

"I don't know what you're talking about. You've got me confused with someone else."

The stress in his voice is clear. I can almost smell his fear.

"Don't play with me," I say. "I can kill you right now. You'll die with your dick in your hand. You know I'm serious."

"What is it you want? I have money, lots of money. Just let me go."

"I don't want your money and I don't want to hurt you, as long as you cooperate. I need information."

"Whatever you want. Don't hurt me."

"This is about Alan Silverman," I say.

"Silverman? But he's dead—"

"This is about the hit, the contract you placed on Silverman."

"What? No, I never—I swear!"

He struggles a bit. I push the knife in deeper and pierce his skin of his neck. He gasps and his whole-body stiffens. I lean in harder from behind, so he doesn't fall down.

"Don't lie to me." I'm in so close and my voice is low. I'm almost whispering in his ear. "You know I'm serious and you know what I can do. I know the whole story. You had your fight with Silverman and decided the only way out was to end it for good, and to have him killed. You placed a hit through the Agency. What I need to know is how you found them and how you contacted them."

"I never—I swear, I don't know what you're talking about!"

"Don't lie to me!" Anger flows through me, and I say this sharply. "I'll kill you now, and I'll come back for the rest of your family. I'll kill Elaine. I'll kill your kids. I'll kill your new grandson if I have to." I would never do this, but I say it without thinking.

"Please, don't!" He's sobbing now. "I hated Silverman. I did. I even wished him dead. But I never did anything about it. I swear to God! Hell, I don't know how I would do it if I did."

My heart is pumping wildly, and my breath catches in my chest. Why won't he tell me what I want to hear? I slam my body into him and force him to his knees. His head is nearly in the urinal.

"Please, don't hurt my family. Please!"

He's begging me, and it feels pathetic. I'm pathetic. How could I threaten a man's family when I know what it means to lose mine? I smell the urine and I'm conscious of his terror. I grip the knife harder and he is gasping and sobbing. I spin him around and stare into his eyes. I can see it, he knows this is the end. He knows he's about to die and there is nothing he can do about it. And he still doesn't say anything. He still doesn't give me what I want, the one thing that will save his and his family's life.

I've heard this kind of pleading before and, when they come to this point in their lives, people will do anything to stop the clock and get another chance. All at once, I know the truth. I can feel it with certainty. He didn't do it. He is not giving me what I want because he really doesn't know. I have the wrong man.

Again.

I take the knife from his throat and step back. He crumples to the floor at the bottom of the urinal and curls into the fetal position. He is sobbing and broken. I broke him. It's my fault and I can't help but feel sorry for him.

"Don't say a word," I say. "Don't go to the police, don't tell your wife. Don't tell anyone or I'll be back, and this will end differently the next time."

I walk away. Out of the bathroom and through the nearest exit, into the night.

Once again, I've failed.

29

Back on the street, I wander. I duck into a bar and have a whiskey to calm my nerves. That doesn't work so I have another, and another. My memory is dim after that. I recall the lights going on and a bartender yelling out last call. As the sun comes up I find myself downtown again, in the central business district. My tie is loose, and my suit rumpled. I'm not sure if I slept in it or walked through the night. My stomach is sour, and it feels like a dwarf is inside my head trying to break out with a sledge hammer. A rough way to start the morning.

It's early and the city is filling up again. The sidewalks are arteries, and the city's blood is starting to flow. The multitudes are on their way in. This is still the first wave, the early tide. Busses and trains are disgorging their passengers. The road is filled with taxis and cars, trucks and buses. It won't be long before all the skyscrapers come to life, filling with light, activity and people. It's morning in the city, just another work day, a part of these people's normal routine. But not for me.

As the sun reflects off the glass of the high rises, bathing everything in its orange-gold light, I squint. I was so sure it was Leach. I'm defeated and deflated.

I walk through the crowd and try to blend in. I've removed my disguise, but I'm wearing the same dark suit I wore the night before. I straighten my tie, and I'm just another guy in a suit on a street filled with guys in suits. I wander aimlessly, no real destination in mind. What will I do next? I can't think of a thing. I still don't know who placed the hit on me or how to cancel it. I tried everything I could think of, and I failed. I'm no closer now than I was at the start. I can't save myself, I can't protect my family. I've failed.

The early morning street noise is a sad song. I've been a fool. All these years I thought I was in control, but I'm just a little cog in a greater machine. I'm a puppet that does what I'm told. I took on jobs and killed people without knowing who they were, or what they'd done. And the truth is, I didn't care. I was paid well. Well enough to buy a nice house, a nice car, and a nice life. I had status, security, love —all the trappings of a good life. I told myself it was just a job. It was what I did, but not who I am. In my mind, I was no different from a plumber or a lawyer or anyone else. I performed a service that needed to be done, but now I know it was a lie. I built a life around violence, lies and deception, and now it's my turn to pay the price. The Agency's not going to stop. They're going to keep coming after me until they get the job done.

I look up and realize that I know this building. I've been here before over the last few days. I try and think why, but I can't concentrate. I'm a mess. I feel like giving up. And then a thought hits me hard.

I can disappear.

Jen hates me now, and she's turned my kids against me. When I saw the look in her eyes, in my heart I knew it was over. What hope do I really have of ever getting her back? And if it's over, what's keeping me here? The Agency has a hit out for Charles Fieldner of Naperville, Illinois, his life is already finished. But I can start over again. I can be anyone I want, anywhere I want. The Agency can't get me if they don't know who I am or where I am. I can disappear and start a new life, free of my father's legacy and free to be whoever I choose to be. I smile for the first time in days.

I'm happy, but only for a moment. If I do this I'll stay alive, but I'll never see my kids again. They'll always wonder why I left, and if it was their fault. I might be alive, but I'll live as a coward, knowing I took the easy way out. My kids will hate me, and it will scar them.

But at least I'll stay alive.

My mind is a jumble and I can't think clearly. I hate myself for even thinking of running, but the thought keeps coming back. How can I help them if I'm dead? I need to get some coffee and Advil to clear my mind. Or maybe another drink. A drink might be better.

Up ahead, a homeless man stands near the curb by the street. He's tall but hunched over. Long ratty hair, a tattered overcoat much too heavy for the weather, and he's wearing sunglasses and holding a cane in his other hand. His head swivels from side to side in an off-kilter rhythm, and he's calling out something in a sing-song way. It might be a Bible verse, but I'm not sure. He has a hat in his hand and he's holding it out, his hand shaking. He's looking for money, but people just pass by, moving out of his way, not even looking at him. I would usually do the same, but now it hits me. I'm feeling sorry for myself, but there are people far worse off than me. I reach into my pocket for some loose bills to give him. As I walk closer, his head swivels my way.

"Bless you, brother. Bless you!"

I take another step forward and reach out to drop the bills in his hat, but as I do, I realize something is wrong. His gaze fixes on me and I realize he isn't blind after all. He can see. Everything around me slows down. I see the world in slow motion. I can't see his eyes, but the way the muscles in his face tense, I know he is about to strike. Beneath the long ratty hair, he wears an earpiece. The hat in his hand moves toward me, and I know he has a blade under there. He says something out loud, but he's not talking to me. There are others nearby and somehow, they were waiting for me.

He lunges toward me, and it feels like I'm out of my body, observing this from a different point in time. The hat drops away, floating softly toward the earth. A glint of sun reflects off the blade. He is moving fast, but it seems impossibly slow.

I react in the same moment, avoiding the blade and blocking his thrust with one hand, and trapping it with the other. With a quick, forceful twist, I capture and break his arm. The blade drops to the ground as he screams in pain. I propel myself at him, knock him off balance and force him into the street. He crashes into the side of a passing car. Brakes squeal. People yell.

I don't know how badly he is hurt and I don't wait around to find out. I run. The crowd parts as I force my way through. I sense someone running from near the entrance to the building, and I wonder if there are others. I break off the sidewalk and into the street. The cars are hardly moving now, and I zigzag between them, running hard. Someone honks their horn and more people yell. The slow-motion feeling has disappeared, and everything speeds up again. My heart races, and my breath is fast. I'm alive again.

I reach the other side of the street, and I'm pushing people and weaving through the sidewalk traffic. I glance back. A man's chasing me. He has short hair and wears a grey suit. He could be a bystander trying to play hero, but I have no doubt that he is with the Agency. How did they find me? How did they know where I'd be?

At the corner, I turn and keep running.

The foot traffic is lighter here. I stand out. There is less opportunity to blend in. There's an entrance to an underground parking garage just off to the side, a big sign above it, and an enclosure covering the stairs leading down. I dash down it, taking the stairs two at a time. I turn another corner and veer around a group of teenagers, all bunched together on the landing, and keep scrambling downward, the walls echo to the sound of my running feet.

I'm not safe.

The man on my tail me might run past the entrance, but it won't take long before he doubles back and pursues me this way. But I have a head start. I can lose him underground.

I crash through an orange door, and I'm in a huge parking deck that goes for blocks under the city streets. I run through it, cross over and move through the aisles. Cars are coming into the garage as the city fills up. I keep on going over to the far side of the garage. I look back. There's no one behind me. I run a little further and take an exit up to the street level.

I slow to a walk as I hit the sidewalk.

Sirens wail in the distance, but I'm blocks away and can't imagine anyone has followed me or knows where I am. Still, I keep looking behind me, scanning the spaces ahead of me and alert to any danger.

I continue walking, letting my breath return to its normal pattern, and my heart slow down to a deep bass beat.

How did they know where I was?

Another block down, I duck into an El station. I buy my ticket and head toward the Brown Line. I take the first train out of the downtown and away from the city.

As the train speeds down the track, it's wheels clacking, the car swaying, I make a decision. The Agency isn't going to stop and I'm not going to run. I will go at them hard and end this, or die trying.

30

I step off the train near the end of the line, out in the boonies south of the city and head for the nearest Dunkin Donuts, a few hundred yards up the street. I order coffee and sit down at a table at the edge of the room with a full view of all the exits. Keeping my eyes and ears open, I review the situation. How did they know I was going to be there? I was wandering aimlessly with no destination in mind. I didn't even know I was going to be, and yet they were waiting for me. They must be tracking me somehow, but I can't figure out how they are doing it.

The shop is bright orange and familiar. A steady flow of new people walks through the door and heads straight for the front takeout counter. I scan their faces and look for any body movements that might signal danger, but everything here seems dull and ordinary. The air is rich with the aroma of fresh coffee and the sweet yeasty smell of the doughnuts. It seems comfortable, safe and familiar. Still, if they are tracking me, do they have someone on my trail now?

A broad-shouldered black man is at a table across the room, near the door. He reads the paper while drinking his coffee, two frosted doughnuts sit on napkins in front of him. I haven't noticed him looking at me, but if he is a professional I shouldn't. Could he be one of them? I'm starting to plan the best way to take him out, when a young girl comes out of the bathroom and slips into the chair next to him. He puts his arm around her shoulders, and she giggles as he slides over one of the doughnuts. I shake my head hard and try to loosen my thoughts. I'm suspecting a dad and his daughter of a being hit men? This is crazy thinking.

The Agency is out to get me, so I'm not paranoid, but they don't know where I am now. Do they? Somehow, they knew I'd show up at that building this morning. How are they tracking me? I climb out of my seat and head for the bathroom. I close the door behind me and take off my jacket. I check my pockets and run my fingers down the lapels, both the frontside and the back. I feel along the lining, exploring every inch of the fabric, but can't find anything that could be a bug or tracking device. I remove my tie and do the same. I'm frantic now. If they are tracking me, it doesn't matter where I go, they will be right behind. I kick off my shoes and see if something has been placed there. Then, my shirt, and undershirt. Nothing. I've taken off my pants and am standing in my underwear, when the bathroom door opens. My blood pressure spikes and I slip into a defensive posture ready to be attacked, but it is an elderly man with thick glasses.

"Oh! Excuse me!" he splutters and immediately closes the door.

I lock the door and stand still for a moment. I'm being ridiculous. I'm imagining things and frightened of my own shadow. After dressing, I splash some water on my face before leaving the restroom and returning to my seat.

I take another sip of my coffee. I'm satisfied that they aren't tracking me, but it still doesn't make sense. If they weren't tracking me, they must have been expecting me. Somehow, I have to turn the tables and take the fight to the Agency. I tried it with Leach, but it only made the situation worse. He didn't contact the Agency, and now everyone will be on alert.

Who else could have placed the hit on Silverman?

Pat Griffin has a strong motive, but she will be on high alert now. I can't catch her by surprise and get the information out of her. The Agency has figured out their mistake, and they are out in force to bring me down. I don't know what they know about me, or where they'll be looking for me. I can't go back home, or see anyone I'm close to. Who can I trust? Who else are they watching? I don't think I can even go back to the hotel to collect my things. So, what can I do to get back in the hunt?

I take another sip of coffee, but it's gone cold. I slam the rest down in one gulp. I must be missing something. Dad knew someone at the Agency. Back in the day, he didn't use technology. He used loose change and a pay phone. I remember him talking, he knew the person he talked with. I try and put myself back in time, I try and remember what he said the times I heard him talking on the phone. Did he say the person's name? I try and focus, but my mind is foggy. If he ever said a name I don't remember it, but I can't help thinking that Dad is the key. He is my last link into the Agency.

What do I do now? It's clear I can't stay here. I have to take the fight back to the Agency, but I can't fight what I can't see. There must be something that offers a clue, something that will help me find my way into the Agency. I need to talk with Dad again. I want to check in and see how he's doing, but if I go to the hospital they'll spot me. I'm sure Dad's being watched. He won't be able to tell me anything either.

I stand, crumple my cup, drop my garbage in the trash can, and walk out the door into the bright morning light. I'm not far from the train station. The whole area is connected by a network of trains and I can go anywhere from here. I head toward the train station, hugging the side of the road, keeping to the shadows. Cars buzz by and I feel the gusts of wind as they pass. I breathe in the dust and the car exhaust, and all at once I have an idea. I know where I need to go.

∽

As I open the door to the storage unit, I smell that familiar mix of dust and cedar, and something I can't place that reminds me of home. I pull the door closed behind me and switch on the light. I look at the stacks of boxes, the furniture, knickknacks, junk and debris, and I'm looking at artifacts from a prior life.

My mother's Japanese makeup desk brings back memories as I run my fingers over the smooth, black-lacquered wood. Mom loved this, and she sat in front of it nearly every morning as part of her daily ritual. Putting herself together, she'd say. She always dressed up and wore makeup, even if she was doing nothing but staying home all day. Even when she was sick, up until close to the end. She'd lost all her hair and wore a wig, but she still dressed and made herself up as if she was going out for a night on the town. The rosy rouged cheeks gave an illusion of health that didn't fit with her sunken eyes. How much did Mom know about Dad's business? We never discussed it, but there had to be clues. Just as Jen suspects me, did Mom ever suspect Dad was hiding a secret? They stayed together all those years. Did she just look the other way? I open the drawers of the table and search for anything I missed before. I look underneath it, and probe for hidden spaces, but the table is nothing more than a table.

I start at the back of the space this time, picking up boxes and going through them one by one. I don't know what I'm looking for, but there has to be something. This place contains all that's left of a past life, and if there is a link to the Agency, it will be here. I open a box filled with old school papers for Beth and me. Beth was a good student and her penmanship was neat and precise. I pick up a report card of mine from fifth grade and see that I was a C student. The teacher's comment at the bottom says I need to show more effort. I don't spend much time on this. I hurry through these papers and go on to the next box.

This one is filled mostly with cookbooks and recipe cards. Mom loved to cook and often tried new things. I can't imagine this will link up to anything, but I go through it carefully, opening the cookbooks and leafing through the pages. I quickly glance through each recipe card. This takes time but leads to nothing. Another box holds Christmas ornaments, and opening this one makes me smile. I keep on looking, going through every box, one at a time. And I don't find anything.

I go over to the stacks of books I'd left on a table. This is where I found the cryptic list, and I know that this connects to something. I go through each book, fanning out the pages, looking for anything that might be hidden. I look in the margins and pull off the covers. Nothing. I take another look at all the furniture. There are two small tables and I inspect them from every angle, looking for something that could be hidden inside. I do the same with an antique wooden dresser. I check the cushions on the chairs. I cut the cushion of one open and spill the cotton filling out on the floor. Other than making a mess, I don't find a thing. I think of slashing apart my dad's big leather chair, but I know this will be a waste of time. I even look at the old bike. The tires have leaked out all their air, and I strip them off the rims to see if something is there. And, of course, I don't find anything.

It feels cramped in this little room. I cough some dust out of my throat and try to see what I'm missing. Dad kept a list of his jobs. Why did he do that? Was this some sort of a personal trophy? A way to remember what he'd done, and a way to keep score? Or did the information protect him from the Agency? If he had something that linked him to the Agency and tied them together, this was valuable and gave him leverage if he ever got caught. Or if the Agency ever turned on him. It would make sense to keep something, but what would it look like and where would he keep it?

I scan the room again. The photo albums are in a big box on the top of a desk, right where I left them. I pick out the first album and page through it. These are all family photos and they picture a happy, smiling family. A fictional family, I think. Was I ever happy? I think I was, but how could I be? Every family is dysfunctional in its own way, but we were uniquely flawed. I grew up in my father's shadow, and over time I was formed in his image. I turn the pages and let the memories flow. There are pictures of me in a little league baseball uniform, proudly holding my bat. In this picture I'm not much older than my son, Jason. What kind of man will he become? I know with certainty I won't make the same mistakes as my dad made. If I somehow get through this all, I won't take him into the family business.

I quickly glance through the albums for anything I missed. I pull some of the pictures out, looking to see if there is anything written on them that will give me a clue, or if anything is hidden between the photos. But everything is as it seems. There are no secrets.

At the bottom of the pile is an album with a red cover I didn't look at before. I open it and see that this is more of the same. Shots of vacations and family outings. This is a hodgepodge of photos, and I'm young in some of them and older in others. While the other books were consistent in time, this looks like an album put together later, photos that were loose and now given a home. There are some Christmas pictures of me when I'm young, and some with me and my sister when I'm older. There is a picture of my mom and Dad in Halloween costumes. She is dressed as a flapper, and he's a 1930s era gangster. I gaze at a picture from a family vacation out west. Dad must be taking the picture and Mom holds Beth, she's just a baby. I'm almost a teenager, wearing sunglasses and trying to look cool. I haven't seen these shots before and I get caught up in them, trying to remember back and take in the context of the time.

I flip the page. I scan these new photos and I catch my breath. One picture stands out and captures my attention. It's outdoors on the bleachers of some unseen ball field. I don't know where this is, but I'm thinking it could be a little league baseball game. A man sits, smiling widely with a toddler on his lap. I focus on his intense eyes, and suddenly it all comes together. Everything starts to make sense.

31

I stand in the darkness at the back of the closet and patiently wait. My surgical gloves make my hands sweat, but I'm used to them, and the dark nylon clothes I'm in won't leave fibers. He'll be here soon. Not sure when, and I don't know who he'll be with, but he'll be here before long.

It's over an hour before the key turns in the lock and the door opens.

Deep in the shadows, I'm hidden behind the rows of coats, my face and body nearly completely obscured. I take in a deep breath and hold it. I will my body to be still and I listen as they step inside.

I don't look out, but I can tell, he's not alone. The footsteps crack on the hard tile floor. I can't tell for sure, but I think there are three—him and two others. My heart beats fast, but it's not fear, it's anticipation. I need to time this carefully. They are all together and I have the advantage of surprise. The longer I wait, the greater the chance they will separate, moving further into the house where my advantage is gone. Or I will be discovered, and it will all be over. Someone kicks off their shoes and sighs. The rustle of fabric on fabric filters through the closet. I wait until the door clicks firmly shut and someone punches in the numbers to reset the alarm code.

My gun is already in my hand and the silencer attached. Someone flips on the hall light and I step out. I take in the scene in a millisecond. There are three men in the hallway, one short and two large. One is facing the doorway, securing the alarm, the other two are nearly facing me, taking off their coats. I point my gun at the larger man, his coat half way off, a stunned expression on his face. He doesn't have time to do anything else. I point and squeeze the trigger.

Thwack!

The bullet leaves a messy black hole in his forehead as he drops to the floor.

The other big man's face contorts. He's spinning around, trying to pull his gun out at the same time. I point at him and squeeze the trigger again.

Thwack!

It's a bad shot and I hit his shoulder, not a clean kill. Still, he drops, his back against the front door. I step forward before he can pull his gun all the way out. I straddle his body with my legs, and kiss his forehead with the barrel of my gun. His face is hard and red. He looks angry but not scared. I know this has ruined his night. I pull the trigger again.

Thwack!

He's done.

I turn to face the last man. He stands statue still in his stocking feet, his hands empty, shock on his face. I step forward and put my gun to his head.

"How did you get in here?" Calhoun asks.

"Is that what you really want to know?"

He shakes his head. Though I know he is shocked, he almost looks amused.

"No, I guess not," he glances down at the bodies on the floor, their blood now pooling on the tile floor, and shakes his head again. "Care to have a seat, Charley? I tell you, my back's killing me. I need to sit down."

Without waiting for my reply, he turns and leads me out of the hall and away from his two dead companions. I'm stunned at his composure. I follow him around the corner to a sitting room. The lights are motion activated and flicker on as he steps into the room. I watch closely but he keeps his hands visible and doesn't try to grab anything. The man knows the drill and shows me respect.

The room is small and octagonal with two big chairs facing a fireplace. It is intimate and cozy, tastefully decorated in an old school, masculine style. I imagine this is where a rich man would go to sip brandy or smoke Cuban cigars. He heads for a big chair next to an ottoman, an orange yellow afghan covering it. He sinks into the chair, letting out a loud sigh. He throws the afghan over his legs and pulls it up to his chest.

"Don't make any sudden moves," I say, my tone light. "Keep your hands where I can see them."

He holds his hands up, then slowly lowers them to the arms of his chair. I remain standing, my gun pointed at his heart.

"Don't worry, I'm not resisting," he says. "I don't know if you're aware of this, but I'm not a well man. Pancreatic cancer. The doctors say I've only got a couple more months and that'll be it."

He looks at me, but if he is expecting sympathy he doesn't get it.

"You know why I'm here."

He nods. "I do, I just wanted to let you know. I guess I shouldn't expect those last few months," he laughs softly. "You're probably doing me a favor anyway."

I don't say anything and let him talk.

"I thought it was you the moment you arrived at my office," he says. "Right after you left, I called and found there was no one under your name listed at the insurance company. That wasn't much of a disguise, and your Dad always sent me pictures, up until recently. You should stick to what you do best, Charley. In spite of finding me, you're not meant to be a detective."

Calhoun laughs, but I don't see the humor.

"I always felt like I knew you," he says. "Even though it's been a long time since we last met. You probably don't remember. You were just a kid then, you used to call me Uncle Jerry. You knew your whole alphabet before you were three. God, but your dad was proud of you." He laughs again as he shakes his head. "You remind me of him, you know."

Anger rises in a hot wave, straight up from the lining of my stomach and I swallow it back. Calhoun is frail, fragile. I don't need the gun. It looks as though he'd blow away in a stiff wind.

"I never had kids of my own, you know. I got a real kick when Charles brought you around."

"So, you're the Agency? It's just you?"

"Just me? God no. I never could have done this on my own. In the beginning it was a partnership, your dad and I."

I'm here for a purpose. I planned to do what I needed and get out, but now I'm curious.

"You were partners?"

"Right from the beginning," Calhoun takes a big breath and closes his eyes. Something passes over his face and I think he is in pain. It passes, and he opens his eyes again. "Your dad never told you the story?"

"He never told me anything."

He sniffs and dips his chin. "Charles never was the talkative one. Let me tell you about it. If you're not in too much of a rush, that is? I'm guessing I won't have the chance to tell it again after tonight."

I nod for him to continue.

"We met back in Vietnam, the first week after I landed. They set us up as partners. He was a sniper, and I was his spotter. They'd identify targets for us, usually some Viet Cong chief or sympathetic local official and then send us after them. The idea was to give them a taste of their own medicine. Pick off their leaders, sow havoc, that kind of thing. Anyways, we were off the grid a lot, deep in the shit. Your dad was the sniper, so he'd pull the trigger. I did the reconnaissance and logistics, whatever was needed to get us in close, so he could take the shot, and we could get away safe."

He looks at me to see if I'm following along, and I am.

"Dangerous work, but God damn, we were good at it. Charles was a natural. He made some damned difficult shots, and he was always cool as an Eskimo in an ice storm. Anyways, we got a reputation for doing this kind of work. And not just with the brass, if you know what I mean."

He looks to me for reaction again. Again, I nod.

"One time, we were in the city for some R and R, and we were approached by this sergeant that had a problem. I won't bore you with the details, but he had a lieutenant in his platoon, a real by-the-books hard ass. He had a suicide wish and wanted to take his men along with him when he went. Anyways, they'd all gotten together and raised some money to get them out of their jam. Charles handled the problem and that was our first job. It was going to be a onetime deal, but it turns out there is a demand for this kind of service. That was my first successful business and it's still going. I owe everything to your dad."

He looks at me expectantly, but I just stare back at him.

"It's hard to believe," Calhoun goes on. "Finding Charles was a stroke of luck. Most people would have called him a psychopath, but I just called him talented. I thought he was one of a kind. Who would've thought he could raise you to take his place?"

Blood rushes to my face. I'm not a psychopath. I'm not like my dad.

"We've talked enough," I say. "Give me the records, and let's get this over."

Calhoun grimaces again. He straightens up in his chair and nods slowly as though finally coming to terms with his predicament.

"Of course. The records."

"Yes, and to call off all your men. Cancel the hit on me now."

"Yes, about that," Calhoun laughs. "That is an interesting story. I don't have any other men, Charley. The Agency was a big success, but it was a franchise. We joined up a few years in. We were part of a network, it covers the whole country and you can get their services anywhere. The Agency provided the systems and the technology, they set up job referrals and the payment systems. They were miles ahead of where your dad and I were."

I stare at him hard and try to read him. Is he telling the truth? I can't tell.

"For me, this was always a small business," Calhoun continues. "We did enough for your dad to earn a nice living. It gave me a good start for my other enterprises, and it was a useful tool to have when I needed it, but this was always just me and your dad. And then, you. I brought in some freelancers for this, but you've cleaned out my inventory, son. No one's coming after you anymore because I've got no one left."

I shake my head and try and keep calm. "Don't lie to me, 'Uncle' Jerry!"

"I'm not. When you showed up in my office, talking about Silverman, that concerned me. I know what you do, and I didn't know why you were asking around about Silverman since I know you killed him. So of course, I figured you were really after me. I didn't know why, but I had to protect myself. I had to reach out to find some people who could do this sort of job. The two men I had guarding my office are gone. One was injured and arrested. The other disappeared. You just shot the last two. I never had other killers working for me. Just you and Charles. It's harder to find people in your line of work than you might think."

This seems like the truth, but in the end, it doesn't really matter.

"You still tried to kill me," I say.

Calhoun shrugs. "Of course I did. Because you were coming to kill me."

"I was coming to find you to stop the hit on me!"

"You got me on that one," Calhoun shrugs and looks genuinely puzzled. "There was a hit on you?"

I'm fully angry now. Suddenly, I want to take my gun and smash the butt against his head. I will myself to relax.

"Yes," I say as calmly as I can. "I got a contract through the normal channels. It was a hit against myself."

"That's impossible. If there was a hit on you, which there wasn't, I would have set it up. But why would I let you know about it?"

I think on this and he's right. It doesn't make sense.

"Maybe someone placed this through a different franchise," Calhoun ponders. "It could have been a glitch with the referral system that it got back to you. Like I told you, I didn't know about it."

I nod. I lower the gun so that he can't see my hands are shaking. I put the gun in my pocket. I don't need it. I never did—not since downing the two big lugs in the hallway.

"Can I get you a drink, Charley? You look like you need one, and I know I sure as hell do."

Calhoun starts to stand, but I wave him back down. There is a bar cart against the wall and I walk over to it without turning my back to him. There are two glasses and several bottles.

"Pour the Macallan, son. That's a special bottle and I've been saving it for the right occasion. There's no point waiting any longer."

The Macallan is in a decorative bottle and it's unopened. I break the seal, and pour a couple fingers full of the amber liquid into each glass. I hand one to Calhoun and I keep the other.

Calhoun raises the glass in a salute. His hands are steady.

"To life," he toasts. "The taking and the giving."

He takes a sip and sets the glass down on the arm of his chair. I drink mine in one gulp. It goes down smooth but doesn't make me feel better.

"The records," I say. "Get me the records and let's get this over with."

Calhoun stays seated. He looks calm and composed. He knows he's about to die, but he doesn't seem concerned.

"About the records," he says, tapping his temple. "They're all right here."

"What, you're telling me you didn't have any written records?"

"Would you? In this line of business that's a stupid damned thing to do. Once you finish a contract, you want to close out the job and forget about it as fast as you can. I wrote down only what I needed to and destroyed it as soon as I could."

I'd searched the whole house earlier and hadn't found a thing. You can hide things anywhere, and if they are electronic, there was no way I could find them. Is he telling the truth? I feel a little light-headed and suddenly, I need to sit.

"I never understood why people keep things they shouldn't. My memory has served me fine all these years."

I plop down on the fireplace hearth. I feel unsteady.

"It's funny. I'm a sick man. I know I'm going to die soon. Even so, I'm not ready to go yet."

"What was in there?" I ask. My throat is tight, and I have to force my eyes to stay open.

"Just a sedative, son. I injected it into the bottle a while back as a precaution. Don't worry, it won't kill you. I'll do that myself after you pass out."

He stands, and he's steadier on his feet now. He walks over to me and leans in close, looking into my eyes.

"It pays to be prepared, doesn't it? I'm going to miss you, Charley. I really am." He reaches into my pocket and takes my gun away. I don't even try to stop him. It doesn't seem worth the effort, but I push against the feeling. I have to concentrate and focus.

"Silverman," I say through dry lips. "Who put the contract on him? Was it Griffin?"

"Griffin?" Calhoun shakes his head. "No, she loved the guy. Not that it matters, but it was me. You can understand why I got concerned when you started asking about him."

I blink and suck in breath. My head is swimming like I've had too much to drink. How will he do it? Will I feel anything?

"Alan had his own way of doing things. There were lines he wouldn't cross, though, and he found out some things he didn't need to know. I had to protect myself. And I thank you for your service, Charley."

He looks at his watch. I'm seeing him in double. I don't have much time left.

"It shouldn't be long now. I'm surprised you're still conscious." He reaches down and picks up my wrist, checking my pulse. "Well, the good thing, Charley, is when they tell your dad, he won't remember. Consider that a blessing."

I feel myself letting go. What will it feel like to die? Will it be like

I'm going to sleep and ust not waking up? Will I feel pain? Will I wake up in Heaven? Nah, more likely Hell.

A spark flashes somewhere deep inside me. I think of Jen and my kids. I picture their faces and I feel pain. I can't leave them on their own. Not yet.

A voice in my head screams,
I don't want to die.

My brain is foggy and slow, but this is my one chance. My last chance. I grab his legs and push myself off the fireplace, lurching toward him. I'm swimming through molasses, I'm clumsy and not sure how I'm even moving, but muscle memory takes over. The voice in my head screams again, *I don't want to die.*

It's a mantra now. *I don't want to die.*

I. Don't. Want. To. Die!

I drive him backwards. He falls to the floor and I'm on top of him. He's fighting back, and his fists pound against my back. But I'm observing myself from a high up place. I'm here, but I'm not.

I don't want to die!

My hands find his neck and I start to squeeze. It doesn't feel like I'm doing it, but I know I am. I squeeze harder and realize he has the gun in his hand. He hits me with it. A sharp pain bites in my neck but I don't stop. He's swinging the gun around and he fires. The gun is next to my ear and the silencer must have come off, the sound is explosive, deafening. I keep squeezing. My thumbs dig into his throat. His eyes bulge, he's wild with fear.

I Don't Want To Die!

The gun goes off again, and then it drops to the ground. I keep squeezing his throat, but my adrenaline has run its course. I can't do it anymore. I push myself up to my feet. I can't stay here anymore. I take a step and trip over my own feet. I fall to the floor and stay there. Have I been shot?

I try and push myself up to standing again, but my eyes close. Everything goes dark.

32

The next day is beautiful and sunny, and I'm glad to be alive. I park my car in the big lot off the main entrance to the community park. The grass here is a vibrant green and the sky a serene blue. I'm thankful to be upright and breathing, and I know how close I came to losing everything.

I inhale the fresh air, heavy with the scents of lilac and fresh mowed grass. The sun warms my skin and I take my time walking along the cedar path. I go around the basketball and tennis courts and past the big baseball diamond. I stop for a moment by the soccer field and watch a group of young girls in bright yellow T-shirts run through their drills. The coach blows his whistle and they sprint to the far side of the field to gather around him. I think of Emily and Jason and how much I miss them, but I can't think about them now. I have one last job to do. I continue along the path and stay in the present. It's good to be alive.

I look around as I reach the playground. The area is filled with kids, from toddlers on up. There are a couple of dads standing by the swings, pushing their kids while they talk. Three boys, around Jason's age, are chasing each other, running in zig zags and yelling as they go.

Benches surround the play area and several mothers look on. I spot Beth at a far bench, sitting alone. I walk toward her.

She is watching her girls play on little horses with coiled spring bases. Beth doesn't notice me until I'm close. When she sees me she jumps up, a look of shock crosses her face.

"Charley! What are you doing here?"

"I stopped by the house. Michael told me where you'd be."

She gives me a warm hug. I feel the emotion and as I hold her tight, my eyes tear up. I blink them back and let her go.

"I've been worried about you," she says, recovering quickly. "You haven't answered any of my calls."

"I've been busy. Mind if I join you?"

"No, of course not."

She sits on the bench and I sit close to her. Audrey and Bria bounce up and down, giggling. They seem joyful and happy. Beth looks at me, puzzled and concerned.

"Dad's going to be all right," she says. "There was a setback, but it's under control now. It was a good thing you were there when he had his heart attack."

I nod.

"When I couldn't get a hold of you, I tried calling Jen. I couldn't reach her either. I was worried. Are you okay?"

I look at her and nod once more. I gaze into her eyes and without saying anything, we communicate. She sees something deep inside me and the expression on her face changes. The concern is still there, but also an awareness. And fear.

"Uncle Jerry," I say as I put my hand on her arm. "He's dead. It's over."

Beth looks away and she is breathing hard. Her face reddens, and I know the panic she feels.

"Charley, look. I didn't mean for it to be like this. I didn't know what else to do."

"Don't," I say sharply. "Don't say it!"

Beth stares at me, and I see the fear take over. Tears flood her eyes. I hold the gaze and she looks away. She drops her head in her hands and the dam breaks open. Her body shakes and quivers.

"Don't do it when the girls are around," she pleads, her voice cracking. "Make it an accident—let them remember me the way I am!"

I stare at her. I'm still not sure what I feel. She tried to have me killed. She wanted me dead. My whole life is ruined because of her. I feel this, but it doesn't come as anger or hate. I feel ... disappointed. How could someone I love so much treat me this way?

I think back to when she was first born. I was in junior high at the time, and already Dad's apprentice. I remember seeing her for the first time, so soft and pink, so small, her eyes closed, hardly any hair on her head. I remember touching my finger to her palm and how she gripped it so tightly. I think of how fragile she was, and I wanted to be her protector. I wanted to be the best big brother, to take care of her and keep her safe from harm.

Beth pulls out a tissue and looks at me once again, her eyes desperate and pleading. She can't speak. I can't speak either. I'm going back in time, watching the movie in my head.

She was only a toddler when I started high school. I loved her so much. I sat with her, read her books, played Lego, dolls, and imagination games. For a time, I was her hero and she followed me around, wanting to do whatever I did.

The movie in my mind flashes forward. As I grew older, I still felt the same way about her, but I'm in the house less and less. I go on outings with Dad, and sometimes, I'm the lead now. I do the jobs when they come up, but they are a chore. I want to be my own man now. This isn't what I want to do with my life. I'm sure as hell not going to grow up to be like my Dad.

In a flash, I make good on my rebellion and go away to school. I'm nearly an adult and out of Dad's orbit for a time. I'm living my own life in a different state, and I'm away from home almost all year round. Just coming back for holidays a few weeks each year. My throat tightens as I think of what this means. When I was gone, I left Beth alone.

Beth is crying harder now, almost out of control. I want to comfort her, but I don't think I can speak without losing it myself. I think back, imagining how it went. When I was away at school Dad still needed a disciple. Beth was only six when I went away. Only six. The same age I was when Dad took me out for the first time.

My gut clenches as I imagine this. My body feels like lead. I picture Dad taking Beth by the hand and leading her out the door. I think of Mom as they leave, a smile brightening her face. I think of Beth, and how excited she must have been. Sweet, trusting Beth. What did she think the first time it happened? Did she scream or cover her eyes? Did she feel sorry for the target, whoever he was, as he coughed the last time and stopped breathing? Did she wet the bed or have nightmares for years after, like I did?

All along I thought this was my secret alone. Beth knew. Did Mom know too? A family secret isn't a secret, if you're in the family. How did Beth feel, all alone back home, trapped with Dad? And me, her protector, so far away? She has Dad's DNA as much as I do. I know that now. She was trained the same way I was, and she has her demons, just like I do.

After Mom died, Beth took care of Dad. While I was the distant son, occupied with my own family and my own life. She remained the close, loving daughter. When Dad's memory began to fade, and Alzheimer's started setting in, she was the first to notice. He told her things. He showed her things, and she knew as much about the Agency as anyone. She was a part of it, and she knew secrets that I didn't know.

"Why?" I ask. "You have to tell me why you did it?"

She looks at me and quickly turns away. She cradles her head in her hands and sobs again. This is the mystery. Why? Is it greed? Is she concerned with the inheritance? I'm prepared for anything, but I hope it's not money. That would be too petty a reason, and I'm not sure I can deal with that.

"It needed to stop!" Beth looks up again, but she can't meet my eyes. "Ever since my girls were born, I've been questioning everything. I don't want them involved in this. I don't want them to know anything about what you did, or I did. I want them to see their grandpa as a good person."

I stare at her and swallow hard.

"Every time I see your Jason, I can't help thinking, he's going to be next."

"No!" I recoil at the thought. "No way I would ever do that!"

She looks at me again, meeting my gaze and this time I look away. I wouldn't bring him in to the business. I shudder as I think the impossible. I haven't become my father.

Beth quivers with fear and flinches when I touch her shoulder.

"It's okay," I say soothingly. "I'm not going to hurt you."

I put my arm around her shoulders to comfort and protect her. She sobs softly, her whole body shaking. Reluctantly, she leans in to me. I fight back the urge to cry myself.

In the playground, the girls are in the big play fort, climbing over and under the bright yellow and green plastic walls, squealing with delight as they play. Beth is bent over, rubbing her eyes.

"It's okay," I say. "It's all going to be all right. I'm quitting. I'm done with all this."

Beth looks deeply in my eyes and nods. She wipes her tears away and blows her nose. I stand and she stands with me. She is still shaking, but I don't think she's afraid. I know she is relieved in a way.

"How did you know?" Beth asks.

"It was the picture," I say. "The one of you sitting on 'Uncle' Jerry's lap. I should have known before. I should have known all along."

Beth nods and wipes her eyes again.

"This will be okay," I say. "We're family. We're going to work this out."

We hug one more time, then I release her. I turn and head toward the parking lot. It's a beautiful day and this feels like a new beginning. I'm a new man, released from my chains and unencumbered by my past. I need to call the detective again. After I've steam cleaned the garage, I'll go in and answer questions, do a full interview. But I'll get through this. I'm a very convincing liar, and I'll cover my tracks.

I think of Jen and the kids, and how hard it's been without them. I think of the way Jen looked at me when I saw her last—the fear and hate in her eyes. I haven't been the best husband. I wasn't honest with her, but I'll change that going forward.

Jen is hurt and angry. She wants nothing to do with me right now, but those feelings will pass. We are meant to be together. I love her and the kids so much and I won't let them go. This won't be easy, but one way or another, I will get her back. I'm a determined man. A resourceful man. A family man.

We are a family, and family is everything.

Made in United States
Troutdale, OR
02/05/2025

28685927R00137